ANOMALY

Peter Cawdron

thinkingscifi.wordpress.com

Copyright © Peter Cawdron 2011

All rights reserved

The right of Peter Cawdron to be identified as the author of this work has been asserted by him in accordance with the Copyright, Designs and Patents Act 1988

First published as an eBook by Peter Cawdron using Smashwords

ISBN-13: 978-1478175551
ISBN-10: 1478175559

eBook ISBN: 978-1-4657-7394-4

US Edition

All the characters in this book are fictitious, and any resemblance to actual persons living or dead is purely coincidental

Dedicated to my wife, Fiona

Anomaly

ANOMALY	1
CLASS	13
CONTACT	29
NEWS	49
HELIUM	61
PIONEER	77
UNITED NATIONS	91
BIG BROTHER	103
HOT CHOCOLATE	113
CARBON	127
DOWNTOWN	137
BLUE SKY	155
WHY?	165
DARWIN	187
NEPTUNE	203
CABLE TV	223
MALL	245
TRUST	283
LIFE	331
AFTERWORD	353
OTHER BOOKS BY PETER CAWDRON	357

ANOMALY

Shortly after lunch, cracks appear in the road, curving in an arc across the intersection. Officer Jimmy Davies directs traffic on the corner of 1st and East 45th in Manhattan. The traffic lights are dead. There's nothing notable about his assignment other than that he's standing outside the United Nations. Davies waves with his white-gloved hand, signaling for the traffic to keep moving.

The sun beats down on him. Regulations dictate long sleeves to protect against UV, but in the midst of a sweltering New York summer, the sweat pours off him. The electrician said fixing the lights should only take fifteen minutes, but it's been almost three hours and his legs are aching.

Around him, impatient drivers honk their horns. Apparently, air conditioning can do that to you, he thinks sarcastically, stopping a line of traffic so he can allow a party of school children to cross from the corner of East 45th. The kids are bubbly, excited about visiting the U.N. building as part of a school excursion.

The smells from the Thai restaurant on the corner waft through the air. A hint of chicken cooked in garlic and ginger, along with the allure of roasted cashews, drives his taste buds crazy.

~~~

A film crew sets up a camera on a tripod outside the gates to the U.N. General Assembly building on a side road adjacent to the T-intersection. The flags of over a hundred countries flutter in the breeze behind them. Cathy Jones stands with her back to the flags, using their vibrant colors as the backdrop for her news segment. Her cameraman, Jimmy Finch, flips his New York Yankees hat around backwards so he can peer through the eyepiece of his camera.

Cathy messes with her hair. If her producer was here she would tell her it looks fine, leave it alone, but Cathy is self-conscious about her auburn locks. Her hair never seems to sit just right. In her mind, American viewers have a love affair with blondes that dates back to the 1930's when moviegoers were in awe of by platinum blonde Jean Harlow and the 50's when Marilyn Monroe first stunned the nation on a grainy black and white television.

Cathy's dad tells her she's beautiful, but all dads say that. Her hair bugs her. She's of Scottish descent, way back on her mother's side, and has Celtic blood. Although her brunette hair is pretty, it has a slight red tinge, something barely visible in the sunlight. It means she can never be a blonde. If she bleaches her hair it goes bright red and frizzy, making her look like one of the witches from Macbeth. And so here she is, a second-string reporter for a small local cable channel, struggling to get her career to take off, reporting on World Education Week at the United Nations. Yeah, she thinks, blondes have more fun.

The jagged cracks in the road grow larger.

"Okay," Finch says, his head still buried behind the camera. "Ready when you are."

Cathy holds her microphone in front of her, ensuring it's low, below her chin, as she speaks crisply.

"In the Western world, education is the norm. No child grows up without the ability to read and write, but for the majority of children born on our humble, old planet, this is not the case. For most, education is a luxury their parents cannot afford."

~~~

Officer Davies doesn't pay any attention to the news crew. He has his hands full keeping impatient pedestrians and irritated drivers apart. From where he stands in the center of the intersection, the cracks are not noticeable, but he notices the cars driving down toward Queensboro shudder slightly as they leave the intersection. It is as though they are driving over a bump in the road, a speed hump or trash fallen from a trailer. Davies doesn't think too much about it, but the cars turning west seem to ride up over a lip in the concrete road about the same distance away from him. It is as though they are riding over the edge of a low curb. Strange, he thinks, the road didn't seem that bad when he drove in.

"How much longer?" Davies yells, calling out to the electricians working on the lights.

"It's not looking good," is the reply. "We just lost all power."

~~~

The earth shakes.

The U.S. Foreign Missions building on the corner of the intersection groans. Panes of glass fall, shattering on the street below. The sound of bending, twisting, grinding metal fills the air. Davies staggers, fighting to stay on his feet. Pedestrians run for cover. A group of school children on the forecourt of the U.N. collapse to the ground, screaming in fear. Several cars rear-end each other in the confusion. Cathy stumbles backwards, but Finch retains his presence of mind. He knows what to do. He swings his camera around, catching the vision of entire sheets of glass falling, and then shattering into a million pieces as they strike the pavement.

"What the hell was that?" Cathy cries, crouching low to the ground. "A bomb?"

Finch is cool under fire. Two tours of Afghanistan have steadied his nerves.

"Nah," he replies.

Cathy watches him panning with the camera, knowing the feed is being streamed live back to the studio. The footage probably won't be used immediately, but the producer will have it by now and, hopefully, she's monitoring the feed.

"There's been no compression wave," Finch says, staying behind the lens. "If this was a bomb, we would have been blown off our feet. And there's no wreckage, no debris, no smoke. I think sweet, little old New York just had herself an earthquake."

Officer Davies steadies himself in the middle of the intersection. The earthquake passes as quickly as it came. Davies gets on the radio, raising a priority call for medics and more police. Several pedestrians lie on the shattered glass, covered in rich, scarlet red blood.

Finch turns the camera on the State Department building. He focuses in on a gash running up the side of the building in an arc. Rather than being jagged, it's smooth, stretching in a curve.

"I don't think this was an earthquake," Cathy says, standing beside him.

"Why?" Finch asks, his head still buried behind the camera as he zooms in on the police officer attending to injured bystanders. The officer herds people away from the shattered building. Several well-dressed businessmen abandon their cars, helping the injured, dragging them off the pavement immediately below the building and out onto the road, away from falling debris.

"Zoom out," Cathy says, seeing his preoccupation with the injured.

Finch pulls back on the zoom, taking in the U.S. State Department building on the far side of the intersection. The damage to the building is cut in a half circle, starting at the third floor and slicing around the side of the building and then up in an arc, reaching toward the rear of the building before curving forward and exiting out the front, just a few floors below the roof.

Cathy mumbles, talking to herself more than Finch.

"Looks like a bite."

The sound of sirens in the distance heralds the arrival of fire engines, paramedics and police winding their way through the heavy New York traffic to the U.N. complex on the East Side.

"I don't get it," Finch says. "What am I looking at?"

"It's not an earthquake. Earthquakes cause damage from the ground up," Cathy says, pointing. The lower stories of the State Department are pristine and untouched.

She struggles, thinking about how to describe what she's seeing. "It looks as though someone's taken a giant ice cream scoop and reached down out of the sky and just sliced around part of the building."

"Ice cream scoop? Seriously?" Finch asks from behind his camera. "That's the commentary you want transmitted around the world?"

Cathy cringes at the thought.

"Maybe it is a bomb," Finch says. "But it was placed on the fourth or fifth floor and blew everything out onto the street."

Cathy isn't convinced. She notes, "Not all the windows blew out, just those along the path of the crack. This is weird."

Finch pans his camera to the other side of the intersection, looking north along 1st Avenue. The offices above the Thai restaurant have also been hit, along with the Institute of International Education and the Turkish Consular office. Like the State Department, they're only affected above street level, with an arc cutting through them from the middle of the third floor.

Directing the camera down East 45th it's clear the fracture moves in a curve that tightens as it rises higher. As the camera takes in more of the buildings, it becomes apparent the curve arcs back toward them. They're standing on the edge of a massive circle, an invisible sphere cut into New York City.

"And look at that," Cathy says, tapping Finch on the shoulder and directing him to look behind them. Finch swings the camera around and sees that the top corner of the U.N. General Assembly building has come apart, but it is the flags that bother Cathy.

"Look at the flags," she says. "Have you ever seen anything like that before?"

Finch zooms in on the Belarusian flag waving gently in the breeze. There is a gap between the lower part of the flagpole and the upper half. The pole has been sliced clean through. They can see through a gap of about four inches to the wall behind the flag.

"Tell me you can see that?" Cathy says. "Tell me it's not just my eyes playing tricks on me."

The gap grows wider. The upper half of the flagpole is suspended in midair, separated from the lower section of aluminum tubing set firmly in the concrete on the ground.

"You're getting this on film, right?"

"A-huh," Finch replies.

"I don't like this," Cathy says. "Whatever this is, I think we're standing in the middle of it."

"What?" Finch says, finally letting his curiosity get the better of his professionalism and coming out from behind the eyepiece of his camera.

"Look down," she says.

"Oh, I have to catch this on camera," Finch says, taking the camera off the tripod and sitting it on his shoulder. "Come on, Cathy. Give us some commentary."

Finch swings the camera up, looking at Cathy.

"Ah, the ground around the United Nations building appears to be experiencing some kind of a bizarre disturbance," she says, tossing her hair back with one hand. "At first, we thought we might be in the middle of a war zone, with a bomb going off, but there was no blast. Then we thought it might be an earthquake or maybe a ruptured gas main. But now, looking at this, it is clear that some kind of strange, physical phenomenon is unfolding before us."

"There are injured people on the far side of the intersection, but they're able to walk. There aren't any bodies. None that we can see."

A tinge of guilt gnaws at her for not running to help, but she quickly talks herself out of any regret. Her role is to report, to document this tragedy.

She walks away from the intersection, walking along the service road leading away from the rear gates of the United Nations. Finch stays with her, filming her as she steps down off the slightly raised slab. She turns and gestures with her hand at the gently curving crack in the concrete. Finch follows her lead as her arm slowly traces out an arc on the ground running north from the gates and swinging around behind the intersection and across in front of the restaurant. The crack traces a giant circle on the ground.

"If this is an earthquake, it's scribed an almost perfect circle through the intersection," she says. "More than likely, we're witnessing the formation of a sinkhole opening up next to the United Nations here in New York. As I speak, the fire department and paramedics are arriving on the scene."

Cathy surprises herself at just how convincing she sounds, and that point about a sinkhole is right on. She's sure of herself. Finch pans around to catch a shot of more police arriving from the south.

Cathy is curious. The massive slab making up the intersection is still on the move. She bends down and picks up an empty Coke can, standing it next to the raised lip of concrete.

The emergency crews evacuate the surrounding buildings. Paramedics focus on setting up an emergency triage point south of the intersection, immediately in front of the United Nations building. Hundreds of dazed office workers and restaurant patrons pour out onto the street. Police clear the area, establishing a cordon some fifty feet further back.

Several other news crews arrive on the scene but they are kept at bay by the police. Cathy and Finch are on the north-east side of the intersection, backing onto the gate to the U.N. complex, well away from the main buildings, allowing them to escape the initial attention of the police. Cathy looks at Finch. He's soaking it up, loving the opportunity to capture so much raw footage.

"Hey, get a shot of this," Cathy says, pointing at the Coke can. Already, the lip of the circular slab has risen higher than the can. "This thing's still moving. Whatever's happening here, it's not over yet."

Finch bends down, getting a long shot of the torn concrete edge. From there, he zooms slowly across the intersection and down East 45th Street where the tilt causes the far side of the slab to dip well below the road.

"What do you make of the flags?" Cathy asks, forgetting for a second that she is still reporting through a wireless lapel microphone clipped on her blouse as a back up.

Finch turns to film the flag poles just twenty or so feet behind them. Several of the severed flagpoles have drifted higher, suspended in midair, separated from the lower flagpoles by over a foot.

"That is some weird shit," Finch says, not thinking about

the broadcast.

"Why don't they fall down?" Cathy asks. "What on Earth is keeping them up there?"

"Who said anything about Earth?" Finch replies, and Cathy feels a shiver run down her spine regardless of the heat.

"How did they get sliced up like that?" Finch asks. "It's a clean cut. It's as though they've been hit with a buzz-saw or a laser beam or something."

The police finally catch up with them, herding them away from the intersection to the northern cordon. The fire department clears the intersection, moving the vehicles and people off the unstable slab.

From a distance, Finch zooms back in. The eastern edge of the slab is now almost four feet above the Coke can, but that isn't what scares Cathy. Dozens of flags are still floating in mid-air, suspended some four or five feet above the severed flagpoles they once joined, and they're moving higher still. On the other side of the intersection, the shattered building fragments are on the move as well, but they're sliding slowly down toward the ground. They jut out of their original positions, slipping toward the concrete, but they don't fall. The whole intersection twists, slowly rotating to the west, following the afternoon sun.

"What the hell are we dealing with," Finch asks.

Cathy doesn't have any answers. Her bluster is gone. She thought she understood what was happening, but now she's confused and bewildered.

CLASS

The East Side Village Community School was started by a group of parents worried about the future of their children. Crime and drugs were rampant in the area, and the government seemed unable or unwilling to address problems in the local public school. To make sure the kids got a decent start in life, the community started its own school. With a mixture of Black, Hispanic and Asian kids, Americans of European descent were in the minority.

David Teller teaches physics and chemistry to all ages, which is unusual in New York City. Normally, these topics aren't taught as separate subjects until high school, but like the parents that founded the East Side Community school, Teller believes in the power of education to awaken young minds.

Originally, Teller didn't have any ambitions to be a teacher.

At college, he studied for a bachelor of science, majoring in astronomy. Stargazing was always a passion. As a young boy, he loved catching fireflies in a jar on a hot summer's night. He'd look up at the moon, dreaming of walking on its surface like Armstrong and Aldrin.

The speed of light always fascinated Teller. His father explained that light takes about eight minutes to travel from the sun to the moon. It would then reflect off the moon and, roughly a second later, young David would see it. The idea of light bouncing around like a cosmic pinball seemed at odds with the instantaneous impression his young mind had of light, and his interest in astronomy grew from that fascination. Teller wanted to see just how fast light was. He'd shine a laser pointer in the bathroom, waving it around like a light saber, but try as he might, he was never quick enough to see the light emerge from his pointer before it reflected off the mirror.

Teller's bedroom walls were covered with posters of astronauts floating in space or walking on the moon, along with images of galaxies and nebulae. As a teen, he saved up and bought his own telescope. It was more suited to bird watching than staring at the night sky, but he could make out the faint smudge that marked the Andromeda galaxy, and he could see the blurred gold and blue sparkle of the International Space Station as it orbited the Earth. For Teller, those blurry images were as good as anything from the Hubble Space Telescope.

College, though, brought out the worst in Teller. Astronomy was no longer fun. With time on his hands, his interests wandered. After his first year, he switched to major in biology. His father thought he was on drugs, but it was a girl that swayed his thinking.

Lisa was bright and bubbly. The world of Charles Darwin, the voyage of the Beagle, the concept of Natural Selection—Lisa made history come alive for him. They had plans—dreams. They were going to travel the world together, fight to protect the rainforests of South America, journey to Indonesia to raise orangutans, move on to Thailand to protect tigers and elephants in the wild, before heading to Australia to protest against Japanese whaling in the southern oceans. Then, one day, Lisa didn't show up for class, she missed her lectures.

Lisa had driven down to Virginia to visit her folks over a long weekend, but she hadn't returned. It took the local police three agonizing days to find her. When they dragged her car from a lake barely four miles from her home they found her body trapped inside, still wearing a seatbelt. It had rained that weekend. Perhaps she was driving too fast, perhaps the road was slick, perhaps she'd been distracted as she approached the bend, perhaps she swerved to avoid a stray dog or a deer. Teller would never know.

He was devastated. Later that week, he drove to the spot where she'd lost control and was shocked to see how little there was revealing the tragedy. There weren't any obvious skid marks.

Lisa had missed the safety barrier leading into the corner by less than a foot. A fraction of a second had made the difference between life and death. The low-lying shrubs and trees along the bank had some bark scraped off them and a couple of broken twigs, but nothing more than that. There was a slight indentation where the wheels of her car had crossed the shoulder of the road, just a couple of errant tire tracks in the soft clay. The drop to the water was no more than fifteen feet, but the lake was deep.

The police said her car would have gone under in seconds. They were considerate and professional. They told Teller there was a mark on the side of her head where she hit the pillar of the door as the car twisted on impact. This, they said, would have knocked her unconscious. She wouldn't have felt anything—no pain, no panic, no fear. Teller wasn't sure if they were just being kind, trying to soften the blow. He hoped they were right. His heart broke to think of her being hurt and alone in those final few moments.

Teller struggled with the senseless loss. The swiftness with which a beautiful life had been lost left him in shock. He blamed himself. He should have gone with her. He should have been the one driving. Things could have been so different. But there are no second chances in life, no re-runs. Teller was left with an immense sense of guilt and loss.

He dropped out of college and worked as a waiter for a few months, trying to find solace in a bottle, but that only made his despair worse. It was his sister who came to the rescue. She was a preschool teacher. She dragged him along on a couple of field trips to help out with the kids. Teller was surprised by how much he enjoyed himself. The kids were little horrors, but that didn't seem to matter. He found a sense of joy in their inquiring minds.

After that, Teller returned to college determined to become a teacher, and he excelled where once he floundered.

It's Monday morning. The East Side Village Community School is his second teaching position, and he loves it.

The anomaly dominated the news over the weekend.

The kids from his fifth grade class pour into the classroom in an avalanche of noise and confusion, yelling and laughing, pushing and jostling with each other. They come from a kaleidoscope of social backgrounds, and he loves their diversity. The world should be more child-like. Kids don't care about the color of someone's skin or the style of clothing they wear. All they care about is playing ball. In their innocence, they haven't learned to separate into religious or social cliques. And the reason is clear, they all have one thing in common, their excitement for life.

Teller sits on the edge of his desk at the front of the classroom. He flicks a switch as the commotion dies down and the overhead projector hums, showing an image of the United Nations building just a few miles north of them. The kids react immediately, pointing at the screen and talking over the top of each other, their eyes lighting up with excitement.

The slab of concrete that previously formed the middle of the intersection lies on a steep angle over against East 45th Street, tilting toward the morning sun rising slowly over the river. Twelve floors carved out of the State Department building are suspended in the sky, hundreds of feet above a gaping hole in the ground. The flags are just a foot or so above the road, but they're slowly moving toward their severed flagpoles still standing inert beside the U.N. building. The flags flutter in the breeze, apparently unaware of how remarkable it is for them to be disembodied and levitating even just a few feet above the ground.

Several trailers have been set up around the roads approaching the intersection, marking portable site offices established for the engineers and scientists who have gathered from around the country, but the largest contingent is just outside the barricade—the media. All the major networks are present. The park adjacent to the U.N. building has become a sea of tents and trailers spilling out onto the road.

"Okay," Teller says. "I'm guessing from your excitement you all saw the news over the weekend. So, who knows what this is?"

Hands shoot into the air as the kids respond to his well-rehearsed routine. They all want to be the first one to blurt out the answer, but for the most part they resist calling out. Several kids call out his name, begging to be picked, but Teller ignores them, picking Johnny, a young black child sitting in the middle of the class. Johnny stands and speaks proudly.

"It's the anom-ma-la-ly. At least, that's what they're calling it on TV."

Teller smiles.

"It's a funny word, isn't it?" he says. "It's a bit hard to get your tongue around. Why do you think they're calling this an anomaly? Does anyone know what the word anomaly means?"

Susan Parker sits in the front row. She is an exceptionally bright student from a Hispanic background. Her father is a drunk, while her mother works nights, trying desperately to raise her family out of poverty. Teller has high hopes for Susan. She has the potential to go far beyond the East Village. He picks Susan. She stands up, beaming with pride.

"An anomaly is something strange or unusual, something that is not normal."

"Good answer. And what do you think? Do you think this is an anomaly?"

Her face glows. She enjoys being asked her opinion. Susan responds with an emphatic "Yes."

"Why is it an anomaly?" Teller asks, trying not to trip over his own words. The phrase "an anomaly" is a tongue twister.

"Because it isn't natural," one of the more impulsive students blurts out.

Teller smiles, saying, "No, it's not. Is it?"

Teller moves his computer mouse and brings up a time-lapse video that condenses the motion of the anomaly over 24 hours down to 60 seconds. The students watch in awe as the slab of concrete, the flags and the building fragments shift effortlessly through the air, twisting and turning upside down hundreds of feet above the ground. Spotlights light up the motion of the slab over the course of the night.

Despite reports to the contrary, the concrete slab within the intersection never turns completely over. At its peak, it tilts down on a wildly unexpected angle, moving in a smooth arc as it swings through the air over toward East 45th Street. The anomaly is moving off-center as it turns on itself, which makes it all the more mesmerizing to watch.

Watching its daily motion compressed into barely a minute, the arc reminds Teller of being at the circus as a child, watching a motorcycle warm up inside the Wheel of Death. The name is overly dramatic—no one ever died. But the steel cage, in the shape of a large sphere some thirty feet in height, was impressive. As the motorcycle inside the cage got up to speed, it would start with small loops. The bike would go faster and faster, climbing higher and higher until it went completely upside down over the inside of the cage, and the crowd roared with excitement. To Teller, the anomaly seems right on the verge of going completely upside down, but it doesn't quite make it. The anomaly moves effortlessly through the air, twisting and turning, but passing just shy of being entirely upside down before sliding back toward the intersection.

By midnight, the slab is several hundred feet above the road, tilting down at the ground on an acute angle. The concrete intersection faces north, looking down along 1st Avenue as it floats above the gaping, concave hole in the ground. The traffic lights and the tree on the levitating slab hang on an angle.

As dawn breaks on the video, the slab twists sideways over by East 45th, slowly sliding down into the hole in the road as the sun rises in the sky. By noon, all the pieces of the jigsaw puzzle appear to have moved back in place before they set off again on yet another circuit.

The clip loops, repeating every minute, always showing the unnatural sight of the flags, the dismembered floors from several buildings and the intersection rotating freely through the air.

"Do you know what it is, Mr. Teller?" Susan asks.

"Oh, I know what it is," Teller says, raising his eyebrows

slightly as he leans forward toward his students.

The class falls silent as he continues.

"I know exactly what it is."

He pauses, enjoying their rapt attention. For Teller, this is what teaching is about—inspiring young minds.

"It's interesting."

The kids look perplexed.

"It's fascinating."

"No," cries one of the children from the back of the room. "What is it really?"

"It really is interesting," Teller repeats, smiling.

A couple of the kids sigh. They are clearly hoping for more from their science teacher.

"You see, science isn't about having answers," Teller begins. "Science is about asking questions. That is what makes the anomaly so fascinating. We don't know what it is. We don't know how it moves the pavement around or why those flags don't fall to the ground or how those sections of the various buildings are suspended in mid-air, all rotating around some invisible point in the middle of a giant imaginary sphere. We have no idea how this could happen and that makes it exciting. Scientists love questions."

"I like answers," one of the Asian boys says.

Teller laughs. "We all like answers. But there are some things in life for which there are no answers, just lots of questions. So how can science help us with this question? What do you think the scientists are doing down there?"

"Are they scanning it?" asks one of the Indian girls.

"Hmm," Teller says. "I'm sure they are scanning it with something. In the movies, they'd have a fancy scanner that could tell them all about the anomaly, but in real life, things aren't quite so simple."

"What else?" Teller asks, provoking some discussion among the children. "What do you think they're doing? What do you think we can learn about the anomaly?"

Johnny stands up. "We can't learn anything about it, because we don't know anything about it."

"Well, not quite," Teller says softly. "There's a lot we do know about the anomaly."

That gets everyone's attention. Teller looks around the classroom. Several of the kids are leaning forward on their desks, their elbows on the tabletops, their heads resting on their palms. He has them eating out of his hand.

"We know how big it is. Whatever this anomaly is, it has a diameter of roughly 130 meters, that's about 425 feet. Can anyone tell me why we describe its diameter in meters instead of feet?"

There's silence. No one wants to offer an answer.

"We use meters, or metrics, in science rather than miles, yards, feet and inches because metrics work in units of ten, making it easy to calculate. Everyone knows how to multiply by ten, right? Scientists are weird creatures. They're really smart, but being smart, they know how easy it is to make dumb mistakes, so instead of using old style measurements, they simplify everything. Isn't that smart? They use a simple measuring system to make hard calculations that little bit easier."

Heads nod.

"So if the anomaly has a diameter of 130 meters, what is its radius?"

Teller can see the kids thinking. Within a few seconds, someone blurts out, "70."

"65," he replies. "But 70 is a good approximation. The diameter is the width of a circle, whereas the radius is half of that. Why is it so important to know the radius? What is it about the radius that makes it important for us to understand?"

Frowns appear on brows around the room as the kids fight conceptually to see where he's leading them. Susan knows. Her arm is outstretched in a flash, but Teller keeps her waiting. He wants to see who else will figure it out. After a few seconds, he points at Susan. She jumps to her feet again.

"The radius is the distance from the center of a circle to the edge."

"And why is that important when it comes to our

wonderfully curious anomaly?"

"Because it shows us where the center of the anomaly is?" Susan ventures, going out on a limb with her answer.

"Exactly," Teller says. He pauses the time-lapse video and points roughly at the middle of the open air between the flags, the building fragments, and the concrete slab.

"And look at that. The center is somewhere high above the ground. It's in this area right here. Everything is revolving around an invisible axis running right through here. On the news, everyone talks about the flags and the concrete slab because you can see them and they look impressive, but the really important part of the anomaly is right here, in this empty bit, because that's the center around which everything revolves."

The kids hang on his every word.

"So you see," he continues. "This is all the math and physics we are doing in the first semester. If the anomaly has a diameter of 130 meters, then its circumference is its diameter times pi, making it almost 400 meters round, so it would take quite a while to walk around the edge. It would be like walking the length of four football fields.

"Oh, and our anomaly isn't a flat circle, is it? We can't see most of it as it's mostly made up of air, but it is a sphere. We can't see all of it, but if we could, it might look like a giant marble or a soccer ball. And objects in three dimensions are much bigger than those in two dimensions. Our anomaly has a surface area of over 50,000 square meters, so if you wanted to wrap it up for

Christmas you'd need an awful lot of fancy paper.

"Remember the concept of volume? That's how much stuff something can hold. Well, our anomaly holds over a million meters cubed."

There are blank looks on the faces of the children. Although it's an impressively large number, it means nothing to them in practice.

"How many of you have been swimming in the Olympic pool over near the FDR on-ramp?"

Hands go up all around the classroom.

"Well, it would take over four hundred of those swimming pools to fill up our anomaly."

The scale of the numbers surprises and fascinates the children. They laugh and giggle at the idea. The local swimming pool puts a million cubic meters in perspective for them.

"Wouldn't it leak out?" Susan asks rather seriously.

Teller smiles, saying, "Yes, it would. But if it was a sealed container, it would hold all that water, and that tells us something important about the anomaly—its capacity. That tells us how large it is. And one of the first things the scientists would have looked for is to see if the anomaly was growing, if its capacity was increasing."

Susan has a worried look on her face.

"But it's not," Teller is quick to point out, realizing none of the kids have considered that possibility before now. "The anomaly has stayed the same size for several days now. You see, all of these small details help us build an accurate understanding of the anomaly, they help us to understand the nature of what we're dealing with."

"And we also know how fast it is moving," he continues. "Who can tell me what speed is a measure of?"

One of the quieter boys at the back raises his hand. Teller nods, signaling for him to go ahead with his explanation.

"I know that one," the boy says. "Because it's like a car, isn't it? It's miles per hour, or how many miles you would go after driving for one hour."

"Very good," Teller says, complementing the young boy. "Whether we are talking about miles per hour or kilometers per hour, speed is the distance an object moves over a certain period of time."

"Our anomaly is actually moving very slowly. Its circumference is 400 meters, and it takes one full day to turn around, so it is turning at 400 meters per day or only 16 meters in an hour. That's about the length of this room in one hour. So in the time you've been sitting in this class, the anomaly has probably only moved past the back row of desks."

Almost in unison, the kids all turn and look at the back of the room. Having a visual yardstick helps them put the anomaly in context.

"I can ride my bike faster than that," cries one of the kids.

"I can walk faster than that," adds another.

"I could wiggle on my belly faster than that," says a third and the kids laugh.

"Yep," Teller says. "As impressive as our anomaly is, it isn't actually moving that fast at all, is it?"

"No," the class replies.

"But do you want to know what I find interesting about the anomaly?"

The classroom is quiet with anticipation, watching as Teller switches between computer programs, bringing up a high-resolution image of the concrete slab. The photo was taken as the slab reached its zenith high overhead, while it was tilting down facing the road. Teller zooms in on the floodlit gutter.

"Look at the litter. Look at the scraps of paper, the leaves and small twigs. Oh, and there's an empty McDonald's shake and a Pepsi can."

The kids look unsure of the importance of trash lying in a gutter.

"Look at the leaves of the tree and the traffic light. They're hanging up instead of swinging down. The most amazing thing about our anomaly is that the trash hasn't fallen. Our anomaly is defying gravity."

There are smiles as a sense of wonder and awe dawns on

the children.

"So what would happen if you are standing there?" asks one of the girls. "Would you fall off? Would your hair hang down?"

"I expect you'd stand there thinking you're the right way up, wondering why the rest of the city is upside down on such a silly, topsy-turvy angle."

The children laugh.

"There are a lot of other interesting things we can learn about the anomaly, and all of them help make it not-quite-so-scary. We can calculate the force with which it's moving. We can calculate the angle on which it is moving, because it's not turning completely upside down as it flips over the top, so it is moving on a slightly different plane to what we'd expect."

"But we still don't know what it is," Johnny insists as Teller starts handing out parent permission slips.

"No, we don't," Teller replies. "But we know it's interesting. And tomorrow, we're going to go and see it for ourselves."

That puts a smile on all their faces.

CONTACT

Less than half of the class brings back permission slips. Only eleven children are allowed to go on the field trip to see the anomaly first-hand, although it seems it isn't for lack of trying on the part of the kids, who enthusiastically plead with Teller to let them go. Teller can't take them against their parents' wishes. He's pleased to see Susan got permission from her mother. Susan says something about her uncle being there with the scientists, but Teller misses it in all the commotion.

With eleven children and two adults, Teller sets out for Midtown East using public transport. News reports say the best viewing spots are along 45th Street, particularly from some of the adjacent buildings, like the Millennium Plaza, which means these are places to avoid. Sure enough, as the bus crawls north along 3rd Avenue, he sees large crowds forming, blocking the streets approaching the anomaly from the west. The kids all peer from the windows of the bus, hoping for a glimpse of the anomaly as they drive by, but Susan is more interested in playing with the gyroscope Teller has brought along.

They get off the bus at 50th Street, walk three blocks east and follow the back streets and alleyways south to the rear entrance of the park beside the U.N. building.

Already, the media circus has halved. Five days in and nothing else even remotely sensational has happened. The anomaly is still newsworthy, but only as a curiosity. It is no longer leading the news, which is fine by Teller as it makes it easier to move through the park and over toward the intersection. He's even more excited than the kids.

Walking into the park just after 11am, they see the United Nations General Assembly building visible through the trees. Apart from the gash on the top corner, marking where the building is ripped open, there doesn't appear to be anything too much out of the ordinary. The slice out of the State Department building is visible above the trees, but as the pieces are set to align around noon, the dislocated fragments look like some exotic modern art display jutting out from the main building.

A large crowd mills around on the grassy field.

There's not much to see. The concrete slab with its lone maple tree and traffic lights, along with the flags and building fragments drift slowly toward their original positions. The anomaly looks almost normal. Almost.

Hot-dog stands, portable coffee machines, and corporate marquees are dotted around the tiny park, sprawling out onto the now defunct road. Street vendors sell balloons and cotton-candy. There's even the occasional beggar asking for money. Most of the kids are more interested in the sideshows than the anomaly, but Susan keeps peering into the distance, staying close by Teller, eagerly looking forward to seeing the anomaly up close.

A couple of the kids want to buy balloons, and it isn't hard to see why. In a testament to capitalism and the speed with which niche marketing can corner an opportunity, helium-filled balloons depicting the anomaly are for sale from numerous stalls.

The balloons are transparent, with the image of the concrete slab on one side, the building fragments just a bit further around and the disembodied flags on the other side. Teller is impressed. It actually isn't a bad representation and will make a handy prop when talking about the anomaly to the kids back at school, so he buys one. A couple of the kids also buy balloons with their pocket money.

Susan doesn't have any extra money. She has a packed lunch and a water bottle, but no pocket money for treats. Her eyes light up when Teller hands her his balloon. She holds the string tight, determined not to let it go. Ah, well, it was worth it to see the look of joy on her face. He knows he can never take the balloon back, but he's confident there will be plenty of them to go around in the days and weeks ahead. Capitalism is nothing if not prolific.

Teller ties a loop in the string, allowing Susan to have the string looped loosely around her wrist so the balloon doesn't float away. Susan is so excited she jumps for joy, proudly showing off her anomaly to the other kids.

A couple of the kids pester Teller for balloons and he laments what is quickly turning into an expensive exercise. There are three other children who don't have any additional money, and they all want a balloon. At five dollars a balloon, Teller decides he won't fall for this again, but he smiles, pays for more balloons and hands them around.

The school group comes up to the police barrier, almost a hundred feet from the outer edge of the anomaly. Security is tight with police and security guards standing just ten to fifteen feet apart behind the wooden barricade, with their backs to the anomaly as they look out at the crowd. There are hundreds of them, which surprises Teller.

Beyond the barricades lie the research trailers and the various observation posts, all blocking the kids' view of the anomaly. But, Teller points out to the students that if they stand in one spot for a while and look carefully, they can just make out the motion of the anomaly. There's a tree on a strange angle, a traffic light with a slight lean that seems to slowly straighten, and the building fragments are moving back together as though the State Department is fixing itself.

Teller pulls out his small gyroscope. It is a kid's toy. He sets the center of the gyroscope spinning and starts fiddling with the outer hoops. He begins explaining to the kids how gyroscopes always point in the same direction no matter which way they turn.

A reporter comes over to him, having seen him talking with the kids.

"Hi, my name's Cathy Jones," she says, reaching out and shaking his hand. "I'm a reporter with Community Channel Four here in New York."

"Ah, hello," Teller replies, not sure what the appropriate response is beyond a simple greeting. "David Teller. I teach basic science at the East Side Village Community School."

Cathy's cameraman mumbles something about finches from behind his camera lens. The camera is impersonal and imposing, like staring down the barrel of a gun.

"Sorry, Finch is a bit of an oddball," Cathy says, gesturing to her cameraman. "Can I talk to you for a few minutes? Now that the initial interest around the anomaly has died down, we're looking for some human interest stories, and I saw you were here with a school group. That's interesting."

"Oh, I guess it is," Teller says, feeling caught off guard. "But, ah. I can't. I'd need clearance from the school and parents before I could let the kids appear on TV."

"Oh, I know," Cathy says, flirting with him. Teller is confused by how she agrees with him and yet still persists in pushing for an interview. "I'd rather be back in the office, but my producer insists that this is my story, so I'm stuck down here, talking to everyone and anyone."

Teller nods, not sure what he's supposed to say in reply but agreeing anyway. Cathy has an all-encompassing personality that seems to sweep him along like a candy wrapper in a storm.

"Finch is a big kid," she says, flipping her hand toward her cameraman in a casual, almost distracted manner. "He's more interested in junk food and specialty coffees."

Teller smiles, saying, "Yeah, it does look like a county fair, doesn't it?"

"Just a few words," Cathy implores him. "We'll keep the kids off camera."

Teller's a sucker for a pretty lady. What harm could come from a short interview? Knowing his luck, the best it will do is a 30 second clip on YouTube. He's not likely to make it onto the evening news.

He nods.

"Great," Cathy says, with a spring in her step. She positions herself beside him, angling her body so she's half-facing him, half-facing Finch and his camera.

"I'm here outside the U.N. with grade school teacher David Teller from the East Side Village Community School, bringing his science class to the streets.

"David, why did you bring the kids here to see the anomaly? What do you think is so special about this bizarre phenomenon?"

Teller smiles for Cathy rather than the camera, even though he feels awkward, still fiddling with his toy gyroscope. He hopes she doesn't ask him about it, but she doesn't seem to notice it.

"Well, the anomaly is unique," he begins, trying to relax and lose himself in his reply. "It is like nothing we, or our parents, or our grandparents, or anyone else on this planet has ever seen before. For these kids, this could very well be the key defining moment of their young lives. Instead of growing up in the dark specter of some catastrophic, epoch-defining event like 9-11 or the assassination of President Kennedy, these kids will grow up talking about how the anomaly reshaped their world."

Teller sees the look of surprise on her face. She seems genuinely surprised by this notion. Like most of the other reporters he's heard covering this story, she probably only sees the anomaly in the sensationalism of the moment. History is never obvious to those caught in the moment.

"Why do you say that?" she asks. The curiosity in her voice tells him she's asking more for her own benefit than that of the camera.

"Scientific milestones are few and far between," Teller replies. "And they normally pass completely unnoticed and remain unrecognized for decades, but this, well, this is something that has seized our attention in a most remarkable way."

"What do you think it is?" she asks.

Teller thinks for a moment before replying.

"What do I think it is? I think it's complicated," he begins. "I don't know any more than anyone else, but I suspect the anomaly is far more intricate and complex than we dare to imagine."

"Well, social media is alive with speculation," Cathy says. "Some think it's alive. Others say it is an alien artifact. Others speculate on it being a portal to another dimension, while still others say it is the result of two parallel universes colliding and collapsing. What do you think?"

"Well, I think those are all very grand and interesting ideas.

It could be any one of those or none of them. The only way we'll find out for sure will be by observing it, by studying it."

The kids are bored with the news crew and disappointed with the anomaly. Having been fed on spectacular images in the media and time-lapse photography, it is a bit of an anti-climax to see the concrete slab sitting low against the ground at this time of day.

"Well, thank you for your time, David," Cathy says, turning to face the camera. "This is Cathy Jones, reporting from what should have been World Education Week at the United Nations, only it seems we're set to learn far more than anyone expected."

She holds a smile for a few seconds before adding, "That's a wrap."

Finch swings the camera down from his face.

"Thanks," Teller says, having enjoyed talking to Cathy.

His assistant teacher has the kids sitting down next to an idle diesel generator, taking a drink break. In an instant, Teller knows something's wrong. A quick head count, and he's missing one child.

Susan.

"Where's Susan?" he asks.

The other teacher gets to her feet, saying, "I—I don't know."

"Stay here," he says, turning and scanning the crowd. Susan was wearing a red jacket and holding a balloon, but the crowd is comprised of adults, making it impossible to see a small child.

"Is everything okay?" Cathy asks, seeing the concern on his face.

"I've lost a child," Teller says, resisting the temptation to say, 'We lost a child.' Teller takes his responsibility for the kids personally. There's no one to blame. No one but himself.

Cathy spins around, scanning the crowd.

"We'll help," she says, and Teller senses she feels guilty, but it's not her fault.

Teller works his way through the crowd, calling out, "Susan. SUSAN!" But the noise around them is overwhelming. Everyone's talking. Cathy follows close behind him. Finch doesn't seem as bothered, hanging back a little, but Cathy clearly feels awful about a lost little girl.

"Where would she have gone?" Cathy asks, pushing her way up next to Teller. "Could she have gone to the bathroom?"

"No, we just had a bathroom break," Teller replies. "At a guess, she wants to get a better look at the anomaly."

Teller pushes through the bustling crowd and suddenly he's standing before a barricade, still holding the gyroscope in his hand, but he's gripping it like a baseball.

"Excuse me," he calls out, getting the attention of a police officer standing well beyond the barricade.

Police officers stand evenly spread some twenty to thirty

feet apart with their backs to the anomaly, carefully watching the crowd.

"We've lost a child," Teller says, but the officer doesn't approach. "A young girl in a red jacket."

The officer doesn't reply, he just shakes his head and continues scanning the crowd. Not his problem, clearly. Teller is patient with kids, but not with adults that are indifferent and uncaring. He finds himself grinding his teeth in annoyance. A little empathy would be appreciated, perhaps directing him to a police command center, but Teller decides not to let the officer get to him. And that's when he sees her. Susan is standing over by the NASA trailer in front of the anomaly. She is talking to an official—a tall man dressed in a dark suit.

"That's her," he tells the officer, pointing. "That's Susan. I need to go and get her."

"I'm sorry," the officer replies. "My instructions are clear. No unauthorized personnel beyond this point."

"Yes, I understand that," Teller pleads, frustrated by the mindless bureaucracy standing before him. "But surely you can see that she's unauthorized and she's beyond this point. All I want to do is to go and bring her back here so she's not unauthorized and not beyond this point."

Teller is more than a little patronizing, but he can't help himself. He has a real disdain for authority when it is exercised without reason. And he knows his smart-ass comment, however subtle, isn't helping things.

"I'm sorry, sir. I cannot allow you to do that," the officer replies, turning sideways so he can see Susan. "I'll call command and we'll get someone to bring her over to you, but you cannot go in there."

"But she's a child. You clearly want to keep people away from the anomaly. She's already halfway there. All I'm going to do is bring her back. I'll be no more than thirty seconds."

The officer rests his hand on his holster as he calls in a request to have Susan escorted back to the barricade. There is no way Teller is crossing the line. At least, not alive.

Cathy flashes her press credentials, saying, "Look, I've been in the restricted area already. I was in there when this all began. How about I go and get her?"

"I can't let you do that, ma'am."

"Susan," Teller calls out, waving his arms at her. "SUSAN!"

Susan looks over at him, along with the man in the suit. She waves back, while the stranger talks to one of the officers next to him, who in turn speaks into a radio. Within a few seconds, the officer blocking Teller's way receives a message through his earpiece. He looks at Teller without any emotion and beckons him with a nod of his head. Teller doesn't need prompting. He ducks under the barricade. Cathy follows his lead, ducking under the railing as well.

Finch remains behind the barricade. He holds his camera by his side, casually recording the whole incident.

"Susan," Teller says on reaching her. "You can't wander off like that."

"It's my fault," says the man standing with her. He holds out his hand. "James Mason, Director of National Security."

Teller shakes his hand, a little confused as Cathy comes jogging up beside them.

"Susan's my niece. Her mother and I grew up just ten minutes south of here."

"Oh," Teller says, surprised.

"Susan's been telling me all about you," he continues with a warm smile. "She says you're the best science teacher ever."

Teller laughs awkwardly, saying, "Kids, huh?"

Mason smiles, rubbing his hand through his niece's hair.

Teller hasn't taken in where they are standing. They're in front of a white trailer with the NASA logo proudly displayed on the side. Several monitors and computer screens have been set up outside the trailer. Scientists mill around, talking with each other. Several of them are standing with Mason.

"Tell him," Susan says. "Tell him about the gyroscope, just like you told me."

Teller blushes.

Mason looks down at the toy in Teller's hand.

He's a burly man. At a guess, Teller pictures him as a

quarterback in college—a jock with brains and charisma. His muscular physique seems to burst out of his suit, while his physical prowess and his crew-cut hair make him look menacing. Being vaguely aware of politics, Teller knows Mason was a personal appointee of President Robert Laver. That Mason is intelligent is beyond dispute, but he's also kind, caring for his niece.

Teller feels intimidated even though Mason is at pains to make him feel relaxed.

"I was trying to tell him," Susan says, looking up at Teller. "I was trying to explain to him that the anomaly is not moving—we are. I told him the anomaly's pointing, but now you can explain it."

Mason smiles. He clearly isn't expecting much from a grade school teacher. But Susan is animated, and Mason seems happy to entertain her enthusiasm. Teller, however, feels like a fool. It is one thing to entertain the imagination of his kids with his thoughts on the anomaly, talking with the Director of National Security, though, is entirely different.

"I gotta tell you," Mason says. "This thing has stirred up a whole lot of fear and uncertainty, but so far we have no idea what it is. We've got scientists coming in from all around the country to examine it, but as you've seen on television, there's not much to it. It just keeps turning over and over again, with no reason as to why."

"Staying still," Susan says, pulling on the leg of his trousers as she corrects him. "It's not moving. It's standing still and pointing into space."

Mason rubs her head fondly.

"So what's it pointing at?" Mason asks. Teller is surprised by his patience, assuming someone at this level of government service would be an all-American action man, firing from the hip and hitting bandits at a hundred yards, but Mason is calm, content to consider the moving/not-moving concept. A couple of the scientists are also listening, a little curious as to who the director is talking to.

"It's pointing at home," Susan says proudly. Teller shrinks just a little. He feels as though he's a fish out of water, especially with the NASA scientists milling around in their navy blue polo shirts. They look focused, determined. He imagines the scoffing and ridicule he is about to face with his petty theory.

"Home?" Mason asks, intrigued. He looks at Teller, saying, "So you think you know why this thing is moving?"

"Well, technically," Teller begins, feeling as though he is tiptoeing through a minefield, "everything is in motion in one way or another. We look at the anomaly as though it's moving and we're stationary, but it is equally valid to say it's stationary and we're moving. It's remaining fixed, always facing in the same direction, while the direction we're facing constantly changes as we rotate around the Earth's axis."

Standing beside him, Cathy looks confused. The scientists, though, are interested.

Teller hands Mason the gyroscope, giving the weight inside the mount a spin.

"It's like this—like a gyroscope mounted on gimbals. The law of the conservation of angular momentum keeps the gyroscope always pointing in the same direction. Only with us, instead of the gimbal frame moving, it's the Earth that's moving. As the Earth turns each day, the anomaly remains stationary relative to the stars, always facing the same patch of sky regardless of which way we turn."

Mason seems lost in thought. Teller points at the anomaly as he continues.

"Look at the bowl of earth beneath the concrete slab. It looks and moves like the dish of a radio telescope tracking a single star over the course of a night.

"We tend to think of ourselves, our homes, this road, those buildings, these trees, as fixed in place. We think of them as stationary, but they're not, they're moving, spinning around as the Earth turns each day. New York is constantly changing the direction it faces out into space as the Earth rotates, so the anomaly is compensating and remaining still, staying stationary, fixed on a certain part of the sky, just like a radio telescope would if it was looking at something interesting in the heavens."

The NASA scientists are intensely interested in Teller's comments.

"Okay," says one of the older scientists. "So you're saying the motion of the anomaly is an illusion, that it's not moving, we are. And the apparent motion relative to us simply allows it to keep station with another celestial body?"

"Exactly," Teller replies, impressed with how quickly he grasped the concept. "Whatever the anomaly is facing is at a right-angle to the slab, perpendicular to it."

He points up into the sky above the slowly moving concrete slab.

"Up there somewhere," Teller says somewhat absentmindedly. "I think it's pointing at something outside our solar system."

"How do you know this?" another of the scientists asks.

"Well," Teller says. "There are reports on the Internet that the anomaly's period of motion is slightly less than a full day, which is what you'd expect from something that is aligning with a point outside our solar system."

"So what's it facing? What is it pointing at?" Mason asks.

"It's pointing home," Susan says, looking up at the grown-ups standing around her, keen to be part of the conversation. To her, it's a simple concept.

"What she means," Teller says, regretting getting his kids so excited with his pet theories, "is the anomaly is facing toward its point of origin. It's pointing at Vega."

No one speaks. The silence feels awkward so Teller continues, trying to break the tension.

"It's a message. It's like a signpost saying, 'Over here.' At least, it seems to be facing the star Vega, it's hard to tell with just a rudimentary sky map and only a vague notion of its direction. So it's a guess, really."

One of the scientists whispers in Mason's ear. Mason says something back to him and he nods.

"Vega," Mason says. "Why Vega? What's so special about Vega?"

"I don't know," Teller replies. "It's a pretty ordinary star about 24 light years away from Earth."

The scientist beside Mason speaks up.

"Vega is in that movie about meeting aliens, right? Contact—with Jodie Foster."

"Ah, yeah, I guess so," Teller replies.

"Don't you find that a little surprising?" Mason asks. "That our first contact with an alien civilization would mirror a work of fiction?"

"It was written by Carl Sagan," another scientist says, coming to Teller's defense.

Teller is out of his depth. He reaches out and takes the gyroscope from Mason.

"Find me a radio telescope and point it in the same direction," Mason commands. "I want to see exactly what this thing is facing."

"I'm on to it," one of the NASA scientists replies, disappearing inside the research trailer.

"It's just an idea," Teller says, regretting saying anything at all, and wondering what he's unleashed. "Ah, we should really be going. The rest of the class is waiting."

"Oh, don't worry about them," Mason says warmly. He takes Teller by the arm and leads him to one side so Cathy and Susan can't hear what he is saying.

"I'm afraid I can't let you go, not just yet. You see, it seems you're slightly ahead of the curve on this one. You've figured out what we suspect. That this is some kind of alien spacecraft, and we're not ready to go public on this yet. We need to get in a position where we can properly manage releasing this information into the public domain.

"We need to confirm your thinking before anyone else picks up on this, as the last thing we need is more wild conspiracy theories. Give us a few hours to run the numbers on this. Let's see if you're right."

"You're detaining me?" Teller asks.

"I'm asking for your assistance," Mason says. Teller knows he's being diplomatic, but has no doubt Mason could be draconian if need be.

Mason continues, saying, "Think of this as an invitation to help. Perhaps you and your friend would like to join Susan and me for a bite to eat."

Teller gets the distinct impression that, if it comes to it, Mason would use force.

"But the kids?"

"We'll make sure they get back to school."

Mason speaks to a couple of the officials.

Cathy is excited, grinning from ear to ear. For someone he barely knows, she seems warm and friendly, perhaps too much so.

He watches as Cathy fiddles with her lapel microphone, trying to hide it from sight. Has she recorded this? He looks over at Finch behind the barricade.

Finch looks bored, kicking at pebbles on the road. Teller goes to say something to Cathy when a couple of the NASA scientists introduce themselves to him, talking warmly with him. Within a few minutes, he's forgotten about Cathy and her microphone, losing himself in discussions about the various observations they've made of the anomaly. Teller is a little intimidated, but he appreciates their expertise. They seem as interested in bouncing ideas off him as he is in learning more about the anomaly.

NEWS

The news conference is held at 6pm in response to the massive public outcry in the wake of the Vega exclusive first broadcast by Community Channel Four in New York.

Mason explodes with anger when he realizes he was recorded off-the-record by Cathy, and the Vega theory was made public. Teller gets the impression he'd love to reopen the prison at Guantanamo Bay just for Cathy, but he seems to have something else in mind, something far more torturous for a reporter.

"Before we start," he begins, sitting behind a long table in the conference/ballroom room of the Millennium Hotel just down the road from the anomaly. "I'd like to introduce you to the discussion panel."

Camera flashes go off in rapid succession. A mob of reporters, cameramen and sound techs all vie for the best shot. Although the ballroom is almost empty, being able to hold over a thousand people, the hundred or so news representatives are packed at the front of the room like they are being pushed forward from behind. The glare of the lights stuns Teller. Even Cathy is taken back by their brightness. Apparently, she's never been on this side of a media gaggle.

At the far end of the table, an aging NASA scientist introduces himself.

"Dr. Bill Anderson, Director of NASA's Ames Advanced Research Center and Chair of the Science Review Board for Harvard."

Anderson has the demeanor of everyone's grandfather. He's slightly overweight, but with a jovial smile that makes him easy to talk to. On meeting Teller before the press conference, he joked about the strands of gray hair growing out of his ears, noting that they'd migrated there from his shiny bald head. As an executive director, he said he's constantly being rebuked by the NASA management board for going too deep into the details of the various decisions being submitted for review, but he can't help it. He's a scientist at heart.

Next to Dr. Anderson sits Dr. Bates.

"Dr. Jonathan Bates, Director of SETI, the Search for Extraterrestrial Intelligence, and founder of the American Astronautical Engineering Society. Adjunct Professor of High-Energy Physics at Princeton."

Bates is fastidious in everything he does. Although he isn't wearing a tie, his shirt is neatly starched and creased. His mustache is meticulously trimmed, looking crisp and sharp. When lost in thought, he has the habit of constantly cleaning his glasses with a soft cloth. Teller figures it's a therapeutic habit. Polishing the glass must allow his mind the freedom to settle on concepts in greater detail.

Mason is next.

Although the Press already know exactly who he is, there is

a point to be made and Mason doesn't miss the opportunity to make it as vivid as possible.

"Dr. James Mason, Director of National Security and Intelligence, Presidential Advisor on Scientific Strategies. My Ph.D. is from MIT where I specialized in aeronautics."

A young African-American woman is seated between Mason and Teller. She introduces herself as, "Dr. Trissa Manias. Head of Astrobiology at Princeton, senior advisor to NASA Life Exploration team, and lead scientist on the instruments team for the Europa Deep Dive Explorer."

Teller is intimidated by the scientists on the panel, but particularly by Trissa. She couldn't be much older than him and already she has a distinguished scientific career.

Teller feels distinctly stupid.

It's his turn.

"David Teller, Bachelor's Degree in Early Childhood Development. Elementary school teacher at the East Side Village Community School."

There's silence.

"Ah," he offers in addition, "specializing in chemistry, physics, and mathematics."

He could crawl into a hole and die of embarrassment.

"Cathy Jones, reporter for Channel Four out of the Village, New York. Bachelor's Degree in Journalism."

Cathy glances back at Mason, trying to visually hand the camera's attention back to him. Teller sees she's as embarrassed and intimidated as he is. Their eyes meet, and he knows she's ashamed to have dragged him into this. In that instant, he feels as though he can read her mind. Here he is, a school teacher trying to find a lost student, and she's propelled him and his ad-hoc, off-the-cuff thinking onto the international stage.

Mason speaks with gravitas.

"Firstly, I'd like to clarify a few points from the unauthorized transmission of a private conversation between myself and Mr. Teller earlier today."

Mister.

Teller clenches his teeth at the stark contrast with the academic prowess of the other panel members.

Cathy sinks in her seat.

"There is no verifiable evidence that the anomaly is alien in origin. At this point, that is a speculative idea being investigated by NASA. Bill? Do you have anything you want to say on that?"

"Sure," Dr. Anderson says. "Although the anomaly appears to be moving to us, rotating and flipping over in the air, it is actually stationary in its orientation to the stars, always pointing at a single point in the sky as the Earth rotates and turns. That leads us to believe that the motion of the anomaly is extraterrestrial in origin, but it is important to note that there is nothing extraterrestrial inside the anomaly itself. This is an ordinary slab of concrete, a couple of flags, and the ruins of several buildings."

Anderson holds out his hand, rotating his palm in an attempt to provide a visual example as he speaks.

"Now, the motion of the anomaly may seem a little confusing at first, but think of the old steam trains you see in a Western movie. Picture the big, old cast-iron wheels that drive the train forward. There's a steel rod connected to the wheel, driving it around. But as the wheel turns, the steel rod always points back in the same direction, it's always pointing back at the piston. That's essentially what the anomaly is doing. As the Earth rotates, the anomaly is always pointing along the same line out into deep space."

A flurry of questions break from the floor.

Mason picks out the closest reporter.

"So is the anomaly pointing at Vega?"

"Trissa?" Mason says, deferring to her with a slight wave of his hand.

"Well, no," she says. "And this highlights the importance of thorough research over speculation and rumors. Vega is visible in the early evening at this time of the year but the anomaly is aligning with something that is roughly twenty five degrees north of the setting Sun."

She looks down at a sheet of paper to make sure she has her facts correct. "The anomaly is static with reference to an empty patch of the sky north of the ecliptic, at Right Ascension 9 hours 17 minutes and 5 seconds. Declination positive 25 degrees 25 minutes 40 seconds."

That seems to shut the reporters up, Teller notes to himself.

"So what is it pointing at?" one of the reporters asks.

"At this point, we are unsure," Mason replies. "There are no visible stars at these coordinates."

Dr. Bates speaks up.

"According to the Sloan Digital Sky Survey, the coordinates match a remote, unnamed but previously cataloged galaxy IC 2450 some seventy-five million light years from Earth. But I need to stress, this is our initial observation. It is not a conclusion and it may be subject to revision. There may well be errors in our calculations or our initial assumptions. It may be that we've read too much into the motion of the anomaly relative to the Earth and there may be no purpose in it at all."

"What constellation is it in?" asks the same reporter, angling for something specific, something tangible against which to peg the anomaly.

Mason says, "Constellations are made up of visible stars that are relatively close to Earth whereas this is so remote as to be visible only to a handful of telescopes. The idea of a constellation, in this regard, is not relevant."

"But it's in a particular region of space? Right?" the reporter insists. "Which constellation does the anomaly align with?"

Teller looks intently at Mason. Furrows appear on Mason's forehead as he considers his options in reply. Teller knows Mason is between a rock and a hard place as whatever he says will, inevitably, be taken out of context, but the media will figure it out sooner or later. Astrology is the bane of astronomy, its pseudo-counterpart. Like it or not, astrology is a part of Western culture and will get dragged into the discussion somehow. Teller bites his lip, wondering which way Mason will play this, hoping he hits any pseudo-science head on.

"It is in the northern region of Leo. But before anyone gets too excited about that, it should be noted that at a distance of seventy-five million light years, saying the point of origin is in Leo is a bit like standing on the shore of the Hudson and saying China is in New Jersey simply because they both lie in that general direction."

There is a flurry of camera flashes.

"Is there anything you would like to add?" Mason asks, turning and looking down the table at Teller.

Teller clears his throat. At first, his words come out too soft, and he finds he has to speak up to be heard properly.

"Ah, no." he replies. "I guess I was a little overzealous about Vega."

"Dr. Teller," another reporter cries.

"Mr. Teller," Mason corrects him.

"Mr. Teller. Is there anything else you can tell us about this alien anomaly?"

"Ah, Dr. Mason is right. There's no verifiable evidence that the anomaly is alien in origin. It could be a misunderstood natural phenomenon, something we've not seen before. For all we know, it could be a coincidence that the anomaly is stationary relative to the stars. It's an observation, not a conclusion. It is too early to tell for sure what the anomaly is, or why it turns as it does."

"But surely," another reporter begins, "you must appreciate the tremendous amount of interest you've generated in the alien anomaly."

'Damn reporters,' he thinks, somewhat exasperated, knowing he's done all he can to hose down speculation about the possible alien origins of the anomaly, only to have the next reporter ignore him and refer to it as 'alien' in the very next question. Sound bites, they'll be the death of civilization.

Teller glances sideways at Cathy who's trying to be as inconspicuous as possible.

Dr. Bates speaks up.

"Science is about testing ideas rather than jumping to conclusions. No one has had the time to properly analyze the anomaly. Being the head of SETI, there's no one that's more tempted than I am to jump to what appears to be the obvious conclusion, that this is indeed alien in origin. But to do so would be folly as we may end up with egg on our faces when the anomaly is shown to be something else. As difficult as it is, we need time to study the anomaly in detail."

"But you must know something," another reporter cries, buried somewhere at the back of the pack.

"We have our best and brightest minds working on this," Dr. Bates says. "But it is important to put the conspiracy theories to rest and realize how little we know about this beyond what has already been reported. There is no record of any such phenomena ever being recorded anywhere, so we are in uncharted territory.

"So far, the interior of the anomaly appears completely normal, but it operates according to some kind of localized gravity rather than Earth's gravity. There's no radiation beyond normal environmental levels. There are no force fields or anything like that. If the slab, flags and building fragments hadn't moved, we wouldn't know the anomaly was even there.

"And for those that speculate on this being an alien spaceship, it is important to note that there is nothing foreign inside or surrounding the anomaly. The only peculiarity we've been able to observe is a small build up of hydrogen at the exact spherical center of the anomaly, almost two hundred feet above the concrete slab. But the hydrogen is in small trace amounts, roughly what you'd find in a party balloon."

"They use helium," Dr. Anderson says, correcting Dr. Bates. The look on Dr. Bates' face suggests he hates being corrected, particularly in public.

Bates tries to smile politely as he continues. "You'll find

more hydrogen in your daughter's bottle of peroxide when she bleaches her hair at the start of summer break."

Dr. Anderson says, "We have no idea about the significance of the hydrogen. It could simply be an artifact, or a byproduct of the process by which this anomaly formed. Again, this is something we need to investigate further."

Mason sips his water before adding some broader comments about the political implications of the anomaly.

"I'd like to address a few comments to the international community. The advent of the anomaly has caused considerable diplomatic consternation. Please be assured that the U.S. will respond to all diplomatic inquiries and, where practical and feasible, will reply to all scientific inquiries being made in relation to the anomaly.

"We would, however, ask for your patience and understanding. Given the significance of this phenomenon, it is our intention to be transparent with the investigation, but this requires considerable logistical and organizational effort on our behalf, and that takes time to establish.

"We have accepted offers of assistance from CERN, ESA, the Russian Space Agency and the Chinese Space Agency, but there are practical considerations that go along with these offers, such as cultural and language barriers, the need for operational collaboration, and even such seemingly minor issues as housing and establishing dedicated laboratories from which to work.

"All research will be subject to standard scientific peer

review which, again, will delay any formal announcement of results, so please, bear with us. Due diligence such as this is an important part of the process that cannot be overlooked in favor of a headline for tomorrow's news."

Mason holds his hands slightly apart, with his fingers poised, lightly touching each other. Teller can see it coming. He doesn't know what Mason's going to say, but he knows Mason is ready to throw Cathy to the lions.

"Ms. Jones," he says. "You broke the Vega story. Is there anything you would like to add?"

Although she looks calm, her hands shake slightly as she holds them on the desk. Her voice quivers as she speaks.

"Ah... I'm so sorry. This is all my fault. It was rash and thoughtless of me to betray what was a casual conversation between a school teacher, one of his pupils, and her uncle. I'm sorry for causing so much confusion."

She starts sobbing.

Mason is stone faced. He isn't finished with Cathy, not yet.

"There is considerable interest from the media about access to the scientific team," he says, "Moving forward, Ms. Jones will act as the media liaison for the anomaly investigation team and will undertake daily briefing sessions for the Press."

Teller's eyes go wide, as do Cathy's.

"It is our intention to provide complete transparency into

our observations of this phenomenon so as to avoid any further speculation. We will not engage in sensational or unsubstantiated claims. I expect Ms. Jones will ensure this protocol is strictly followed so there is no repeat of the confusion that occurred today."

Cathy nods. Her head hangs low as she clenches her teeth. Teller can see she has a fiery determination to redeem herself.

HELIUM

Teller walks up to the NASA trailer with Cathy.

"You too, huh," Cathy says, seeing Finch looking despondent. His camera sits idly beside him on the ground.

"Oh, yeah," Finch replies. "A cavity search would be more fun than what I've just been through."

Cathy flinches. "That bad?"

Finch is quiet. He holds Susan's balloon, poking it with his finger like it's some kind of boxing speed bag. He clearly isn't in the mood for idle chatter.

Susan sits next to him in a deck chair, watching the slab of concrete in the distance as it slowly rises up on one side. The concrete is almost at a right-angle to the ground, appearing like a large circular wall casting a dark shadow over the United Nations building by the river. Susan sits there tossing a football idly from one hand to the other to stave off the boredom. The anomaly is supposed to be exciting, but she seems to find it slow.

Mason, Bates, Manias and Anderson walk up behind them, stopping to talk with a few of the NASA scientists some ten feet away. With the news conference over, there's a lot of discussion about the next steps. There is a general agreement that they've learned all they can passively, watching the anomaly from a distance. At some point, they need to probe the interior of the anomaly, but the question is how?

"What about our guests? Dr. Anderson asks Mason.

Both Teller and Cathy can hear the conversation, but Teller is conflicted. On one hand, he wants to hear what's being said, on the other he's horribly embarrassed by what's happened and wants nothing more than to disappear into the cracks in the road.

"He had some good points, some good insights," Dr. Anderson says. "A fresh perspective."

"We have no room for amateurs," Dr. Bates says in a voice that sounds hostile.

Mason says, "We're all amateurs when it comes to First Contact."

Dr. Bates protests, saying, "You're thinking about keeping him around? You can't be serious. Think about how this will look to the public. We need scientists, not school teachers."

"Earth isn't a planet full of scientists," Dr. Trissa Manias says, keeping her voice low. "We could do with broader representation."

Dr. Anderson says, "Remember the Challenger space shuttle disaster. Group-think dominated within NASA, and we couldn't see the forest for all the damn trees—until we lost seven astronauts. A little diversity in decision making is a good thing."

Dr. Bates shakes his head in disagreement.

"Trissa?" Mason asks.

"I agree with Anderson. We're in uncharted waters. An extra pair of eyes on the look out for rocks has got to be a good thing."

"I disagree," Dr. Bates says. "He's not qualified to be here."

"He might not be qualified," Mason says. "But he's sharp. He thinks laterally."

"He was wrong about Vega," Bates says.

"He was," Mason admits. "And yet for all that, it's still been a productive afternoon."

Dr. Anderson adds his support. "I say, we keep him around."

"Me too," Trissa says.

Cathy pretends to talk to Teller, but she's listening and aware he's listening as well. She raises her eyebrows knowingly as Mason walks up behind Teller. Mason's right hand lands on Teller's shoulder with a thump.

"We'd like you to stick around a little, okay?"

Teller goes to say something in reply, wondering if 'Sure,' or 'Thank you,' would be appropriate, but Mason keeps walking. An answer isn't needed.

Mason crouches by his niece.

"I got hold of your mom," he says, bending down beside her. "She's going to be home around eight, so we'll get one of the police officers to drop you off then. Okay?"

Susan's eyes lit up at the prospect of a ride in a police car.

"Can I turn on the siren?"

"I don't know about that," Mason says, rubbing her head fondly. "Hey, where'd you get that football?"

Finch raises his hand. "Guilty, as charged. I found it in the trailer, behind one of the filing cabinets."

Susan tosses it to her uncle and he tosses it back with a smile. She passes the ball to Teller.

"Have you thought about ballistic trajectories?" Teller asks, passing the ball to Mason.

Mason grins, saying, "Are you thinking what I'm thinking?"

"I sure am," Teller replies. "All in the name of science."

"Your thoughts?" Mason asks, gripping the ball like a quarterback as he speaks to Dr. Bates.

"Well, I don't think it's going to be harmful or anything like that. I'd expect its arc would follow localized gravity, so as it passes through the anomaly it's going to fly sideways, falling toward the slab."

"Galileo would be proud," Dr. Anderson jokes, recognizing the historical precedence for the simplest of experiments when it comes to gravity.

"Boys," Trissa says, shaking her head, but she's smiling.

Like the others, she's curious too.

"Notice how the flags rustle in the breeze," Bates says. "The wind is already blowing through this thing without any adverse effect at all. We've had a couple of birds fly inside the anomaly, they pretty quickly hightailed it out of there after tumbling and struggling to orient themselves, but they were fine. I think we'll be fine."

"If anything," Dr. Anderson says, "a football is a good choice for our initial probe into the interior. It's low-tech so nothing can go wrong. It's aerodynamic and has a well understood trajectory. And it's brief. It'll give us some good metrics."

Teller likes the way they can rationalize something so childish and make it sound scientific, but they're right, it is a good, simple, first step, and it's fun.

Mason speaks into his radio. "Can you get one of those guys from the National Guard over on the south side to turn around? Tell him we're going to throw him a football."

The reply over the airways is one of surprise. The radio operator asks for confirmation.

"It's okay," Mason replies. "You heard correctly."

Teller laughs. "This is what I love about science. It can be fun if you want it to be."

Mason takes off his suit jacket and drapes it over one of the deck chairs. He loosens his tie and rolls up his sleeves. It's humid, even with the sun setting. Sweat soaks his armpits.

Together, the group walks over toward the anomaly. As he stands before the vast, circular hole in the road, Teller feels small, in awe of the size of the invisible sphere before them, distorting a portion of their world.

The concrete slab that once made up the vast intersection, with its white lines marking the road, its curb and trash can, along with the tree and the traffic lights, are almost perpendicular with the ground. They look like some crazy advert raising awareness for some obscure conservation group trying to make the concrete jungle all the more jarring to the mind by displacing it and sticking it sideways on a billboard. Teller half expects to see a Greenpeace logo somewhere near the bottom right.

The U.N. flags are hundreds of feet above him, floating effortlessly in the sky, waving in the breeze. The shattered remains of several floors from the State Department have slid into the hole in the ground. The world has gone topsy-turvy, it is as though someone has handed the architecture of the city to Dr. Seuss.

"Come on, Finch," Cathy says joining in the moment, "This is history in the making. Start the tape rolling."

"Absolutely," Mason says. "Make sure you get a good shot of this. We've got to give your buddies on the news desk something for the late edition."

On the far side of the intersection, beyond the gaping hole

in the ground, a soldier stands facing them. He yells out, "I'm open."

"How far do you think that is?" Mason asks, turning to Teller.

"Oh, I'd say it's around 40-50 yards. How good is your arm?"

"It's good enough," Mason replies with a wink. "And where should I throw this thing? On what angle do you think?"

Teller likes being asked. Mason has a way of making the people around him feel important.

"Dr. Bates is right. The football is going to fall that way, over toward the slab, so don't worry too much about height, you'll have plenty of height once the ball passes into the anomaly. Be sure to throw to the right and the ball should arc back to the left as it falls sideways toward the intersection."

"And you're sure this will be fine?" Mason asks, looking one last time at Dr. Bates and Dr. Anderson. They both nod, grinning like school kids.

Finch lines up so he can catch a side profile of the director throwing the football and then pan to follow the ball as it passes through the anomaly.

Susan is excited. She is holding her balloon, jumping up and down, saying, "Do it, Uncle James. Do it."

Mason slaps the ball hard into his right hand, and cocks his arm back. He takes a few steps and unleashes a Hail Mary pass, aiming for the spot Teller pointed at.

Deep inside, Teller wants to see something spectacular as the ball passes into the anomaly, something like sparks or St. Elmo's fire, but the ball sails effortlessly through the air. Its arc changes, though, as it passes through the air within the anomaly. Instead of following a curve toward the ground, the football holds its height while curving to the left, falling toward the near vertical slab of concrete that once made up the busy intersection.

Teller cheers, as do several of the scientists watching. It is silly, stupid really, but the sight of a football defying the gravity of an entire planet brings out the sense of wonder in all of them.

"Kids," Cathy says, winking at him and smiling.

The ball passes out the far side of the air surrounding the anomaly and then drops down toward the ground. The soldier has to run backwards to make the catch before yelling, "Touchdown."

They all laugh.

Dr. Anderson turns toward the NASA trailer, looking at the gaggle of scientists monitoring the anomaly, and holds his arms up in a gesture, posing the obvious question.

"Nothing unusual here," comes the reply.

"Throw it back," Mason yells across the pit. The soldier winds up his arm, determined to do himself proud, and throws the ball back, but he doesn't allow for the unusual dynamics of horizontal gravity within the anomaly. The football arcs to the left, falling sideways toward the concrete slab. It might have made it out the other side had it not struck the traffic light sticking out of the concrete almost parallel with the Earth.

"Oh, did you see that?" Finch cries from behind the camera.

"I hope you got that on film," Cathy says.

"Sure did."

The football bounces sideways on the concrete slab and rolls to within a few feet of the edge, coming to a rest and looking like it has been glued in place on a wall.

"Damn," Mason cries.

"Not the most scientific of investigations," Dr. Bates says, "But practical."

Dr. Anderson says, "Good confirmation. Nothing there we didn't expect."

"That was so much fun," Susan says. "We should do that again."

"Sorry," comes the cry from the other side.

Mason holds his hand up in acknowledgment.

Well, that would keep the journalists off their backs for a while, Teller thinks, knowing they love a bit of unique footage, and the vision of that football defying normal gravity was quite something to behold. Then a thought strikes him.

"Why don't we just go and get it?" he asks.

"What? Go in there?" Dr. Anderson asks. "Are you mad?"

"No," Teller says. "Think about it. This thing emits no radiation. It doesn't do anything other than turn over on itself. It should be perfectly safe."

"I can't let you do that," Mason says. "It's too risky."

Trissa settles her hands on her hips, saying, "And this from the man that just played football with what could very well turn out to be an alien entity."

"Think about it," Teller says. "What's the risk? We know there were people inside the anomaly when it first appeared. Both Cathy and Finch were in there. No one was harmed by it, except for a fender bender and a bit of flying glass. What could go wrong?"

Cathy confirms his point, saying, "We stepped in and out of the anomaly several times without noticing anything at all when the slab was close to the ground."

"But that was when it was aligned with Earth," Mason replies. "This is different."

"How?" Anderson asks. "I'm with Teller on this. Are we being overly cautious simply because the anomaly appears more sensational when it's on a steep angle?"

"In principle, it is just the same," Teller says. "Think of this like climbing over the next door neighbor's fence to get your ball back. It's nothing more than that."

Dr. Bates jokes around, saying, "Only your neighbor is The Thing from Outer Space."

"Can I have your balloon?" Teller asks, turning to Susan.

"Sure," she replies, handing it to him with a smile.

Teller turns to Anderson and Bates, saying, "I'll use this as a reference point for local gravity as it will always face up, pulling tight on its string regardless. And its thin membrane is ideal as an early warning of any violent change. If it pops, I'm out of there."

Cathy looks worried, which surprises Teller as they barely know each other, but given she landed him in this mess, she probably feels a little responsible.

"I'll be fine. It's only a big deal because we think it is a big deal. The reality is, the anomaly was completely stable both times the football passed through it. And that slab weighs several hundred tons, if not more, so I'm hardly going to cause an imbalance. I'll be like a fly landing on an elephant."

Teller walks over toward the U.N. building as the slab of the intersection rises up before him like a wall. The sun is setting. Already, spotlights light up the near vertical concrete intersection.

"Bates?" Mason asks.

"It's a go from me," he replies, holding his hand over his radio. He's been talking intently with the NASA team back at the trailer.

"Trissa?"

"I'm okay with it. I think we're talking ourselves into this being a big deal when it's not. It only appears that way because of the sensational motion. The football. The flags. Everything suggests he'll be fine."

"Anderson?"

"It's a go from me, too. I don't think we're going to see anything other than Teller switch between gravitational planes—just like the football did. There was no physical contortion or deformation of the ball, so I think he'll be okay. And he's right. The balloon is a good canary in this mineshaft. Keep your eyes on that."

Finch continues recording, moving around and changing his angle, trying to capture everything that's being said.

Cathy stands beside Finch, whispering, "I can't believe they're serious about this. And they said we were irresponsible. So it looks like humanity's first interaction with an alien civilization is going to be as the result of a game of backyard football."

Finch laughs.

Teller walks up to the edge of the slow moving slab, holding the balloon out in front of him as though he were offering it to an invisible stranger. Everyone else stands back. Finch lines up his camera angle, kneeling on the concrete road beside the anomaly.

Teller's vaguely aware the others have stepped back as he inches slowly forward. There's nothing like people backing nervously away to provide reassurance. It's not like he is going to get sucked in to some kind of vortex or something, is it?

The size of the slab is daunting, and Teller finds himself wondering if this is such a good idea. But there's the football, less than ten feet away, resting gently on the vertical section of road.

He holds out the balloon, allowing the breeze to catch it and watches as it drifts closer to the anomaly. As the balloon passes into the imaginary sphere stretching out from the upturned intersection, it turns and pulls sideways, pulling toward East 45th Street. Teller is pleased to see that the balloon doesn't pop. The balloon made the transition between different gravitational orientations with ease. This might actually work.

He crouches as he approaches the vertical mass of concrete, rock and dirt, seeing the stratified layers beneath the road base on the side of the massive structure. He reaches out with his hand, reaching through what he thinks of as an invisible barrier, but there is nothing unusual. His hand feels no different at all. He touches the intersection on the other side of the elusive boundary between his world and the anomaly, feeling loose bits of grit and dirt beneath his fingers. The road feels like a rough, unfinished concrete wall.

Teller kneels and leans inside the anomaly. Immediately, he has to put his hand out to stop himself from falling head first into the wall that is the slowly moving intersection. Gravity sucks, he reminds himself. With both hands on the concrete, he climbs awkwardly up and onto the slab, falling forward clumsily on his shoulder, but he is in.

"Are you okay?" Mason calls out, already seeing he is fine.

"Yeah, I'm good," Teller replies, turning around and sitting inside the anomaly on the concrete.

For a few seconds, he feels disoriented, a little dizzy. The world looks strange. He feels like he is sitting upright, with the balloon still pulling taut above him, but the rest of the world is now sideways. He stands up slowly, steadying himself. His inner ear is spinning slightly.

"You guys look weird," he calls out.

"You look pretty weird yourself," Cathy replies, excited at seeing him standing sideways within the intersection. At a guess, he must look like some bizarre kind of Spider-Man walking along a wall.

"The whole world looks like it's falling over," he says, picking up the football. "The buildings look like the under-hang of some giant, surreal cliff at the beach. And all you guys look like you should be falling down."

"Hah," Mason cries.

"How does it feel to live your whole life sideways?" Teller asks, trying to be funny.

Susan is jumping up and down giggling with excitement, only to him, she's jumping sideways and then flying feet first back into a wall.

"How does gravity feel?" Trissa calls out. "Should feel normal."

Teller copies Susan, jumping in the air a few times. Finch catches the motion on video. From where they are standing, it must look like he is jumping horizontally and flying back into what looks to be more of a concrete wall than a once bustling road.

"Feels fine," he says. "It's not like walking on the moon or anything. It feels entirely normal. No different to walking on Earth."

Hmm, there's an interesting thought, he realizes. He's talking about the anomaly as though it were something that isn't on Earth.

Teller tosses the ball out of the anomaly and watches as it rolls along the ground on the other side. To him, the ball looks as though it's rolling up a wall.

"Okay, Neil Armstrong," Mason replies. "I think we've had enough excitement for one day. Time to come home."

Teller looks at the balloon still pulling upwards on the string.

"You said there's a concentration of hydrogen in the center of this thing?" he calls out.

"Yeah," Dr. Anderson replies.

"I have an idea," Teller says, turning away from them and walking toward the center of the massive, circular slab.

"What are you doing?" Mason cries. "Get back here."

"Just a moment," Teller says. "I have a simple experiment in mind. Watch closely. Hey, Bates, make sure the mass spectrometer is running."

"Teller," Mason yells, while Dr. Bates talks frantically with the NASA team over the radio.

Teller stands in the middle of the intersection. He reaches up on his tiptoes with the balloon stretched high above his head and lets go. The balloon sails up from his perspective, sideways from their perspective. On reaching the center of the anomaly, it pops, bursting in a flash. The string, along with a few bits of rubber fall slowly back to the concrete slab beside him.

Teller looks up. There, in the center of the anomaly, is a soft glowing sphere. He smiles.

For Teller, at least, this is no longer an anomaly.

PIONEER

"What the hell have you done?" Mason cries as Teller jumps down off the slab.

Teller lands a little awkwardly, falling sideways and almost crashing into the ground. That is going to take some getting used to. He's so excited he barely realizes Mason is angry with him. He looks up at the Director of National Security, saying, "What?"

"What do you think you were doing in there?" Mason demands again.

"Saying hello," Teller replies nonchalantly. He's more interested in what Bates and Anderson have to say. They are both on the radio.

"So, is it lithium?" he asks.

"It's lithium," Anderson replies with a smile.

"I knew it," Teller cries, pumping his fist in the air. "We've made contact!"

"What?" yells Mason, but his phone is ringing. He looks at it, saying, "It's the White House."

Mason walks off to one side to take the call. Bates and Anderson start walking briskly back toward the main NASA observation trailer, Teller and the others race to keep up.

"What just happened?" Susan asks, seeing her teacher's

excitement and becoming wrapped up in it herself, but not understanding why.

"Yeah, what was all that about?" Cathy asks. Finch is still filming the soft glow at the heart of the anomaly as it lights up the growing darkness like a campfire.

Mason runs back after finishing his phone call. Whatever the president has to say it is short and sharp.

"Teller," he says. "Tell me you haven't done something stupid."

"On the contrary," Bates replies, speaking on behalf of Teller. "I think our elementary school teacher has had a stroke of genius. We might actually have some answers for you and the President."

"Really?" Mason says, and Teller knows he's not sure whether he's more curious, more angry, or more confused by what just happened. Bates and Anderson already understand what is happening at the heart of the anomaly, as do several of the other NASA scientists. They're excited, talking madly with each other. Finch makes sure he's capturing the discussion on video.

"Take a look at this," Teller says. "It will explain everything."

He sits down in front of one of the computers set up in front of the research trailer and brings up a Google image search for 'Pioneer plaque.'

"What we have here," Anderson begins, pointing at the anomaly and unable to contain himself, "is a probe, more precisely, a Von Neumann probe."

"Exactly," Teller says.

"Okay, back it up a little," Mason says.

Teller points at the image of an engraved golden plaque on the screen before them, saying, "In the early 70s, we sent out probes to explore the solar system. Pioneer and Voyager."

The image on the screen is an etching of a man and a woman, both naked, carved in front of the rough outline of the Pioneer space probe. To one side, a series of lines with dots and dashes all converge on a single point, marking the location of the Sun in relation to nearby pulsars. Above that, are two circles, while below the star map there is a crude depiction of the planets in the solar system, with the path the Pioneer spacecraft flew as it left Earth and swung by Jupiter on its way into deep space.

Teller composes himself, wanting to speak clearly and not end up tying his tongue in knots.

"When we became capable of interplanetary space flight, the first thing we did was to send out a bunch of probes to explore the solar system on our behalf. But that's not all we did. On both the Pioneer probes and the Voyager probes we included messages, token gestures really, but messages intended for an alien intelligence."

Mason asks, "How is this relevant?"

"Ah," Teller says. "Along with those messages, we included a key, something that any technologically advanced civilization would be able to decipher. After all, what good is a message if the recipient can't understand it?"

"I don't see what this has to do with the anomaly," Mason says, rather impatiently.

"You will," Trissa replies, walking over and joining the conversation.

Anderson smiles, grinning from ear to ear.

"Okay," Teller says. "Look at this image. Look at what we sent out as a message to any aliens passing by."

Mason looks, but from the blank stare on his face it's clear he doesn't see anything significant.

"The key," Teller continued, "is these two small circles at the top. To us, they're the least interesting aspect of the plaque. But, in reality, they're the most important part of the whole message because they're the key to understanding all the measurements in all these other diagrams."

Bates asks, "And what key did we use?"

"Hydrogen," Mason says, as the answer dawns on him.

"Exactly," Teller replies. "We used the transition state of an electron in orbit around a single proton—we used an excited hydrogen atom. We used hydrogen as our starting point to communicate with any extraterrestrial intelligence that might be out there. We used something every alien civilization would recognize simply because it is the most abundant element in the universe, because it's the most simple, basic element, and because it represents a common point of understanding between us and them."

"And so the anomaly," Mason begins.

"The anomaly is using the same principle to communicate with us."

"I still don't get it," Cathy says. "There's a world of difference between a golden plaque and a slab of concrete floating upside down."

"I'm a teacher, a grade school teacher," Teller says. "At times, I come across kids that can't read when they first come to school, so I start teaching them from the most basic of books. A is for Apple, and that kind of stuff. It has to be something easy to understand, a primer. And from there the child will learn and grow. One day, they'll be able to read Shakespeare, but not on that first day.

"In the same way, the anomaly is communicating with us using a primer, the most basic book that describes the universe around us—the periodic table of elements. The anomaly is using the ABCs of the universe to talk with us. Only in this case, A is for hydrogen."

"Whoa," Mason says. "You're saying it's alive."

"Not alive," Teller replies. "At least, I don't think so. Not in the sense we would use of organic life, but there is intelligence. This thing, whatever it is, it's speaking to us in the simplest language it can, saying, 'One proton, one electron.' It's asking a question. Asking us for a response.

"By releasing the balloon, we answered with helium, the next element in the periodic table, so it has responded with lithium, the third distinct element in the table."

"So it's tit-for-tat," Mason says, trying to get his head around the concept.

"Essentially, yes," Teller says. "What's the next element after lithium? Isn't it one of the noble gases?"

"No," says one of the scientists standing by them. "It's a while before we start hitting the nobles. The next element would be beryllium. If we respond to lithium with beryllium, the anomaly should respond with boron."

"Ah, yes," Teller says, scratching his head as he tries to remember the early sequence in the periodic table.

"It's playing Twenty Questions," Trissa says, "Quizzing us about our knowledge of the natural world."

"I guess so," Teller says.

"And you don't think this thing is alive?" Mason asks, repeating his earlier question in a different manner. "Why not?"

"Well, robotic probes are capable of going so much further than a manned spacecraft. They're much simpler and lighter, so they can reach further. And, really, there's not that much need for an alien to be physically present, not with advanced machinery like this, especially given the phenomenal distances and the sheer amount of time involved in traveling from one star system to the next, not to mention the risks associated with prolonged exposure to radiation while traveling. So they'd avoid a lot of headaches by sending a probe, something like an advanced version of Pioneer or Voyager."

"Makes sense to me," Bates says.

Anderson nods in agreement.

"You're getting all this, right?" Mason asks, looking at Finch.

"Oh, yeah."

"So that," Mason says, pointing behind himself at the soft glowing sphere at the center of the anomaly, "that's not something to be worried about?"

"Not at all," Dr. Anderson replies. "It's just the lithium reacting with moisture in the air, and it's small, it's contained. It's roughly the size of a basketball but quite diffuse."

"We've got to get more elements together," Dr. Bates says with a burst of excitement.

"I'm on it," one of the NASA scientists says, disappearing into the trailer and jumping on the phone.

"You said it is a probe?" Mason adds, turning back toward

Teller.

"Yes, sir."

"So what is it probing? What does it want?"

"I don't know," Teller replies.

"Guess," Mason says. It is an order, not a question.

"Well, at a guess, it's going to start off by establishing a baseline with us. The anomaly is probably going to keep working up the periodic table until we can no longer reply."

"Why can't we reply?" Mason asks.

"Ah, once you get into the heavy elements there are gaps. We can produce most elements in a reactor core or a particle accelerator, but some of them have such short half-lives we'd never be able to stabilize them long enough to get them to the anomaly in any kind of reasonable volume.

"And then there's a whole bunch of elements we've never seen. They're theoretically possible, but we haven't been able to produce them. So the probe will pretty quickly come to understand our limitations, which makes sense, from its point of view."

"How?" Mason asks.

He is asking a lot of open-ended questions, but this is good. Even if it is still largely speculative, at least they are starting to make some progress, exploring the possibilities.

"Probes like this would be sent everywhere," Bates says, expanding on the principle of a Von Neumann probe. "Their makers would understand that they would inevitably intersect with other civilizations at various stages of their development. This thing could have arrived during the Iron Age, or the Bronze Age, or during the Age of Enlightenment, long before we had reached a level of technical innovation where we could interact with it. Hell, it could have as easily landed during the age of the dinosaurs as now."

"Yeah," Anderson says, seeing where Bates is going with this. "So it would have to have a lot of patience. It would probably be content to stay in its initial turn-your-world-upside-down novelty stage for millennia as it waits for the inhabitants to reach the point where they stop worshiping it as some kind of deity and start talking to it. The anomaly is probably programmed to wait patiently until the host species can isolate hydrogen and helium as distinct elements and start an intelligent conversation."

"And we're still quite young," Trissa says, picking up where Anderson left off. Teller loves listening to these distinguished scientists filling in the gaps in his understanding. "From the point of view of an interstellar civilization, we've only just taken baby steps into orbit. We've walked on our moon, but everything else we've done within our solar system is robotic, carried out at arm's length, at the very limits of our technology."

"Precisely," Teller says, excited about how all these points are coming together into a coherent concept. "So the anomaly is trying to figure out exactly how much we know. It wants to know where we are at in terms of progress. It's asking as many questions of us as we are of it."

"And what happens then?" Mason asks. "What happens when it finds out our limitations?"

There's silence for a few seconds.

"Well, once it knows," Teller says, venturing out on thin ice. "When we get to the point where we can no longer complete elements in the periodic table, the anomaly will understand precisely how advanced we are in terms of technology. And it will work with us according to what it thinks we can understand."

Mason is silent, almost brooding, thinking deeply about what is being said. Anderson and Bates nod in agreement.

"You've got to remember," Teller says. "This really is a two-way conversation. As we learn about the anomaly, it also learns about us. This is a meeting of two civilizations separated by tens of thousands, if not millions of years of technological advancement. We just don't have any parallel. It's not like Columbus discovering the American Indians. The inequality that exists between us is such that it would be more like Jane Goodall working with chimpanzees in the wild for the first time, only we're the chimps. I suspect the anomaly is learning more about us than we're learning about it."

The furrow on Mason's brow shows he's worried by that concept.

"Fuck!" he cries. "How the hell did all this fall in my lap?"

He holds his hands up to his face, running his fingers over his temples and up through his hair.

"All right," he begins, "This is no longer a scientific investigation. This is now a military operation."

"What?" Anderson cries.

"You can't do this," Bates says.

"Are you serious?" Trissa cries.

Mason is already on the radio calling for troops to take over from the police and secure the inner area.

"What the hell are you doing?" Anderson demands, yelling at Mason with the veins in his neck bulging. "This is not right."

Teller is silent. Susan is scared. She hugs Teller's waist. Teller crouches down beside her, wanting to reassure her everything's going to be okay.

Cathy and Finch back slowly away, trying to be inconspicuous. They aren't trying to run. Teller can see they just wanted enough distance to be able to talk, so he edges toward them, wanting to hear what's being said.

Cathy whispers to Finch. "I thought this already was a military operation."

"Apparently not," Finch replies. "I don't like where this is going."

"Be sure to make copies," she begins, not wanting to say

any more.

Troops begin running around the area, stationing themselves beside the trailer.

"Why are you doing this?" Bates asks. "This is possibly the most significant interaction in the history of humanity and you want to start us off on a war footing."

"I'm not starting anything," Mason replies. "But if Teller is right and that thing figures out our weaknesses and exploits them, we will be defenseless. We need to learn more about it before it figures out anything else about us."

"There's no reason to assume hostile intent," Anderson cries.

"You don't get it," Bates replies, fuming with anger. "Teller is right. This is not a meeting of equals. This is not some diplomatic mission between different countries or different cultures. The differences between us and them are so vast as to be incalculable. I mean, look at it. The damn thing can defy the laws of gravity. Hell, we don't even know what gravity is!"

Mason looks intently at Bates, listening carefully to his argument.

Teller tries to make sense out of what's happening.

Mason isn't ignoring the scientific concerns. He's going on gut instinct, and his gut clearly tells him they've already gone too far. Mason is, after all, appointed to support a political position, not scientific inquiry. Mason is throwing on the brakes before the train runs off the tracks.

"Oh," Bates continues, "Newton gave us some vague notions about the strength of gravity being the inverse square of the distance between two masses, but that's like saying two plus two equals four. Einstein takes the concept further to suggest gravity is a consequence and not a force. But the reality is, if the universe behaved the way we think it should, according to our understanding of gravity, the damn thing would fly apart. Entire galaxies exist in defiance of what little we know about gravity, and this thing toys with it, the anomaly flaunts its ability to control gravity like it is child's play."

Bates is in full flight. Mason is going to hear him out if it's the last thing he does.

"The anomaly has such a mastery of gravity that it can simulate our own gravity within a precisely defined area. Not only that, but it completely negates and defies the normal gravitational attraction of an entire goddamn planet at exactly the same time. That's a double-whammy. That's a level of technological innovation we cannot even dream of attaining.

"And you think it's a threat? If it is a threat, there's not a damn thing we can do about it. For us, it would be like an Amazonian tribe taking on a fully armed nuclear aircraft carrier with a bunch of half-naked natives in canoes. If the anomaly wants to attack us, to exploit us, it could do so in a heartbeat and there's nothing we could do about it. Nothing. Not a goddamn thing. You're not thinking this through."

"He's right," Teller says, impressed with his argument.

"You need to listen to Bates," Trissa says.

Mason turns to a Marine captain standing beside him, saying, "No one goes anywhere, does anything, or talks to anyone without my express permission. Cut all transmission with the outside world. You will provide food and bedding and detain all personnel on-site until I have met with the National Security Council. Understood?"

"Yes, sir."

Mason bends down next to his niece, putting on a fake smile as he says, "Looks like you get to have a sleep-over tonight with the scientists. I'll call your Mom and see if that's all right with her. Okay?"

Susan doesn't seem too sure what to think, but she trusts her uncle so she nods in reply. Anderson and Bates continue to protest but Mason walks away.

Without saying a word, Mason holds out his hand to Finch.

Finch pops open the camera and drops a still-warm recordable HD disc into his hand.

Teller can guess what's going to happen next.

Mason is taking this to the President.

UNITED NATIONS

The next day, the President of the United States of America sits at the front of the U.N. General Assembly building with the Vice President on his right and James Mason, the National Security Director, on his left. Teller, Bates, Trissa, and Anderson sit to one side at a second table with Robert Gaul, the United States Ambassador to the United Nations.

From the seating arrangement, there is no doubt in anyone's mind that science is taking a back seat to politics. They swap handwritten notes with each other, reflecting on what they think as they look out across the sea of delegates from over two hundred member states and territories. Teller feels distinctly out of place, but he has the outermost seat, and he figures the pecking order is quite appropriate in his case. If he had his way, he'd watch the whole debate from back at the NASA trailer. Or better still, from home.

Initially, there was some resistance to meeting in the General Assembly building as the top corner at the rear of the building is missing, dragged off into a slow orbit by the anomaly. The actual segment isn't that large, only about twenty feet or so in length and less than five feet wide, but it keeps the anomaly rooted firmly in the minds of the delegates.

Structurally, the building is sound, but the sight of the sun streaming in through a hole torn in the side of the assembly hall is unnerving. Once a day, when the anomaly aligns, the corner looks almost normal, but most of the time the wind swirls in through the gap, defeating the air conditioning.

Several diplomatic representatives initially refused to attend the assembly, notably the Chinese and the Germans, but after a flurry of late night phone calls from the State Department, everyone is in attendance.

Dr. Yani-Villiers, the Secretary-General for the United Nations, addresses the audience.

"The events of the past few days are unprecedented in human history. For the first time, we have verifiable evidence that we are not alone in this vast universe. That the creation we call our own is shared with other sentient, intelligent beings."

"The appearance of the anomaly has confirmed our greatest hopes while unmasking some of our deepest fears. Our world will never be the same again.

"We have awakened, as if from a deep slumber, one in which we only ever focused on ourselves, to find ourselves as part of a greater universal calling, one in which intelligence reaches out to find companions.

"There are many questions, few answers. Today, we have not arrived at a destination, we are undertaking the first steps of an epic journey. And this is a journey that must be made in peace and understanding."

Teller is genuinely surprised by the depth of the Secretary-General's comments. His speech captures Teller's hopes and dreams. But Teller isn't naive to the reality of international politics and he's sure there are competing agendas muddying the waters.

The Secretary-General rounds out his comments and introduces the President of the United States.

"My friends," the President begins. "We are living through the most profound of historic events. The significance of contact with an alien intelligence is singularly unique and without parallel in human history. It represents a profound turning point for Homo sapiens as a species. We are no longer the only known sentient species in the universe. There is much we can learn, much we want to learn, but through all of this, we stand to learn the most about ourselves."

It is a good point, and one Teller hopes is not lost on the audience.

"Already, the interest in the anomaly is overwhelming. We are working to provide scientists around the world with raw, unfiltered, transparent access to the results of our scientific investigation."

And that is as far as the President gets through what is supposed to be a carefully crafted, twenty minute speech. The floor of the General Assembly erupts in protest, with delegates from all quarters crying out to be heard. The Secretary-General calls for order. As the unrest abates, the Secretary-General addresses the U.S. President.

"You can appreciate, Mr. President, that the very nature of

publishing results itself implies a degree of processing and filtering. Your results are, by definition, yours, not ours."

The President replies calmly.

"Dr. Mason has personally overseen the research team and can describe the protocols that are in place. Dr. Mason?"

From the look on his face, Mason didn't expect to be thrown to the wolves quite this early. He clears his throat, and starts talking off-the-cuff.

"We are broadcasting both raw metrics and internal discussion points directly to CERN in Switzerland to ensure neutrality and complete accessibility to the scientific community."

Again there is a flurry of protests from the floor. The Secretary-General calms the delegates before settling on a question from the German representatives.

"What about the rumors of military control?" someone yells.

"They're rumors," Mason quickly responds, dismissing the point and looking to move onto something else.

"We don't want access to the data, we want access to the anomaly itself."

"In time," Mason says, before being swiftly cut off.

"Your timetable does not interest us, Dr. Mason. We want access now, just as you have."

"You have to understand," Mason replies, determined to have his say. "This is a discovery we are sharing with the world. By virtue of the fact that we are providing transparency to all, we cannot allow exclusivity to a few as that would be prejudicial to everyone else.

"The United States is determined to share the anomaly research fully and equally with all member states and that necessitates avoiding partiality, even to close allies."

"But you have the privilege of direct access," the German diplomatic representative says. "Why should you be afforded that opportunity and not others?"

"We can guarantee our own transparency. We cannot guarantee the transparency of others," Mason replies bluntly to scoffs from the floor of the General Assembly. "We have accepted offers from ESA and several other national space agencies to form a scientific review board. Most of these foreign scientists will have on-site access to the anomaly, but they will be using our systems, reporting in accordance with our protocols, and answerable to our authority."

"Why should we trust you?" the Russian ambassador snaps. "America has a reputation of being transparent only as far as it serves her own national interests. What transparency is there over your illegal activities in Cambodia during the 60s? What insights did you share with the world during the Iranian crisis in the 70s? What visibility was there into the War on Terror? Edward Snowden, Julian Assange and Chelsea Manning would all attest to a lack of transparency. Why should we trust you now?

When the stakes are so high? When there is the possibility of harvesting radically advanced alien technology."

The Russian ambassador stands, addressing his comments to the assembly at large. "This is the country that champions freedom and justice, but will not ratify its membership to the International Criminal Court. And why? Because it fears its own illegal activities will be exposed. America protects its citizens from the illegal actions they undertake in the name of the United States. My fellow ambassadors, we cannot trust those that do not trust in the transparency of international justice."

A wave of murmurs rise through the audience as the translation teams pass on the message to the various representatives through their earpieces.

"That is not true," snaps Mason, losing his cool.

"Oh, but it is true," replies the Russian coldly. "The only American ever convicted of a war crime is Lieutenant William Calley for the massacre of five hundred civilians at My Lai, and your President Nixon ensured he only ever served one day behind bars as a convicted felon. Hah! You talk about freedom and justice, but only ever as it suits you.

"And what about President Bush condoning torture following September 11th?

"What about when Private Manning was held incommunicado for over a year in defiance of international human rights? Held simply because he aired your dirty laundry? And now you have imprisoned Manning, locking the door and throwing away the key.

"You make a mockery of justice. You will not ratify the most basic provision of international law and yet we are to believe you will somehow honor us with unfettered access to the anomaly. What do you take us for, Dr. Mason? Fools?"

Mason goes to speak, but the Russian continues at a blistering pace.

"The anomaly appeared here, before the gates of the United Nations—not in Washington D.C. It is a message of hope directed at the world as a whole, not just at the United States of America."

He turns, addressing the assembly.

"No, we cannot trust the Americans. They will abuse this trust, just as they have abused their world power time and again over the past century. The anomaly must come under the control of the United Nations."

The assembly breaks into an uproar.

Mason tries to respond, but the noise within the grand hall is overwhelming. The Secretary-General calms the delegates, allowing Dr. Mason to respond.

"This," Mason begins, pointing at the gaping hole in the side of the Assembly building. "This is not about the United States of America. This is not about the United Nations. This is bigger than politics, bigger than any of our petty disputes or the mistakes of the past. This is about science. The anomaly speaks the language of science."

Mason is sweating, struggling to counter the ferocity of the arguments put forward by the Russians. But Teller was there when the President and his advisers warned Mason that this would probably happen. They were expecting a backlash and warned Mason that under no circumstances would the United States surrender its access to the anomaly, or in any way compromise the integrity of the research. Mason is walking a tightrope.

The President will not weigh into this debate and Teller knows it. Mason is on his own. The President can't step in even if he wanted to. His authority is absolute. The pride of an entire nation demands that his comments are binding. Negotiations are for those with room to maneuver, to posture and debate. The President has no such luxury and Mason understands that better than most. Teller can see that in the way Mason carries himself. Mason has to weather this storm on his own. If it comes to it, the President would veto any further discussion and simply walk out.

"You represent a democracy," the Russian counters, "where the majority establishes the rules, and yet you say you champion science where the majority has no rights at all, where the number of people that believe in something is immaterial to reality. So which is it? You cannot have it both ways, Dr. Mason. If it is science you represent, then you cannot be answerable to an American President!"

Mason is losing the assembly. Teller clenches his teeth, clamping his jaw shut. He wants to yell out a couple of points to help Mason, but he would only make things worse. Mason has to wrestle the argument away from the Russians. He can't go on reacting to their logic. He needs to drive his own agenda forward.

"Mr. Ambassador," Mason begins, deliberately slowing down his response as a means of forcing the Russian to listen. "Neither the U.S., nor the Russians, nor any other country has a clean history when it comes to matters of state, so we should not get bogged down in such recriminations.

"You are correct when you say this is a matter of trust, so let's talk about trust."

The President moves uneasily in his seat, as does Teller. A frank admission of American shortcomings isn't going to help things.

Teller whispers under his breath, saying, "Come on, Mason."

Mason needs to move to a different angle. Teller finds himself fidgeting nervously with his pen as he listens to Mason's reply.

"Allow me to put forward an example, if you will."

Mason is stalling. It is obvious to all, but it's working, taking the heat out of the Russian's argument.

"Canned food was first invented in France, and used by the armies of Napoleon, but do you trust the French or the science? Powered flight was first invented in the U.S., but do you trust the Americans or the science?

"Whether we like it or not, whether we are conscious of it or not, whether it supports our beliefs or grates against them, the reality is we trust science regardless of where it originates. We drive safely in cars, fly tens of thousands of feet above the Earth in airplanes, turn on light switches, and even eat fresh caviar imported directly from Russia—we can do all this because of advances in science.

"This is not about America. America is merely the vessel carrying the load. This is about the science. If the most capable scientists in this regard originated from Somalia, we would welcome them with open arms. Our goal here is not one of priority but transparency."

A rumble of discussion echoes around the room as the delegates talk among each other. The President seizes the opportunity to close things out while they are ahead. He stands, taking his cue from Mason's words, and speaks without a microphone, projecting his voice from the stage.

"We are here today because we welcome debate. We are here because we are being transparent, because we will not hide behind diplomatic overtures, because the anomaly is something that is to be shared by us all. The practicalities of implementing this are no small task, and so we ask for your patience and understanding. This is our commitment to the world. Thank you for your time this afternoon. That is all."

And with that short statement the discussion is over.

The assembly breaks in an uproar, but the President turns

and walks off stage followed by the Vice President. Dr. Mason, Teller, and the others follow suit as the delegates within the hall erupt in protest. Teller feels sorry for the State Department. They have their work cut out for them with both the Russians and the Germans.

BIG BROTHER

Although it is only a couple of hundred yards from the General Assembly building, it takes Mason, Teller, and the others almost three hours to make their way back to the NASA research trailer beside the anomaly. The sight of the anomaly, with several stories from the U.S. State Department and several other buildings moving freely through the air makes for a spectacular backdrop to the diplomatic discussions, and everyone wants to talk to those involved in the discovery of an alien intelligence. Security is tight, but no one seems to notice. The allure of the anomaly is overwhelming.

The dozen or so amputated flags and their severed flagpoles, along with the fractured corner of the U.N. building are at their zenith as the sun begins to set, floating high above the crater that was once a busy intersection. By rights, the flags should be hanging down, but they fall sideways toward the concrete slab, facing over toward the river in the distance, as they flutter in the gentle breeze. Their draped fabric betrays the peculiar gravity within the anomaly.

Insisting that the assembly meet on the U.N. grounds, well inside the security zone and in full sight of the anomaly, is a stroke of genius on the part of the President. It refutes the notion that the U.S. is somehow deliberately restricting access to the phenomenon, undermining the position of their detractors. Following the meeting, no one is in a rush to leave.

Mason jokes with Teller as they walk back to the NASA trailer, saying, "Do you know what's the most remarkable thing about the anomaly? It's that hundreds of U.N. delegates all feel the pull of its gravity without actually going inside the damn thing."

They walk past police lines and behind barricades. The military presence didn't last long. The State Department got wind of what Mason was doing the night before and demanded the troops withdraw, replacing them with police, fire fighters, and paramedics, making security seem far more innocuous than it really is.

Mason says, "Appearances are more important than paranoia," noting Teller's curiosity.

"A word of advice," he says as they walk along. "Don't ever go up against the Vice President. You'll lose."

Teller laughs, saying, "Not sure I'll ever need that, but I'll be sure to take your advice."

As they walk around the anomaly, skirting the area by fifty feet, Teller asks, "So no army at all?"

"None that are visible," Mason replies. "I've got a rapid response Marine team dressed up as army medics in the park, and a bunch of Navy SEALs working alongside the engineers inside the security perimeter, but the State Department insists the SEALs remain unarmed while working with civilians."

He doesn't seem too pleased with that decision, but he's

going along with it.

Mason walks up to the main NASA research trailer and sees a familiar face beaming back at him.

"What the blazes are you still doing here?" Mason asks, seeing Susan sitting in one of the deck chairs eating a hot dog and drinking a coke. "Why haven't they taken you home yet?"

Susan looks up with a smile, saying, "I asked them if I could stay."

Cathy speaks up. "Her mother called, saying she'd been dragged in to work an extra hospital shift, so I said we'd look after her. I thought Susan could have dinner with us."

Finch is recording the conversation of a couple of scientists setting up some equipment next to the slow moving slab within the anomaly. His camera is mounted on a tripod, allowing him to swivel around and catch shots of the remaining few diplomats leaving the United Nations in the distance.

"Well," Mason replies, with a smile, picking up Susan and giving her a hug, "as much as I'd love to have you stick around, I think you need to go home. I'm surprised your mom didn't send your father over to pick you up."

"I talked to her on the phone," Susan replies. "She says it's okay."

"I'm sure she did," Mason replies with a wink.

"Can I watch the show first?" Susan asks.

"The show?"

"Yeah, it's on in a few minutes," Cathy says, sitting down next to Susan. "Oh, you haven't heard, have you?"

"Heard what?" Mason asks, somewhat wearily. Teller listens in, wondering what Cathy is talking about.

Finch swings around, making sure the camera is on Mason's face so he can catch his reaction, and Teller suspects the director is about to get sucker-punched by something, but he isn't sure what.

"Ah, hasn't any one told you?" Cathy asks.

Teller is surprised Cathy has the jump on Mason, as he always seems to be one step ahead of things. Cathy dances around the issue, which makes things worse.

"Told me what?" demands Mason impatiently.

"Didn't the State Department tell you?" Cathy asks, but from the grimace on her face, it's clear she knows they haven't and she's stalling, trying to get out of the firing line.

Mason stares at her with his beady eyes. Words aren't necessary to convey the anger brewing inside. She's making things worse by not coming clean.

"Ah. You know they've set up a live feed with CERN?"

"Yes," Mason replies.

"They've got four continuous feeds. One of them is from

Finch's camera."

Finch waves from behind his camera.

"The others are a wide angle shot of the anomaly, the inside of the research trailer, and the last one is a close up of the slab."

Teller thinks that's pretty innocuous. He can't see what the big deal is until Cathy drops the bombshell.

"And?" Mason asks, leading her on.

"And they're royalty free. Broadcast with sound. Finch has been told that, under no circumstances, is he to stop broadcasting. It's 24x7 coverage, so I guess when we turn in for the night we leave his camera on and point it at the anomaly or something. But they're serious about this whole transparency thing. Finch has to keep his camera on at all times. No censorship. That's the mantra."

"And?" Mason repeats. Teller intuitively knows where this is going. This instruction must have originated with the Vice President. Mason and the VP don't see eye to eye.

"And the networks have picked up on it," Cathy admits. "They're calling it the reality show of the century. ABC and NBC have both announced hour long reviews of the anomaly footage every night."

Mason is silent.

"They've been running commercials all afternoon. Showing clips from tonight's show."

Mason's lips tighten.

Finch zooms in.

"Teller and I are polling all right, as is Susan. But they're fielding a lot of complaints about you."

"What the?" Mason stops himself. "This is outrageous! This is a serious scientific investigation, not a goddamn episode of Survivor."

"It's the networks," Cathy confesses. "You give them a video feed with no qualification and they're going to repackage it into anything that will attract viewers and sell advertising."

"FUCK!"

And that was the money shot Finch was waiting for. He grins from behind the lens.

"I do not believe this," Mason says, all of a sudden becoming acutely aware of Finch.

"It's not just the international community you need to worry about," Cathy adds, "It's the American people."

"I guess that makes sense," Teller says, trying to hose things down. "I mean, ultimately, we're here to represent the people on this planet. It is only fair that they see exactly how we're representing them."

"Don't," Mason says raising his finger, a sense of rage building within him. He's been KO'd from behind, and he knows it.

"Hey, it's on," Anderson says, pointing at one of the computer screens. A couple of the scientists have NBC streaming through their internet browsers.

They all gather around, turning up the sound. All except Mason who stands quietly at the back.

"Hey, this is so recursive," Finch says, videoing the scientists watching themselves on television. "Tomorrow, I'm going to try to get a shot of us watching a shot of us watching ourselves."

Cathy laughs.

Mason is on the phone to the President. Teller can hear him trying to contain his voice. The volume is up so loud, Teller can hear the President's distinct voice sounding rather tinny in reply. Mason points out that it is demeaning to the research team to have their efforts trivialized into some bizarre form of Big Brother. Although the President is sympathetic, he is firm on two points. There will be transparency. There will be no censorship or political limitations placed on how the footage is used. The President tells Mason it's their job to investigate the alien presence without respect to any other consideration, and without being distracted. But it is a distraction, Mason protests. To which the President suggests he switch off the television.

"At least there are no evictions," Finch jokes as Mason ends the phone call.

If looks could kill, Finch would be a dead man. Although Teller didn't catch everything the President said, he caught enough to have a pretty good idea the big man has been scolded.

Cathy's standing beside him. She whispers, "Twitter will be going off. They'll be loving this."

Mason watches quietly as footage of the major events from the day are spliced together with a running commentary. At times, the audio is simply their comments replayed and broadcast without editing. At other points, a panel of experts sits in critique of their actions. The unspoken assumption is that the experts know better. Mason comes across like a bully.

Privately, Cathy says, "Mason's an easy target. It won't be hard to isolate footage, remove it from its context, and portray him as a megalomaniac."

"No," Teller says, agreeing with her. "It won't."

But the concept is quite clever. As much as Mason hates the idea, and as bad as Mason comes across on television, the broadcast actually works in his favor. Even though the American networks are butchering the footage looking for controversy, something to grab a headline, the footage demonstrates to the critics that there's no political interference in the investigation. Mason just has to keep his mouth shut and his nose clean.

"So this is what we have to work with," Mason says, leaning forward and switching off the monitor. He's seen enough.

Teller figures Mason knows full well he'll come out looking worse as the days go by. That's the nature of leadership. Leadership isn't about building consensus, it is about getting things done.

"You, young lady," Mason says, pointing at Susan. "We need to get you back to your family.

"And as for the rest of you, we don't have time to be sitting around watching ourselves on television. There will be time for that later. Back to work. Come on. We've got an alien intelligence to talk to.

"I want to know what's next. I want scenarios. I want options. I want possibilities.

"Personally, I think it's a mistake broadcasting all this, but it's not my call so we've just got to live with it. And that means we need to be sharp. We can't be sloppy. The world is looking over our shoulder. Now is the time to shine. Let's do what we do best and focus on the science."

And with that, Mason walks away with Susan, determined to make sure she doesn't spend another night sleeping in the tents with the rest of the team.

HOT CHOCOLATE

Over the course of just a couple of days, the research group triples in size, and that means the logistics supporting the effort has also grown in size and complexity. The army brings in air conditioned tents for the team to sleep in and provides portable amenities, including showers.

Considerable effort is invested in the mess tent to ensure the quality of food is high and healthy. Mason is concerned with morale. Everyone puts in long hours in a tense environment and he says food is an important part of keeping them happy and productive.

An on-site medical facility is established along with a quarantine area in case the need should arise. A section of the park beside the Marine post is cleared for use as an impromptu helipad. Much to their disgust, the networks are pushed back into the side streets.

All in all, the effort is impressive. Support structures have grown out of nothing. Someone has even arranged for a state trooper to pick up some of Teller's clothes, his laptop, and a few of his books. He didn't ask how they knew which books he was reading at the time, but someone has obviously thought long and hard about what things to bring from his home.

Teller wonders how they got in. On second thought, it was probably quite easy. They'd have called out a locksmith and been inside within minutes, which is a scary realization in itself.

The sound of diesel generators fills the night. Although the research group is working in the middle of New York City, tapping into sufficient power is proving difficult, and there's a concern about power surges. Computers and electronic equipment run off grid power, but everything else, including lighting and air conditioning is run off diesel generators.

Teller is bored. Everyone has something to do. Even Cathy and Finch have set roles, but he's a grade school teacher. He floats between workstations, peering over people's shoulders, trying not to distract them, but he quickly realizes it's not possible to drop into some of these conversations. The scientists might as well be speaking another language when they talk about the results of their tests.

The detached concrete slab making up the intersection has passed overhead and is now arcing down again, so it is some time after midnight. Teller's too tired to be bothered looking at his watch. An approximation of time is all he needs. The evening has been spent running through scenarios for exchanging elements with the anomaly, double-checking observations, and preparing for the next phase of their interstellar conversation.

"Hot chocolate?" asks one of the Army chefs wandering around and making sure everyone has everything they need to put in the 16 to 18 hours most of the team are investing in their research.

"Sure," Teller says, taking a break from reviewing a log file he barely understands.

Dr. Anderson has broken down the anomaly research into a number of sections to allow for various teams to focus on different problems. There's the gravitation partition team investigating the physical characteristics and motion of the anomaly for clues as to how it functions.

The core team runs scenarios on the next steps in communicating with the anomaly. They're also considering how to handle the heavy metals problem when it arises.

The contact team is tasked with lateral thinking about ways in which communication with the anomaly could branch off beyond basic chemistry. They are considering how to discuss aspects like relativity and quantum mechanics with the anomaly, as well as more esoteric subjects like history, art, and literature. One suggestion is that certain types of music might be universal, being based on harmonic breakdowns and natural rhythms, so thought is being given as to how communication could proceed along those lines.

When it comes to quantum physics, one of the brighter young scientists has, tongue in cheek, suggested placing a cat in a box with a vial of cyanide linked to a radioactive counter to see if the anomaly will resolve Schrödinger's paradox for them.

The engineering team is on the slab itself, and they clearly love their assignment, getting to ride the inverted intersection through the night. They are constructing an impressive set of scaffolding reaching up over a hundred feet in the air to make it easier to reach the core. Several soldiers work alongside the civilian construction group. They are raising, or is it lowering, equipment to the slab by rope as the anomaly moves slowly throughout the evening. Teller marvels at their courage being upside down several hundred feet in the air, stuck to the intersection. Vertigo would get to him. It was one thing venturing onto the slab while it was close to the ground, but riding it through the night and working up there must be disorientating. The world would appear upside down.

The liaison team is the interface between the research teams and scientists from around the world. In some ways, they have the toughest of all tasks, filtering thousands of requests and connecting scientists with each other. The investigation is highly organized, and that raises his confidence in the research being undertaken.

Someone must have raided a nearby apartment or a furniture store, as smack in the middle of the road, right in front of the anomaly, they've placed a couch along with three comfortable armchairs and a coffee table. It's as though the anomaly is the ultimate in wall screen TVs or in-home theaters. Teller thinks the impromptu lounge setup is strangely appropriate. Seeing a couch and armchairs plonked in the middle of the street is as much out of place as the anomaly itself, leaning to the surreal atmosphere surrounding the alien presence. This gives "front-row seats" a new meaning.

Cathy sits down next to him on the couch. A couple of marshmallows float on top of her hot chocolate, betraying her sweet tooth. The cool of the night has settled, and she snuggles in, rubbing her shoulder gently against his to stay warm. Teller feels as though she is the only one he knew prior to all this madness, even if only by a few minutes. That she led him into this maze of mirrors escapes his thinking.

Finch hovers in the background. He has a sound man and a back-up cameraman working with him, but he is determined to film as much as he can himself. Professional pride has kicked in.

Trissa, Anderson and Bates walk over and sit down as well and enjoy the comfortable armchairs. It is just after one in the morning and the thought of a nice cup of hot chocolate before heading off to bed is just too tempting.

"It's been a long day," Cathy says, with the emphasis on drawing out the word "long."

She asks, "Have we learned anything else about our intergalactic friend?"

Teller thinks about it for a second.

"Kind of," he replies.

Out of the corner of his eye, Teller sees Finch ensuring he's catching the conversation on camera. Teller wonders who would be watching the telecast this late in the evening. For the most part, the live feed must be boring, akin to watching grass grow. It's daylight somewhere, so someone will be watching this live.

Cathy sips her drink, as does Bates and Anderson. They seem interested in his opinion, as amateur as that may be.

Mason is nowhere to be seen. He must have turned in for the night.

"It's quite clever, really," Teller begins, describing something he's been thinking since the U.N. meeting. "The way they've chosen to interact with us is ingenious."

He sips his hot chocolate.

"I mean, we have no way of detecting the anomaly directly. All we can see is how it manifests itself. We have no idea what it is actually made from. I read one comment on the Internet that suggests it's made of non-baryonic matter."

Cathy turns her head to one side, not understanding the term.

"Dark matter," Bates says, clarifying Teller's comment. "If it is, we may leap frog hundreds, perhaps thousands of years forward by learning how this works."

Teller is aware his comments are being broadcast so he tries to stay as objective as possible.

"The anomaly might be made of dark matter. But it could just as easily be some kind of technology that can exist at a subatomic level, below what we can register, or in some other dimension. Certainly, that glowing ball of lithium is an example of manipulating matter at a subatomic level. It should burn out within seconds, but it is constantly being replenished."

"How?" Cathy asks.

"Oh, I have no idea," Teller replies. He looks over at Bates who shrugs his shoulders.

Anderson says, "Remember E=mc2? The amount of energy required to continually create matter in this fashion is phenomenal, and yet we see no evidence of the energy itself, no radiation at all, but there it is regardless, glowing like a gas lamp."

"They're showing off," Trissa says lightheartedly.

Teller smiles, saying, "Oh, they're certainly doing that. The whole flip-the-world-upside-down does that quite effectively. But I've been thinking. We can't see the anomaly directly. We can only see what it does, like moving the intersection and the flags, or the vaporous ball of lithium, but we can't actually see the anomaly itself. And I think that tells us something important about it."

"What?" Bates asks, intrigued by the point.

Teller sips his hot chocolate before continuing.

"I think Mason was right in his address to the U.N.

"This is all about trust. Whoever made this probe could have set it up to actively investigate any foreign intelligence it comes across, and it could have done that without us ever knowing anything about it, but it hasn't. They wanted this to be a discussion, a two-way conversation. They wanted this to be respectful, not forceful. And I think that's quite profound.

"Look at the patience involved. I released that helium

balloon almost thirty-two hours ago, and the anomaly responded with lithium in a fraction of a second. Now it's just sitting there waiting, knowing full well the flurry of interest it has generated among us ignorant savages."

Anderson adds his thoughts. "I remember reading about how Jane Goodall first enticed wild chimpanzees into the open. She sat on the edge of the forest every day for a year, waiting patiently, watching as her presence challenged their social order. And finally, one day, a brave young male came out and made contact. Then, slowly, over several days, others joined in."

"Yeah, it's interesting, isn't it," Trissa says. "I think patience is a sign of higher intelligence. And it seems this thing could wait centuries for us to give it some beryllium. And yet it could interrogate our facilities at CERN, or the reactor at Indian Point, and find out exactly how advanced our nuclear technology is in a heartbeat. If it wants to know our strengths and weaknesses, it could go out and probe them and we'd be oblivious—but no, it's asking politely."

"Perhaps," Teller says, "This is an example of intergalactic etiquette."

Cathy laughs at the thought, saying, "So this is like the alien equivalent of not talking with your mouth full, or keeping your elbows off the table?"

"Something like that," Teller says with a smile. "With anything disruptive like this, there's always bound to be some fear. That's only natural. But when people stop and look at how gentle the anomaly is, and how respectful it is, I think they'll realize there's nothing to be afraid of."

Teller hopes these comments are something the media pick up on.

Anderson is falling asleep in his chair. He's trying to stay awake, but his eyelids clearly have other ideas.

"I'm beat," Trissa says, getting up. "Goodnight all."

Teller stands up as well, saying, "Yeah, it's time to hit the sack."

"Yep," Bates replies, stretching his arms and yawning.

Slowly, they disband, saying their goodnights.

Finch turns the camera on the Navy SEALs working with a couple of the engineers to set up some more fast ropes running up to the intersection high overhead.

It's a counter-intuitive view. Teller and Cathy see Finch's preoccupation with the soldiers and stop to watch for a while. The soldiers drill anchor points into the concrete road beside the intersection and throw their ropes up inside the anomaly, watching as the coils of rope fall up toward the inverted slab above, well away from the tiny glowing core.

Several of the SEALs are upside down facing them as they ascend the ropes. They're falling upwards toward the slab in their climbing harnesses. The unarmed soldiers are carrying equipment down to the team already on the slab. At least, it's down from their perspective. For Teller, the sight is bizarrely counterintuitive. The rope pulls taut from the street up, only to go slack and loose above the two soldiers as they slide backwards on toward the slab. Above them, below them—it's all a matter of perspective, and Teller is so tired his head is starting to hurt trying to figure it out. It sure looks impressive, though.

They talk idly for a few minutes as Finch sets up his camera on a wide angle shot, leaving the back-up crew to film through till dawn.

Finch wanders off, talking about ordering additional equipment, leaving Teller and Cathy alone. They turn and start walking the hundred yards or so to the sleeping tents in the adjacent park.

"Do you really think it's friendly?" Cathy asks.

Teller hasn't actually used that word, but she is right, that is the implication, that the anomaly is peaceful. Far from the Hollywood blockbusters, humanity's first contact with an alien species appears to be friendly.

"Yeah," he says. "I think it is. And I think it is far more aware of us than we are of it, and it knows how difficult this is for us."

Without looking down, Cathy reaches out and takes his hand in hers. Her fingers are warm. He responds, gently holding her hand.

"Are they like us?"

"I don't know," Teller says honestly.

"Yes, you do. If anyone knows, you do."

"It's all inference," Teller says, feeling more awkward holding her hand than speculating on the anomaly. "Guesswork, really. I suppose there would be similarities. Here on Earth, we have what's called evolutionary convergence, where things like eyes evolved fifteen to twenty different times, all independently, for the simple reason that eyes are so darn useful. So, could they have eyes? Based on how successful eyes are on Earth, I'd say, yes. I'm not sure you could reach the stars if you couldn't see them."

As they walk, their arms swing in rhythm. Teller feels like a school kid on a first date, which is silly. They're both adults, and yet holding hands brings out the child in him.

"So they can see us?"

"I really don't know. Maybe. Probably. It depends on how transparent their atmosphere is, I guess. Bats and cave fish have no need for eyes, so it's hard to know without knowing more about their home world. Certainly, you'd have to imagine they look up at the stars like we do—with a sense of wonder and awe."

Cathy glances up at the stars just visible through the light pollution thrown out by New York City. Teller follows her gaze.

"But are they like us? Do they have feelings? Emotions? Do they care about each other?"

Teller squeezes her hand gently, appreciating her question

on another level. It is nice to see Cathy as someone other than a reporter. From what he's seen over the past few days, she has a good heart, she just got a little too excited about Vega. She and Finch were out of their depth, something that's equally true for him.

Cathy leans into him, running her hand up his arm. He likes being touched by her. There's something fundamentally human about touch, especially when faced with something as alien as watching a portion of an intersection defy gravity, rotating freely through the air.

"Yes," he replies, thinking about it. "I think they are a lot like us. Nature is brutal. Nature is indifferent to cruelty, but to be civilized is to be civil, to be courteous and kind. Everything I've seen suggests they're civil in a way we should aspire to. So, yes, I think they have feelings. I think they care about each other. I think they care about us."

Cathy says, "It's interesting, isn't it? Everyone's interested in the science, or they're afraid ET will wage war against us, but no one stops to think they may be motivated by concepts like love, compassion, and mercy. I think those are far more interesting aspects to consider than hydrogen, helium, and lithium."

"Huh," he replies, appreciating her perspective. "Yes, we do tend to get a bit preoccupied, don't we. From what we've seen so far, I suspect there's every reason to think they are considerate. But there's also the danger of reading our own emotions into their actions, projecting our concept of love onto them, so we'll have to wait and see to be sure."

"You know," she says, sliding her hand up his arm. "You're kind of sexy when you talk geeky science."

"Hah," Teller cries, taken off guard, realizing she is looking into his eyes.

She pulls playfully on his arm. Cathy has a beautiful smile. Her pupils are dilated in the soft light. To Teller, she's stunning.

"Ah," he begins, feeling rather awkward. "I've never been good with the opposite sex."

"You don't have to be good at everything," Cathy replies, toying with him.

At an intellectual level, he knows what she's doing, and he can see how she enjoys playing with him, getting the upper hand. He's defenseless. Falling in love is not something that's subject to intellectual analysis. Try as he may, Teller cannot help being drawn to her.

Cathy says, "I've always hated that phrase—the opposite sex. I mean, how exactly do we oppose each other? How exactly are we opposites? I think we're complementary."

Without really thinking about the implications of his words, Teller says, "I guess, opposites attract."

It is only then he realizes quite what he is saying.

"I mean, men and women are complementary, not opposites. I wasn't trying to say you and..."

Cathy cuts him off, putting her finger on his lips.

"Sometimes," she says, "you talk too much."

And with that she leans in and kisses him.

CARBON

Teller sleeps in.

It's almost ten in the morning before he's showered, shaved, and dressed. Someone has laid out a freshly-pressed NASA polo shirt for him. It is something he wears with pride.

"Not bad for an elementary school teacher," he mumbles to himself.

He wonders how quickly the novelty will wear off and when he'll start to miss the kids. He wonders what they think of him, wondering how well he comes across on television. He thinks about several of the kids individually, picturing their responses, their enthusiasm, and their sense of pride in seeing their teacher working with NASA. He can just imagine their heartfelt support and encouragement. They're going to be so excited when he gets back to school, and that's a sobering thought for him. It's easy to become lost in the moment and assume things will continue as they are, but everything comes to an end. In some ways, Teller will be glad to leave the circus. And the kids are going to want to know everything—every last detail. That brings a smile to his face.

He grabs a bagel from the mess tent and walks the thirty yards over toward the command center that has grown up around the main NASA research trailer. Even from a distance he can see Mason in full flight, his arms pointing as he commands what, for him, is Patton's Fifth Army. If he was a musician, he'd be a conductor. None of this blowing on a bassoon at the back of the orchestra for Mason. He'd be first violin, at least.

Cathy and Finch walk back from the morning media briefing. As usual, Finch is filming everything, even the walk back from the outer barricade. Cathy sees Teller and darts over to him with a spring in her step, leaving Finch behind. Teller smiles as she comes up to him holding two cups of coffee.

"Is that what I think it is?" Teller asks.

"Double latte," Cathy says, handing him one of the cups. "The coffee here is lousy, but I've got contacts on the outside—an old friend that works as a barista in Midtown. She's set up a portable station and is making a killing from the media."

"Oh, thank you."

He sips at the coffee through the disposable plastic lid. The milk froth is smooth and creamy. The coffee is a little cool, but quite refined, and not too bitter. After two days of military mud, Cathy's latte is refreshing.

"We're going to have to get security clearance for your friend," Teller jokes.

Cathy is beaming. She reaches out, brushing her hand playfully against him.

"I must admit, I have an ulterior motive in bringing you some coffee."

"Really," Teller replies, enjoying her contagious enthusiasm.

"Can you help me?"

She looks quite coy.

"Sure," he replies, smitten.

"Mason's given me the assignment from hell. Well, that's probably a bit of an overstatement. I shouldn't call it that, but I've definitely drawn the short straw."

"Oh, really?"

"Yeah. I get the religious debate. They're sending a car over in a few minutes. I've got to go and meet with the Interfaith Commune Group down in lower New York. Would you like to come? Keep me company? Help out if the discussion gets overly technical?"

"Sure."

"You mean it?" she asks. "You'll come? Really?"

"Really."

"It's not too late to say you're too busy," she says.

"Me? Busy? I'm a school teacher. There's nothing for me to do here except get in the way."

From the radiant smile on her face, Teller can see his company on this assignment means a lot to her, so he is happy to go along. She is quite quirky, and he likes that about her.

"I'd love to come," he says as they walk into the command tent. She gives his hand a little squeeze, trying not to draw too much attention to them, but wanting to reach out and touch him. She is flirting, but he knows she's trying to avoid making it too obvious to anyone else. Nothing much happened last night, nothing beyond a fleeting kiss, but they both seem drawn to each other all the more.

"Oh, here's another headache," Mason says with a smile, reaching out and shaking Teller's hand. "Sleep well?"

"Too well," Teller replies.

"Good. The core team has a list of questions for you, and the contact team wants to run some scenarios by you. The scaffolding's complete, so we're ready to proceed with the beryllium. Anderson has that scheduled for lunchtime when the intersection aligns. Oh, and you're going to love this, they're going to throw a few isotopes at it, try to mix things up a little and see what it makes of that."

"Nice," Teller says, liking their thinking. "I'll be interested to see how it responds to that."

Anderson walks over, seeing Teller talking with Mason.

"Hey," Anderson says, patting Teller on the shoulder. "You're going to love this. Beryllium, boron, carbon. We get carbon!"

"Really?" Teller replies, his mind racing with the possibilities.

"Oh, yeah. And we're going to have some fun with it. Give it some purified 12C and separate dumps of the isotopes 13C and 14C. I've got buckyballs, graphite, even a few diamonds. We've sourced some carbon nanotubes from Berkley. A couple of the guys are really pushing the bounds of the fullerenes on this one, putting together an absolute smorgasbord of the different types of carbon molecules. Don't ask me how, but Bates has got his hands on almost a kilo of buckminsterfullerenes—that's purified 12C in an arrangement of 60 atoms that looks like a bunch of mini soccer balls. What do you think our little green friend is going to make of that?"

"Damn," Teller says. They've taken the concept of communicating via chemistry and are running with it. The science team is about to ask some serious questions of the anomaly. Teller begins to regret saying he'll go with Cathy. She's standing beside him, apparently reading his mind. He glances at her. She frowns a little—his childlike excitement is clearly evident.

He says, "I suspect our friend is going to get very excited about taking things beyond the elementary level. Twenty bucks says he shows us some new fullerenes in response."

"You're on," Anderson says, shaking his hand. "This is one bet I wouldn't mind losing."

"He?" Cathy asks, somewhat amused at the assumption of gender.

"It," Teller says, conceding ground.

"How are you going to present?" Teller asks.

"The idea is to use the scaffold to drop-feed from just above the core," Anderson says. "So we're avoiding the possibility of introducing any foreign elements during the delivery process, minimizing any possibility of contamination. I want to keep the tone of our conversation pure, so to speak."

Teller nods.

Anderson points at the rigging on the concrete slab as the anomaly sits on a 30 degree incline. The framework appears stuck to the slow moving intersection, rising out in a hook-like shape that reaches above the softly glowing core like a giant question mark.

"Now is when the real science begins," Teller says, aware Finch is broadcasting their conversation. "I wish I could stay for the drop, but I'm speaking at the Interfaith Commune Group this afternoon."

Mason looks at Cathy. She tries to hide her delight.

"Are you sure you want to go?" Mason asks, turning toward Teller. "You know what you're getting yourself into? Right? It's a very different world out there. It's not the same world you left a few days ago."

Teller is surprised to hear Mason talking like this. He isn't sure what to make of Mason's comment.

"The anomaly has changed everything. The rule book has gone out the window. The whole planet is scrambling to keep up.

The implications of contact with extraterrestrial beings is earth-shattering. I don't think you realize just how sheltered you've been in here. Things are moving at a rapid pace out there. This whole fiasco has upset the apple cart."

Mason leads Cathy and Teller to one side, saying, "Cathy's a reporter. She's used to hostile interviews. You, I'm not so sure."

"I appreciate your concern," Teller says, surprised to hear this from Mason. "But I'll be fine."

"It's not just the obvious fringe groups and conspiracy nuts you've got to watch out for," Mason says. "This thing has rattled everyone's cage. Governments, churches, corporations, they're all struggling with what's been termed The Upheaval. They're struggling because the assumptions they built their lives upon are being questioned by the advent of an alien intelligence. And they're reacting in different ways. Some are embracing it, others are in denial, while still others are raging against it, but make no mistake. No one is indifferent to it."

Mason pauses for a second.

"There's a reason I asked Cathy to go. And, no, it's not to throw her to the wolves."

Cathy clenches her lips as she focuses carefully on what Mason is saying.

"For us, the anomaly is fascinating. It's impartial and unemotional. It's just another science experiment, albeit on a cosmic scale. We just want to have a crack at it and analyze the results. We're all quite happy to lose ourselves in the details. For the rest of the world, though, this thing is disruptive, it's upsetting. The anomaly's very existence threatens everything. It threatens the religious status quo, it challenges the old political order, it forces a rethink. Everything is being re-evaluated."

"So why did you choose me?" Cathy asks. "Am I the dumbest? Or am I expendable?"

"Not at all," Mason says, laughing at her choice of words. "I chose you because you're the closest one to them. Out of all of us, you're the best one to relate to the challenges they face.

"For you, this isn't about hydrogen and helium. For you, this is about the awe, the intrigue. For us, the anomaly is a chance for discovery. But for you, this is about change. And you have a unique advantage—you've seen all this through our eyes, and you've seen it without any fear."

Teller is genuinely surprised. For a hard ass, Mason has some depth of thinking behind his reasoning.

"Well," Mason says, addressing Cathy, "I guess that means I am throwing you to the wolves. But the point is, you're street-smart, you're used to people driving a hidden agenda. You're a reporter. You know the angles. Just don't commit to anything and I think you'll represent us quite well.

"The organizers have assured me the debate is not going to be technical or speculative. I've told them we're not willing to entertain any kind of scientific discussion, or any announcements outside of the established channels, so they're not after an inside scoop. They just want an inside opinion. They want to hear from someone that's been here on the ground. The less technical the better. That's why I chose you."

Cathy nods in agreement.

"Are you sure you still want to go?" Mason asks, looking at Teller.

"Yes," Teller says.

As intriguing as the element drops are, there will be plenty of time to go over the results when he gets back. And, besides, he's surprised by Mason's comments about the outside world. Teller hasn't given the rest of the world a second thought. He assumed everyone would be as excited about the anomaly as he is, so he is curious to see what other points of view there are out there and understand their reasoning and motivations. Besides, deep down, Teller feels as though he falls into the same non-technical category as Cathy. He's an elementary school teacher, not an astrophysicist. It's time to let the real scientists get on with business.

"Then go," Mason says without any hesitation. "I've got enough headaches to deal with.

"Do you know what this bloody anomaly did when it ripped apart those buildings? It tore through the office of the Consular General for the country of Turkey. It tore the roof off the mission for Bosnia Herzegovina, and cut through a storage room belonging to the Embassy of the Republic of Korea. They all want to claim territorial sovereignty over the damn thing, saying its presence on their diplomatic territory is akin to being present in each of those countries."

Cathy laughs.

"You laugh, but I'm happy to hand the religious debate to someone else. I've got enough to deal with."

Cathy and Teller turn to walk out.

Mason calls after them.

"Hey, take no prisoners."

DOWNTOWN

The drive to the town hall takes almost an hour even though it's only four miles away.

Teller and Cathy sit in the back of a Marine Corps Hummer. The police have cleared the road immediately around the United Nations so they can drive out with ease, but the rest of Manhattan is a mess. The military Hummer is provided with a police escort, but the traffic is chaos. At first, it seems like the classic New York City gridlock on a Friday afternoon, with everyone wanting to head upstate for the weekend, but it doesn't take long to realize something's horribly wrong.

Garbage has begun to pile up in the streets. It's bagged, but birds and animals have torn at the uncollected waste. Police sirens sound in the distance a little too often.

Union Square has been the site of a riot. Several buildings have been burnt out. Storefronts have been ransacked. A bus lies overturned, having been used as a barricade, forcing the Hummer onto the side streets. Broken glass is strewn across the footpaths.

The historic Grace church, on the corner of Broadway and East 10th Street, is in flames. Smoke billows from its ornate marble steeple. Several fire engines are in attendance, battling to contain the blaze. The streets are chaotic. People are everywhere, all of them carrying something, but mostly bags of food and fresh produce.

"What happened?" Cathy asks, leaning forward from the back so she can talk to the driver.

"A couple of days ago, it was just panic buying," the young Marine says from behind the steering wheel. "They said people were hoarding, that there was no need for panic, but the stores couldn't restock fast enough. People got angry. The mayor sent in the police to break up the protests, and hey, presto, instant riot. A couple of young kids were killed in the melee. One of them was the daughter of a union boss, or something like that, so the unions shut down the city, stopped the trains, refused to pick up garbage, closed the ports. The whole city has ground to a halt. Everyone's gone loco. Since that thing appeared from outer space, the place is like a powder keg. One spark, and boom!"

He stops talking as they approach a barricade of burnt-out cars blocking the road. The young Marine reverses the Hummer, turning around so he can try another route.

"This anomaly is making people go crazy. They're acting like it's the end of the world."

They drive on for a few minutes before the driver asks, "It's not the end of the world, is it?"

"No," Teller says confidently. "It's not the end. It's a new beginning."

It is only then Teller notices Cathy has moved over next to him. Rather than sitting on the far side of the Hummer, she's moved to the middle seat. Somehow, she feels a little safer being close to him. Teller rests his fingers on her hand. She squeezes his fingers in response. She's afraid. She looks in his eyes, and he can see she deeply appreciates the gesture on his part.

Slowly, they drive through a noisy, angry crowd. Police struggle to contain the protestors.

Teller is alarmed by what he's seeing. He has an irrational sense of invulnerability that says, "Nothing will happen to me." Only, he knows it's without any basis in reality, and that leaves him wondering just how bad things could get out here.

Flander's Square, immediately outside the town hall in lower New York, is full of protesters waving placards. Teller catches sight of them as the Hummer is directed to the rear entrance at the back of the adjacent courthouse.

Roswell Was Just The Beginning.

No Police State.

They Have Been Lying To Us For Decades.

Our Rights Are Not Subject To Alien Interference.

What About Life On Earth?

Beam Me Up, Scotty. There's No Intelligent Life Down Here.

U.N. = World Domination.

Lizard Men Run This Country.

No More Military Cover-Ups.

Free E.T.

Teller and Cathy are ushered through the rear door into the town hall auditorium. The discussion has already begun. One of the stagehands escorts them to their seats behind a long table on the raised stage.

There is a mixture of cheers and boos as they sit down. The public is packed in tight. Teller doesn't like this, the auditorium is clearly beyond capacity. Any panic in here would be fatal, he thinks, noting that people are already blocking the aisles and standing pressed up against the fire escapes.

"Sorry, we're late," Teller says, addressing the moderator.

After a round of introductions, it's clear the other panel members are disappointed, if not insulted, that Mason has sent a school teacher and a reporter to represent NASA in the forum. The chair for the meeting directs the first of several prepared questions to them.

"Do you see the alien as incongruous with religion?"

"Ah, that's quite the open-ended question," Cathy replies, not realizing it's a closed question demanding either a "Yes" or "No." She seems determined not to rely too heavily on Teller. "Regardless of their historical or regional origins, all religions are concerned with humanity. They are concerned with us, with people, with how we live life here on Earth, with our morals, our ethics, our sense of duty. So, no, I don't see the anomaly as incongruous with any of our religions. I think it is distinctly separate and operates outside them—without contradicting them."

Cathy has to rush to add that last comment before being cut off. Teller likes her style. She's trying to avoid the obvious confrontation to come. It is a nice try, but he doubts it will work. And, besides, it really was a closed question.

Reverend Barbara Johnson replies swiftly, representing the Worldwide Church of God. She's the only person dressed informally, which Teller finds interesting. She's wearing a polo shirt and jeans. With her thick black hair sitting just off her shoulders, she looks confident and relaxed.

"I agree. Although some would have us believe otherwise, citing examples like the church persecuting Galileo, the reality is, Christianity has always been supportive of scientific endeavors.

"Newton was a devout Christian, as was Benjamin Franklin. Ralph Waldo Emerson was an ordained clergyman.

"Although Darwin was agnostic toward the end of his life, he was raised in a Christian family and studied to become ordained with the Church of England. There's no doubt this influenced his academic career and his various discoveries.

"Niels Bohr, the father of quantum mechanics, was a Lutheran.

"So there is a strong precedence for Christianity supporting scientific research.

"For me, the appearance of intelligent extraterrestrial life is simply another step in our emerging scientific understanding of the universe. There's no conflict with the scriptures. There's no need for the anomaly to fit into the framework of the Bible."

Archbishop Chambers replies, saying, "I beg to disagree. The Bible speaks clearly of angels and demons, of the seraphim and the cherubim. These are celestial beings of differing orders within creation, creatures that did not originate on Earth. Today, we'd call them aliens. They're extraterrestrial in origin, and yet they are subject to the Almighty. The LORD God is above all and is worshiped by all. The anomaly is part of creation, therefore it must be subject to the Creator."

Although Teller appreciates Reverend Johnson's opening comments, he doesn't like where the archbishop is going with his point. Teller knows this is going to be a seesaw debate, but he isn't sure which way the panel will end up leaning. It could go either way.

The Hindu delegate speaks up, swinging the balance back with his strong Indian accent. "We see no conflict. The anomaly is in harmony with our religion. It is, in essence, an example of the Dharma, the force or power that holds the universe together. Rather than challenging our notions, it reinforces them. Its very motion is shown to be in harmony with the cosmos."

Rabbi Stills adds his thoughts. "We look at this anomaly

like it is something new, but it is not. The scriptures speak of Moses and the burning fiery bush, the bush that burned but wasn't consumed by flames. That sounds remarkably similar to the events we saw unfolding before us when you released that balloon full of helium."

"But the balloon was consumed," Teller says, confused by the Rabbi's point.

"Ah, yes," the rabbi responds. "But my point is that such supernatural manifestations of power are not unprecedented in human history."

"This isn't supernatural," Teller says rather aggressively, surprising himself with how forceful he is on the issue.

"Oh, but it is," the archbishop says, agreeing with the rabbi. "It is not natural. It defies the laws of nature, does it not?"

The archbishop doesn't wait for an answer, cutting Teller off before he can reply.

"You must agree it is supernatural, something that is beyond nature. You yourself pointed out that we only see the manifestation of this power, we don't see the source. Just as Moses could see the burning bush but not the LORD God Himself."

Teller raises his palm, wanting to interject something, but the archbishop continues at a pace.

"And Moses commanded the waters that they stood in a heap. Is that not what we see with this anomaly? The very laws of gravity being defied. And in both cases, no reasonable, rational, scientific explanation can be provided. You see, the anomaly is in the realm of both science and religion."

"Now, wait a minute," Teller begins, finally able to get a word in. "You're portraying science as though it is a philosophy or an alternative theological notion, but it's not.

"Science is the discipline to investigate the world without regard to any preconceived ideas, be they religious or traditional beliefs. Science looks for reasons. And it asks but one question. Why? In this case, the technology is beyond our understanding, but that does not mean it is beyond all understanding."

The archbishop goes to speak, but it is Teller's turn. He cuts him off.

"There are television screens in this hall, projecting and enlarging our image for all to see. And yet to someone from the Bronze Age, when the majority of the scriptures were written, these would be mystical, magical, supernatural, but that doesn't mean they are supernatural. It just means there's a gap in understanding that needs to be bridged. And, when it comes to the anomaly, we are bridging it. We are investigating this remarkable alien artifact to understand its science."

"If I may add something," Cathy says. "The anomaly was sprung upon us all. A week ago, none of us would have thought we'd be sitting here today having this discussion. And it is surprising. It's alarming. We want to understand it. We want to be able to reconcile it with our beliefs, and we will, but we need to be patient, to give the process of investigation more time. We shouldn't be hasty to jump to conclusions, religious or otherwise."

"I agree," says Reverend Johnson, her southern twang hanging on her syllables. "Christianity has always been about compassion and understanding. It hasn't always lived up to those ideals, but they are at its foundation. When it comes to this alien entity, these must be the guiding principles. We need to understand the anomaly, as what you don't understand, you invariably fear. And fear has no place in our first contact with an extraterrestrial intelligence."

Teller nods. He likes Reverend Johnson's style.

"It is an abomination," the Reverend Stark cries, ignoring her entirely. "Ye shall worship the LORD your God and Him only shall ye serve. But look at you. You worship the anomaly. You adore it. You set up your little research centers. You focus your attention on it. You lavish your praise on it. You marvel at how it defies gravity. But it is to be condemned. You are deceived by your science. Professing yourselves to be wise, you have become fools."

"Now, hang on," Teller says, but Stark keeps going.

"Oh, I don't care what it is," the Reverend Stark continues. "I don't care if it's from Vega or Las Vegas, from Mars or New Orleans. What I care about is what you've done to it. You have turned it into an idol, a modern day golden calf. You've set the anomaly up on a pedestal. It may be from an alien world, but it cannot save your soul from the depravity and folly of your own sinful nature. You have magnified this alien artifact above God."

"I have to agree," says the imam at the end of the table. "Islam is also clear on the subject of idolatry. There is only one God and that is Allah. Mohammad is His prophet, blessed be his name. If this was the burning bush of Moses, of whom we, the Christians and the Jews all honor, then there would be a message from Allah in this abomination. If this was the parting of the waters, enabling the exodus from Egypt, there would be great deliverance to the people of Allah. But your anomaly is mute. The angel speaks from the burning bush, but the alien is silent."

"But it speaks to scientists," Cathy cries, frustrated by their closed minds.

"So it speaks to you?" the archbishop asks. "Are you now to assume the role of our apostles and prophets?"

"Do you presume to speak for Allah?" the Imam asks.

"Are you our new high priests?" the Reverend Stark asks. "Is it only scientists that can enter into the Holy of Holies to hear from the anomaly?"

Teller is horrified, but he isn't the only one, Reverend Johnson is clenching her teeth. She tries to say something, but she is cut off.

"You have no idea what you're dealing with," the archbishop says. "We should evacuate the city. If this alien of yours turns out to be hostile, we need to be ready to respond."

"With force?" Teller asks, understanding precisely where the archbishop is leading them. Teller thinks such a notion is absurd. "Don't you see? Your assumptions are all wrong. You're imagining the worst."

"You assume as much, if not more than us," the Reverend Stark says. "Can you not see the folly in your own naive position? When has First Contact with another culture ever not degraded into war?"

"Prudence demands caution," the archbishop says. "We should err on the side of safety."

"We need not err at all," Teller replies, feeling exasperated.

"I see only suffering," the Buddhist monk says. "The Buddha taught us about the Wheel of Life. The turning of the anomaly is like the continual rebirth of life, with each cycle offering the hope of change, rising up before us, but it only ever turns back to where it began. It is a false hope.

"You crave knowledge, but you don't understand that suffering is caused by your lust to know more. You crave a level of understanding you will never achieve. You are not content to let the anomaly be—to let the wheel turn. You are driven, consumed by your desires, and so your desire for knowledge will wound you. It is karma. Everything you do to understand this anomaly will only drive you further from true enlightenment. For what you seek cannot be found in a test tube or a telescope, it can only be found through the cleansing of the soul, through mantra and meditation."

Teller wants to storm out in disgust, but the cameras are watching, broadcasting his reactions to the world. The religious leaders are goading them, ganging up on them. Teller doesn't want to say anything he's going to regret, but sooner or later his anger is going to spill over.

"This is an age-old debate," he begins, finding an opening and vainly hoping he can steer the conversation in a positive direction. "It reaches back to the days of Copernicus, if not further. This debate is clearly not about the anomaly. This is not a discussion, as it should be, about the prospect of talking to an alien race. This is about the religious distrust of science."

"Are you an atheist?" the Reverend Stark asks.

Teller is exasperated. He squints as though he's trying to look right through the tiny man.

"How is that question even relevant?" the Reverend Johnson asks, coming to Teller's defense. "We're here to discuss the proposition of humanity talking with an alien intelligence, not to stir up strife."

Teller appreciates the way she stands up for him.

"I want to know who I'm talking to," the Reverend Stark says with disdain.

Teller looks at the archbishop, the rabbi, the Hindu and the Imam, before turning to look at the Buddhist monk and the minister sitting beside Cathy. Reverend Johnson shakes her head in astonishment. The others are silent. For once, they actually want to hear what he has to say, but Teller isn't about to let the debate degenerate into a personal attack.

"Listen to yourselves," he begins. "Just stop and think about what you're asking and how irrelevant it is to any discussion about the anomaly."

"Oh, it is very relevant," the Reverend Stark insists.

"Really?" Teller asks. "And I suppose the fact our Buddhist monk here does not believe in any kind of god at all is of no relevance? Doesn't that make him an atheist? Ah, but he's sincere in his religious convictions so you'll tolerate him."

Teller feels the adrenaline surging in his neck as he speaks. His hands are trembling. He's surprised to see how deeply stirred he is by the debate, and speaks with conviction.

"And I suppose your refusal to acknowledge the Hindu gods also has no relevance? Even though, from their perspective, it is you that is the atheist!"

"How dare you?" the Reverend Stark snaps. "This is an interfaith commune group. We have respect for each other's beliefs."

"Respect?" Teller replies, feeling the reverend is being disingenuous. He struggles to find something to say that won't inflame the situation further. Cathy grimaces.

Reverend Johnson tries to calm things down, saying, "Let's take things back a step or two."

But the Reverend Stark will have none of it. "I did not come here to be insulted," he says. "Answer the damn question!"

"To be fair," Cathy says, interrupting, "I think there is a valid point here. Religion is, by definition, exclusive. If I believe in God according to your definition, then I'm an infidel according to everyone else at this table. To believe in one religion is to exclude the others."

"Are you an atheist as well?" the reverend asks, staring down the table at Cathy.

"I am ashamed of you," the Reverend Johnson says, cutting into the argument in defense of Teller and Cathy. "You're obsessed by this. You've got to put everyone in your little, fundamentalist box. You just don't get it, do you? This is an opportunity to learn, an opportunity to explore, an opportunity to grow, but you'd rather descend back into the Dark Ages where your faith is unchallenged."

Damn, Reverend Johnson has moxie.

"Don't you see what this is?" Teller asks, seizing on the lull to bring the conversation back to the anomaly. "We have the chance to talk to an intelligence beyond our own."

"Some of us already do that," the Reverend Stark replies coldly. "It's called prayer."

"Do you see our concern?" the archbishop asks, picking up on the train of thought started by the fundamentalist minister. "We have our God. To us, this anomaly is being presented as a false god—a deity promoted by science. When the Spanish first landed in South America, the Aztec worshiped them as gods. It seems this same trend is unfolding before us again, and that's dangerous. It's wrong."

"To you scientists," he continues, "this might seem like a petty concern or an irrelevant, irrational fear, but the scriptures foretell of the end times. They speak of lying signs and wonders. They speak of a strong delusion that causes the elect to believe a lie. To us, the anomaly is a godless wonder bewitching the people."

"But it's not," Teller pleads, wondering how he can get them to see reason. He implores with his hands as he speaks. "It's the opportunity for a new beginning."

"And that's blasphemy," the Reverend Stark counters. "The only new beginning will come when Christ returns as the King of Kings to start his reign of a thousand years."

Teller responds instantly, without missing a beat, almost jumping out of his seat.

"And that's blasphemy to him, him, him and him," he says, pointing at the Hindu, the Buddhist monk, the Imam and the Rabbi.

Reverend Stark simmers in silence. His teeth clench in anger.

"When you get in an airplane," Cathy says, turning the topic around quite innocently, "Do you care about the religious beliefs of the person that built it? Or do you care about the science behind flight?"

Teller likes how she shifts the argument. It is a legitimate point. She may be soft spoken, but she's sharp.

"And these days," he says, picking up on her logic, "most planes are held together with little more than glue. There are few welds. There's not a pop-rivet or a nut and bolt in sight, and yet we trust them. But why? Neither you nor I have read the scientific reviews, we haven't studied the methodology or even seen the test results. And yet we inherently trust the science behind an airplane. Why? Because we trust progress. We trust the rigor of scientific expertise constantly refining and correcting itself.

"And that's the key. We don't trust science because it gets everything right. We trust science because, regardless of whether it gets things right or wrong, it measures, it records, it calibrates, it learns, it changes, it refines, and it corrects. And that process of transparency and open review has transformed the world in which we live for the better."

"We have to be willing to learn," the Reverend Johnson says. "We should be excited about the times in which we live, not afraid. There's too much uncertainty already, too much fear. Our people look to us for comfort, for stability, for assurance. We need to embrace the future, not rebel against it."

Cathy leans forward, wanting a better view of the participants further down the table.

"Will we make mistakes with the anomaly?" she asks. "Sure.

It would be surprising if we didn't. But we will ensure there's transparency. We will ensure the world shares in each discovery. The research into the anomaly isn't being conducted to threaten religious values, or to overthrow the role of religion in society, it's being undertaken with a sense of adventure, like the explorers of old, like Magellan and Columbus."

Out of the corner of his eye, Teller catches movement back stage. The Marine that drove them to the meeting walks out on stage and whispers in his ear as Reverend Johnson pleads with Reverend Stark for understanding.

"If we spend our time fighting each other, we're failing to understand each other. Is that what Christ would want?"

"I'm sorry," Teller says, interrupting Reverend Johnson. He puts his hand gently on Cathy's forearm as he stands up. "We've been informed we're needed urgently back at the research center.

"Thank you for the opportunity to be here today. I apologize for arriving late and for leaving early, but we'll have to continue this debate another time."

The Marine directs them toward the backstage area. Cathy smiles, waving at the restless crowd, trying to instill one last act of openness and kindness into the torrid debate.

Teller smiles for the crowd before whispering in her ear. "We need to get the hell out of here. Now!"

The chair of the debate starts recapping the main points as they leave the stage.

"What is going on?" Cathy asks as they hurry out the back door and into the waiting Hummer.

"The crowd outside is getting violent," the Marine says as they climb in the vehicle. "The police have started firing tear gas to disperse protesters, but it's getting ugly. The police chief is concerned about your safety. I need to get you out of here before things get any worse."

"Where is our escort?" Cathy asks, noticing their police detail is gone.

"They're not due back until the close of the conference. We can't wait that long. We need to get on the road and get you back to base."

And with that their Hummer heads north, riding up over bricks and broken bottles scattered across the street.

BLUE SKY

Within a few minutes, they're heading north along 6th Avenue and past the Holland tunnel. Before long, burnt out vehicles block sections of the road, making progress slow. The driver cuts across to Hudson St., driving away from Midtown, moving on an angle away from the U.N. building on 1st Avenue.

"Where are we going?" Teller asks, leaning forward from the back of the Hummer. "Why don't you just take Houston over to the FDR?"

"I'm sorry, sir," the young Marine says. "I didn't want to worry you. Command has re-routed us through the Village and up around Hell's Kitchen. Midtown's a powder keg. They want me to bring you in from the north. Apparently, it's quieter up there."

"So we get to tour New York City," Cathy says, realizing their four mile journey has just been extended to ten miles and God knows how many hours.

A burnt out semi-trailer blocks the road, forcing them onto a side street and over onto Greenwich St., but they're making better time than they did on the more direct route to the town hall.

The streets are quiet. The ride is rough. Rocks, stones, and the odd tear gas canister litter the concrete roads. Dark smoke rises over several parts of the city. There are few cars on the road now, just the odd emergency vehicle. Gangs of youths walk the streets.

Reports come in over the radio of a riot at Penn Station, so they cut across to 10th Avenue, all the while moving further away from 1st Avenue. As they approach the Lincoln tunnel, Teller realizes they are roughly level with the U.N. complex on the East side. He looks East, out over the haze toward where he knows the anomaly is located even though it isn't visible at this distance. He figures they have to be ten to fifteen blocks away, at most. He could walk that in the time they've already been on the road.

"How much further north?" Cathy asks, also realizing where they are.

"I've been told to head up to 59th before heading East."

"That's right on Central Park," Teller says, surprised.

"Affirmative," replies the Marine.

"Is this really necessary?" Cathy asks.

"Yes, ma'am. It's for your safety."

"But not your comfort," Teller jokes.

Cathy smiles as she settles back into the seat beside him.

"This seatbelt is designed for men," she grumbles under her breath, although Teller doubts that. It's probably just utilitarian.

The material is coarse and cuts across her chest at an uncomfortable angle. For his part, Teller notes that the U.S.

Marine Corps hasn't heard of inner springs, feeling the hard metal bench below the thin foam mat covering the seat.

"What's your name?" Teller asks, realizing he doesn't even know the name of their driver.

"Corporal John Davies," the Marine replies.

"How long have you been in the Marines, John?" Cathy asks.

For Corporal Davies, it's clearly strange to be called by his first name while on duty, but he seems to like it. "Four years," he replies.

"How did you end up on the anomaly detail?" Teller asks.

"I'm a heavy lifter, sir," the corporal replies. "Working closely with the SEALs. Assisting with—"

He never finishes his sentence.

In a blinding flash, the windscreen erupts in flames, bathing the inside of the vehicle in brilliant strands of crimson, burnt orange, and fiery yellow. From where Teller sits in the back of the vehicle, he can feel the searing heat lash at his exposed forearms and face. The Marine swings the Hummer hard to the right, clipping the side of a parked car before plowing headlong up onto the curb.

The Hummer slams into the corner of a ten story brick apartment building.

For Teller, everything happens in slow motion. The vehicle

comes to a thundering halt, but his momentum continues forward and it feels as though he's thrown out of the seat. The seatbelt locks. Teller twists sideways as the anchor point holds him back. He feels his hip catch as the belt cuts into his waist, drawing blood. His hands fly forward, as does his head, whipping down and back.

Cathy screams. Her hair lashes out before her. And as quickly as the collision began, they come to a painful stop.

Fire dances across the crushed hood of the Hummer.

Bricks fall on the smoldering vehicle, drumming out a crack and boom as they pelt the sheet metal.

Cathy groans.

Teller pops open his seatbelt and falls forward. His ears ring with a high pitched whine, while his forehead throbs. It's as though he's been hit on the back of the head with a baseball bat.

He turns to Cathy. She's dazed, struggling to comprehend what has happened. She releases her belt as Teller fights to open the door. Fire laps at the tires on the Hummer. Black acrid smoke wafts through the air.

Stumbling out onto the road, Teller falls to his knees.

Cathy looks around as she steps out into the bright sunlight behind him. They are on the far side of an intersection. People run back and forth, yelling, screaming. It takes a few seconds for them to realize the crowd is moving in unison, surging up and then back down the road. They've driven through a riot, coming into it from the side.

Teller struggles to his feet, dazed, looking at the rioters throwing bricks and rocks at police. The men are all young and fit. Probably in their late teens or early twenties. And he shakes his head, trying to make sense of the situation. The young men are wearing bandannas over their faces. At first, he thinks it's because of the smoke, but then he realizes they're hiding their identity as they hurtle rocks and Molotov cocktails at the approaching police.

Turning back toward the Hummer, Teller realizes the Marine hasn't moved. He wrestles with the front door of the vehicle, prying it open. Corporal Davies lies slumped over the drab olive-green steering wheel. Blood drips from a gash on the side of his head. His seatbelt sits coiled to one side, ready to be pulled down and into place. Bad habit. Teller grabs at the Marine. The heat from the flames radiates outward, scorching his hands, but he can't leave Davies. He pulls the corporal out of the vehicle and drags him away from the burning Hummer, breathing heavily as he staggers backwards, dragging the Marine along the street.

Tear gas canisters bounce through the intersection, leaving a trail of smoke curling behind them as they skid past the burning vehicle. The crack of rubber bullets being fired cuts through the noise and confusion around them.

More youths join the fray, coming in from a narrow alley and catching the police line from the side. They hurl rocks at the cops. The police begin falling back, dragging their injured with them.

An armored personnel carrier with a water cannon hoses down the youths, but the burst of a Molotov cocktail forces the vehicle to retreat. The tank-like carrier covers the retreating officers as it takes repeated fiery hits from home-made grenades.

Cathy is overwhelmed by the noise, the screaming, the yelling. She has her hands up, covering her ears. Teller lies the corporal down some twenty feet further along the road, away from the burning wreckage of the Hummer.

A gang of youths spot them. Rocks and stones begin raining down upon them. A brick catches Cathy on the side of her head, opening up a gash. Blood runs down her cheek. Teller tugs at the holstered sidearm on the corporal, pulling it out and pointing it at the oncoming horde. He snatches at the trigger several times, but nothing happens.

"The safety," Cathy cries as the mob charges at them.

A Molotov cocktail sails overhead, striking the building behind them and erupting into flames. The explosive heat wave causes them to cringe. Fire lashes the wall, rippling across the brickwork.

Teller fumbles with the 9mm Beretta, flicking the safety catch off as rocks strike him on the shoulder and forearms. A chunk of brick ricochets off the curb, bouncing up at him and colliding with his right shin. The rock tears through his trousers, stripping the skin off his leg and causing him to fall to one knee.

He points the gun at the gang running in hard toward them and squeezes but again, nothing happens.

"You've got to cock it," Cathy yells, snatching the gun from him.

She pulls back on the slide on top of the Beretta, loading a round from the magazine into the chamber, and fires, striking one of the rioting youths in the center of his chest. The young man drops to the road barely ten feet away, a bloodied machete still clenched in his twitching right hand. With that, the others scatter, darting for cover.

Cathy fires again and again, firing at an overturned, burnt out bus, making sure the rioters get the message loud and clear. Teller rests his hand on her arm, getting her to stop. She looks at him in a daze.

The young man rolls to one side, clutching at his chest. Brilliant red blood stains the street. No one comes to his aid.

"We've got to get out of here," Teller says, grabbing the corporal and lifting him up, hoisting him over his shoulder into a fireman's lift. He begins running along the street before turning down a side alley. Cathy keeps pace with him, constantly looking behind them to see if anyone's following.

"Why do they make Marines so heavy?" Teller asks, panting hard, almost collapsing under the weight of the soldier.

His lungs are burning. The muscles in his legs ache, but he pushes on. His feet feel as though they are going to give way beneath him, but he gets to the end of the alley and turns away from the intersection, trying to get as much distance between them and the riot as possible.

Cathy looks around at where they are. Teller can't look. It takes everything he has just to keep his legs pumping. His run slows to a clumsy jog under the weight of the Marine, but he pushes on. All he can see is a glimpse of green grass next to the cracked pavement.

They've come out into a small park bordered by several apartment blocks.

Teller can go no further. He has to stop. He has to catch his breath. He tries to put the Marine down gently but the corporal falls the last foot or so as Teller tries to stop his head from hitting the pavement. The corporal groans. Teller slumps to the ground beside him, struggling to breathe. His lungs are screaming for oxygen. He rolls over on the hard concrete path, looking up at the clouds in the blue sky above.

Cathy is shaking. The gun hangs from her fingers before falling to the concrete. She's crying, sobbing. She falls to her knees and sinks to the pavement beside him.

Teller leans forward, putting out his hand to touch hers.

"It's okay," is all he can manage.

He's disoriented. He's unsure where they are in relation to the police and the rioters. They can't stay here, but he isn't sure whether they're moving toward the police lines or away from them.

Yelling echoes down the alleyway. They have to keep moving. Teller tries to get back to his feet but his body refuses. The initial surge of adrenaline has faded and now all he is left with is the pain wracking his body. His muscles seize. He pushes himself up, kneeling beside the corporal.

"Got to keep moving," he says, trying feebly to pull the corporal up again, but he's too weak. He falls to his knees beside Cathy, exhausted.

"I killed him," Cathy sobs, sitting beside Teller on the concrete. The realization of what happened has only just registered.

"No," Teller replies softly. "You saved us. You did what you had to."

She turns to face him. Her hair is matted with blood, while her face has been marred with soot. Tears streak down her cheeks.

"It should have been you," she cries, thumping her hands on him, beating at his chest. "It should have been you that fired that shot. It shouldn't have been me."

He pulls her close, putting his hand on her head and pulling her into his shoulder as she sobs. The blood in her hair is warm and sticky, but nothing matters any more. Her chest heaves as she cries. There is nothing Teller can do, nothing he can say, so he holds her close. Tears well up in his eyes.

A basement door opens down a handful of stairs, just below ground level. An old man stands there in the doorway of a fire escape, beckoning Teller to come to him. Without saying a word, he motions him to come inside.

Teller is dazed. He feels as though he's in a dream—a nightmare. For a second, he just stares at the old man, wondering if he's real.

He gets to his feet, which startles Cathy. She turns, seeing the aging African American with his receding, gray hairline, standing there in the shadows. Teller grabs at the Marine, pulling his arm up as he swings his shoulder down to gain some leverage. Teller staggers over toward the door with the Marine hanging from his shoulder.

Cathy follows Teller in a daze, leaving the handgun lying there on the pavement amid the splotches of blood.

WHY?

Teller staggers down the narrow hallway, putting his bloodied hand out to steady himself under the weight of the Marine, leaving deep red streaks on the cream-colored walls.

The old man is talking, but Teller can't hear anything, just muted, indistinct sounds. He isn't even sure if Cathy has followed. In his mind, he is steeling himself to leave the Marine somewhere safe and then trudge back out to get her. He's moving on instinct, self-preservation. It's a matter of pushing through whatever pain there is in order to survive. If they can last a few more minutes, they might make an hour, if they can make an hour, they might make it through the day.

The frail old man leads him up a flight of stairs.

Each step is a mountain to climb. Teller's back aches, the muscles on his neck and shoulders shake in spasms of agony, his thighs burn under the strain. He grabs at the banister, pulling on the steel railing. His feet are on the verge of giving way. The old man tugs at him, urging him on, trying to help him bear the load.

A young family stands at the top of the stairs. It hurts to look up. Sweat drips from his brow, stinging his eyes. He's only barely aware of the young lady that reaches out to help prop him up. There are kids in the way. He stumbles into them as he clears the last step. The old man beckons him into an apartment on the far side of the hall.

Teller staggers into the living room and collapses, falling forward and dropping the Marine on a couch as he crashes to the carpet floor beside him. He fights to get back to his feet, to go back and get Cathy, when a soft hand rests on his shoulder. He is staring right at her, but it takes him a moment to realize it's her smiling face staring back at him. And with that, he slumps back against the couch, exhausted.

"Thank you," Cathy says, turning to the elderly man standing beside his aging wife.

"Sarah is a nurse," the old man says, gesturing toward a woman barely out of her teens. She has a first aid kit and is already looking at the Marine lying on the couch.

The two kids can't be more than eight years old. They stand to one side, staring at the bloodied strangers, filled with a sense of curiosity and caution.

The old man hands Cathy and Teller a glass of water each. Teller is surprised just how refreshing the first sip is. He hadn't realized his throat was so parched.

"No, granddad. You can't give them water. They may have internal wounds that require surgery."

"You worry too much," the old man says. "Water is good."

Teller drinks it anyway. He moves to one side, allowing Sarah more room to examine the soldier.

"What kind of nurse are you?" Cathy asks, regaining her sense of awareness far quicker than Teller.

"Maternity and delivery, I'm afraid," Sarah replies. "I'll do what I can for your friend, but it's been a long time since I worked triage."

Sarah pushes two fingers hard up against the soldier's jugular and takes his pulse, watching her old-fashioned analogue watch as she quietly counts out the beats.

"His pulse is running at 58 beats per minute, which is low, but his heart beat is regular. I just hope there's no internal bleeding."

She pulls open his eyelids, looking at his dilated pupils. Then she reaches gently around the back of his head, comparing the two hemispheres of his skull as she works her fingers delicately around to the front of his skull.

"There's no cranial damage, which is good. But he has suffered a nasty concussion. It's troubling that he hasn't regained consciousness. That tends to suggest there's some swelling on the brain, which is not good. We need to get him to a hospital. This isn't something we can treat here."

"Phone's still out," the old man says.

Sarah tries her cell phone.

"No signal," she says. "Grandma, can you get me a couple of buckets? One with a little warm water in it. Oh, and some towels, plenty of towels."

Sarah unbuttons the soldier's shirt, exposing deep purple bruises forming on his chest. She pushes gently on his ribs, looking for any give while also looking for a response that shows some level of consciousness. The Marine groans.

"He's got a few broken ribs, but they're not detached, which is good. It means they won't have gone on to cause any further internal damage to his lungs."

Teller is feeling better with each passing minute. Physically, he's in pain, but the love and kindness of these strangers is healing.

"Please," the old man says. "Have a seat."

The old man helps Teller to his feet and over to a large armchair. Cathy sits down on the broad arm of the chair, leaning up against its back. Teller can't blame her for wanting to stay close to him. He wants to be close to her. There's something about rallying together that gives them both strength. He puts his hand on her thigh. She's shaking. He isn't sure if it's from the injuries she sustained in the accident, or from the shock of firing on the rioter.

"How you doing?" he asks.

She runs her hand up through her hair, saying, "I'm fine," only to pull away her sticky fingers, realizing her hair is matted with blood.

Grandma returns with several buckets, one with some warm water sloshing around in it. Sarah pours a little disinfectant in and swirls it around before soaking some hand towels and dabbing at Cathy's forehead.

"Can you put the other bucket over by the soldier, grandma?" Sarah says. "It's not uncommon for head injuries to cause vomiting, so we need to keep a close eye on him."

Cathy sits up a little as Sarah begins cleaning her wounds, and Teller can see she appreciates being cared for. The trembling in her hands subsides. Sarah alternates between the wet hand towel and a dry towel, slowly cleaning her wounds.

"Feel better?" she asks, as she wraps a compression bandage around Cathy's forehead.

"Yes, thank you."

She turns her attention to Teller. The disinfectant stings, but Sarah is gentle as she daubs at a cut on his forehead.

"Grandma. Can you get them some painkillers? Some Tylenol or something? But write down exactly what you give them and the time you give it to them. The medics will need to know that at the hospital."

The young girl calls out, "Sarah, the soldier. He's moving."

The corporal rolls to one side. His eyes open briefly. Sarah is already rushing over next to him. She holds the bucket low beside him, resting her hand on his shoulder. He convulses, bringing up a small amount of bile that she catches in the bucket. Raising his hand to his head, he groans before rolling back and turning his head away. Sarah wipes his lips with a towel.

"This is good," she says, looking over at Cathy. "Well, it's not great, but he's doing better than I thought. When it comes to head injuries, everything's relative and better is good, not as good as being normal and healthy, but it's a really positive sign. He's slipping in and out of consciousness, but that's okay. It means the swelling isn't getting worse. And he moved his whole body when he spewed so there's little or no serious spinal damage. That's really good to see. I think he's going to be all right."

"Thank you so much," Teller says, relaxing and letting his head sink back into the armchair. Sarah comes back over and begins washing his forehead with a damp cloth.

They introduce each other, with Sarah naming everyone in the family. Teller isn't that good at remembering names at the best of times, let alone now. He just smiles politely.

"What happened out there?" the old man asks.

"We were returning from lower New York," Cathy says, "I don't know quite what happened. One minute we are driving along talking, and the next all hell broke loose. I think we were hit by a homemade bomb."

"You're soldiers?" Sarah asks as she finishes up.

"Oh, no. Scientists," Teller says, pausing for a second as he corrects himself. "Well, actually, I'm a school teacher and Cathy's a reporter, but, these days, well … we seem to be somewhat out of our depth."

Cathy smiles at the massive understatement in his words.

"I knew I'd seen you before," the old man says. "You're that guy on the TV. The one with the balloon."

Teller raises his hand in acknowledgment, embarrassed.

"He's a little unconventional," Cathy says.

"We need to get back to the NASA research team," Teller says. "Is there any way we can get hold of the police or the army?"

"Our son," the old man says.

"My dad's a police officer," Sarah says, completing the sentence for her grandfather. "But he didn't come home last night. We got a message from the wife of one of his buddies saying they had to stay on duty at the station until the state of emergency is over."

"Do you have an Internet connection?" Cathy asks, turning toward Teller as she adds, "Maybe we can get a message out to them."

"Sure," Sarah replies, pulling a laptop from the bookshelf. She turns it on and hands it to Teller. "But I don't know if our internet connection is working."

The television is on, with the sound turned down.

"Do you mind if we listen to that?" Cathy asks.

NBC News is replaying an address by the President from earlier in the day.

The old man turns up the volume on the television.

"... the deployment of the National Guard to restore order in New York City in support of emergency services is to take effect immediately. Members of my cabinet are in discussion with Governor Rosenthal of New York state to make the necessary logistic arrangements. The first units are expected to be deployed shortly after 1 pm Eastern Standard Time."

"In regards to U.N. Resolution 2721—that the anomaly is under the jurisdiction of the United Nations—it is the position of the United States of America that the United Nations does not have the authority to dictate to permanent members of the U.N. Security Council. The United States has exercised its veto over this U.N. Resolution and has rejected the notion of United Nations peacekeepers operating on American soil. This decision is final."

"Well," the news commentator continued, "There you have it. America stands in defiance of the International Community and the U.N. resolution to station so-called peacekeepers in New York."

"At this point, only the United Kingdom and Australia are supporting the U.S. Even Canada has joined in the growing chorus of international condemnation for the U.S. position on the alien anomaly. China, France and Germany have all called for the immediate cessation of U.S. interaction with the alien, stating it represents a danger to world stability."

Cathy swears, unable to contain herself.

"Riots broke out in Brussels late last night," the news anchor says, "when what began as a peaceful protest in front of the U.S. embassy turned ugly. With five dead and hundreds injured, it seems the upheaval caused by the anomaly is spreading like a wildfire throughout Europe.

"Protesters have converged in most capital cities, including London, Paris, Madrid and Berlin, but a heavy police presence has ensured these protests have remained largely peaceful, at least for now. There is no doubt, however, that European governments are under increasing pressure from their electorates to do something about what is seen as American arrogance over the discovery of an alien intelligence.

"In Iran and Pakistan, effigies of President Laver, draped in an American flag, have been burned in the streets.

"Japan, normally the epitome of conservative diplomacy, has ordered American warships to depart from its territorial waters, while the Congress of South America has formally requested the United States withdraw its economic missions from all Latin American countries in protest at what they describe as the American hegemony.

"In the United Kingdom, the Linnaean Society, along with the International Council for Science, has called for the establishment of a non-governmental organization to act as the arbiter for scientific research into the anomaly, calling on the U.S. government to relinquish control over the Manhattan site, but the Laver Administration has remained resolute."

Cathy turns to Teller, saying, "I don't like where this is heading. This is getting out of control."

Teller barely hears her. He acknowledges her but he's busy

tapping away on the laptop keyboard. The phones might be down, but the internet connection is up.

"Any ideas on how we can get out of here?" she asks.

"I've signed into a video chat room and posted contact details on the CERN forums. I only hope someone from the liaison team is monitoring them. Certainly, they won't be expecting to hear from us via Switzerland."

"Hey that's us," Cathy says, pointing at the television screen. The old man, his wife and his grandchildren all gather around. There, on the screen, is a shot of Teller and Cathy in the back of the Hummer as it pulls out of the parking lot behind the town hall.

"This just in. Officials have confirmed that two members of the anomaly investigation team have gone missing en-route from a meeting in lower New York."

"David Teller and Cathy Jones were last seen heading north on 6th Avenue. The military has dispatched helicopters and ground units to search for the missing scientists lost somewhere in the Broadway/Union Station area. Anyone sighting the team should notify the New York Police Department on…"

"Oh, no," Cathy cries. "They'll never find us. They're looking too far south and east. They're going to miss us by about ten city blocks at least."

Granddad tries the phone again, typing in the number on the screen, but the phone is still dead.

Grandma wanders out into the kitchen and returns a few minutes later with some ham and cucumber sandwiches on rye bread.

"No, grandma," Sarah says, and Teller realizes she's resorting to her medical training and the nil-by-mouth policy for anyone that might require a general anesthetic.

"You worry too much," grandma says. "They need their strength."

"They could have late-onset injuries," Sarah protests. "Like a damaged kidney or slow, internal bleeding."

"Look at them," granddad says. "They're fine."

Teller is famished. The sandwiches are moist and seasoned with a little cracked pepper. The bread is fresh, which surprises him. He looks up, as if to ask, only to have the lovely, aging old lady preempt his question by telling him she baked the bread this morning.

The old man sits down across from them. Cathy turns the television down. Like most emergency coverage, it has started to repeat itself, playing the same clips over again.

"You can leave that on," the man says.

"Oh, it's okay," Cathy replies. "News is only ever so new. By the time most people hear the news it's old. Working in the industry, I know the real art of news is in regurgitating the sensational rather than providing new information. They'll repeat this for the next few hours without really adding anything."

Sarah checks on the corporal, taking his pulse and wiping his forehead.

"How is he?" Teller asks.

"He's stable. His pulse is a little higher, 65 beats per minute, which is good."

She checks his dilated eyes. There's a weak, gradual response to light, just enough to give them a glimmer of hope that he's improving. Sarah finishes up with the soldier and sits down at the kitchen table, pouring herself a glass of water.

"Is the alien friendly?" the little boy asks, taking everyone off guard.

"George," Sarah says. "Don't be nosy."

"It's okay," Teller replies. He leans forward toward the young boy and, despite his aches and pains, smiles as he says, "Yes, it is."

"What does it want?"

"Well," Teller says, thinking about how to respond to the boy. "It's curious. It wants the same thing we do—to learn about life elsewhere in the universe. Only elsewhere for the anomaly is home for us."

"Is that why it came here?" the boy asks.

"Yes."

"Where did it come from?"

"Hmm, a long time ago, in a galaxy far, far away," he begins, but no one else seems to pick up on his weak attempt at a reference to Star Wars. Timing's everything, and now is not the time. Teller clears his throat. "Where the anomaly came from is not quite as interesting as when it came from. We think it may be from somewhere out beyond our galaxy. If that's the case, then it has been traveling for millions, if not billions of years, so it has been traveling for a very, very long time."

Young George looks a little befuddled and Teller's school teacher habits kick in as he tries to put the time involved in context.

"The anomaly has been traveling through outer space for longer than you or I have been alive. It may have been traveling for longer than there have been people on Earth. It was probably sent out long before dinosaurs walked the Earth. And so, whoever sent this probably knew they'd be dead long before the anomaly arrived, and yet still they sent it."

"Why?" Sarah asks, packing up her first aid kit. "Why would someone send something they'd never hear back from?"

"That's a good question," Teller replies. "Why would you send out a probe you'd never hear from again? Personally, I think this is the most intriguing aspect of the anomaly. And the answer is simple when you think about it."

Teller looks around the room.

"What's the most valuable thing in this room?"

The little boy speaks up first.

"The TV."

Teller laughs.

"Nope, that's not it."

Sarah looks around her grandparents' apartment. Teller follows her gaze. The furniture is old. The pictures on the walls are faded. Dust sits on the bookcase. There is a black-and-white photo of grandma and granddad getting married, along with a photo of her parents wedding day. There's a photo of her mother when she was six months pregnant with her and, next to that, a photo of her graduation from medical school. Little George is right. The most expensive thing in the room is the television.

"I don't know," Sarah says.

"It's you," Teller replies, gesturing with his hands toward each of them.

"The most important thing in life is life itself. People always look for meaning in life, as though meaning is somehow missing, but it's not, it's all around us. Your granddad, your grandmother, your mom and dad, your brothers and sisters. There's nothing more valuable than them. There's no dollar figure you can place on them."

Everyone's silent, hanging on his every word.

"And so why did some alien species millions of light years away from us send out these probes? To find the most valuable commodity in the universe. Life.

"And it didn't matter to them if they never found anyone. It didn't matter to them that they'd never live to see their probes make contact. It didn't matter if their entire civilization had collapsed and disappeared. They still chose to reach out. Life reaches out to find life.

"They must have sent out thousands, perhaps millions of these probes into space, and all on a whim, on a hope. They sent them out not knowing if they'd ever find anything, but knowing that if they existed, then there must be others out there too, and so they sent out probes to find them, to talk to them, to communicate with them, to help them. And the 'them' is us."

Teller leans down toward George saying, "Those aliens sent out probes for the same reason your granddad opened the door to a bunch of scary strangers lying on the pavement all covered in blood, because that's what intelligent life does. Life cares."

The old man smiles with pride.

"And most of these alien probes wouldn't have found any life at all. While those that did might have sat idle for millions of years waiting for intelligence to evolve. We don't know a lot about the anomaly, but what we do know is that it was built by someone that wanted to reach out and share their knowledge. They wanted to share their lives with other intelligent beings in this cold, lonely universe. They want to show others that they're not alone among the stars."

Sarah's laptop chimes. The message on the screen reads,

"Dr. William Anderson, NASA, wants to start a video conference with you. Answer Yes/No."

"Yes," Teller says, filled with excitement. He clicks the button and the webcam brings up an image of Anderson in his blue NASA polo shirt.

"Teller? Cathy? Is that really you?"

"Yes," Teller cries. "It's us."

Cathy leans into the video from the side. The rest of the family huddle around looking over the back of the armchair at the small computer screen.

"What the hell happened to you guys?" Anderson asks. "Where are you?"

"That's a good question. Where are we?" Teller asks the old man.

"Westfield apartments, West 47th Street, just off 10th Avenue. We're in unit 104."

Mason is looking over Anderson's shoulder, writing down the address on a notepad.

"We'll have someone out to get you ASAP," Mason says, leaning into the video for a second before disappearing off screen.

"Damn, Teller. You look like shit," Bates says, standing behind Anderson.

"Yeah, it's good to see you too," Teller replies, laughing.

"Hey, tell Mason we're going to need paramedics here as well. We need to get Corporal Davies to a hospital. He got busted up pretty bad."

"Will do," Bates replies, disappearing in the same direction as Mason.

Cathy catches a glimpse of Finch in the background, filming the video chat.

"Hey Finch," she calls out, but he keeps filming, ignoring her. She turns to Teller, saying, "Bloody typical. Not so much as a word from him to ask how we are."

She turns back to the camera on the laptop, seeing Finch standing behind Anderson, and she calls out, "I'm getting a new cameraman, Finch. You're fired. Do you hear me?"

Anderson laughs. Finch seems unfazed by Cathy's comments. He waves in acknowledgement without appearing from behind the lens.

"Your little friend has been pretty busy today," Anderson says. "We fed him a couple of kilos of carbon in all different varieties and he turned on the fireworks."

"Really?" Teller replies, losing himself and his aching body in the prospect of learning more about the anomaly.

"Yeah. Right after we finished feeding in ten different types of pure carbon molecules, a pin-prick of blinding light appeared in the center of the anomaly. The boys in Geneva reckon it was sub-millimeter in size, probably down to the micron level. Damn thing started glowing like the sun. It was casting shadows in the midst of a bright noon day sky. We couldn't look at it. That tiny dot fired up like an arc-welder. It was fusion, Teller. A goddamn controlled fusion reaction smaller than the head of a pin."

Teller is quiet, listening intently.

"Then we start noticing a fine powder falling to the ground. It was carbon. The bloody thing was simulating the triple-alpha process required to produce carbon in the heart of a star! Bloody show off. I'm still waiting for the final analysis, but that would mean temperatures of over a hundred million Kelvin in a controlled spot, so the anomaly now holds the record for the highest temperature ever achieved on Earth. Bloody thing could have set the atmosphere on fire if it wasn't careful. How the hell it insulated us from the heat is beyond me."

Teller smiles. There are lots of "bloody's" in Anderson's description. He is clearly over-excited. Teller doesn't know quite what the triple-alpha process is, but he understands the basic principles behind fusion and the formation of heavier elements from lighter ones.

Anderson must read the look on his face.

"They were temperatures and pressures normally only found at the heart of a super-giant star. Our sun can't get anywhere near these extremes. In one afternoon, we've leapfrogged fifty years of fusion research. The anomaly has given us temperatures, pressures, electromagnetic energies, densities, composition, magnetic field strengths for containment, the whole nine yards. The damn thing has given us a blueprint for a fusion reactor! It could take us centuries to replicate something like this, but we now know it's possible. Scientists will be studying this footage along with our monitoring log file in college physics labs for the next couple of decades at least."

"Nice," Teller says, appreciating the broader ramifications, especially for energy production.

"The whole show lasted about half an hour and then the anomaly got bored and moved on to nitrogen, so we responded with liquid oxygen, and we've been chatting back and forth since then."

"Bates has a theory," Anderson says. "He thinks the anomaly is working through the periodic table as a primer before constructing something out of these elements, some kind of device. What do you think?"

"Makes sense," Teller replies. "There's got to be a next phase in the cycle of communication, and it seems reasonable that the initial discovery phase would lead to something that's related. Does he have any ideas about what?"

"Nope. But it scares the crap out of Mason. He's been pleading with the President to cut the live feeds, but with all the diplomatic pressure, the President is more determined than ever to make sure there's complete transparency."

"It won't be bad," Teller replies. "Whatever the anomaly is working toward, it will be in keeping with what we've seen so far. It will be an extension, an improvement, something that takes our conversation to another level."

"Yeah, well, Mason wants you back here. At the current rate of element exchange, we'll be up to radium by midnight, if not sooner. He wants your thoughts on all this."

"My thoughts?" Teller replies, still getting used to the attention. "I don't know anything about fusion or triple-whatevers. I think I may have outlived my usefulness."

"Nonsense," Anderson says. "We're in uncharted territory, so it's a level playing field for all of us, elementary school teachers and astrophysicists alike."

Anderson gives him a wink. Teller appreciates his kindness, but he really does feel out of his depth. It was one thing to come up with the idea of initially introducing helium, but when it comes to atomic isotopes and high-energy physics, Teller is a dead weight and he knows it.

"Bates says we're going to run into trouble once we hit Fermium. It's bloody nasty stuff. Even Bates is struggling to get his hands on more than a few hundred milligrams of the crap. After that, we get Nobelium, and that's worse. It has a half-life of only ten days. There are no known stockpiles of the stuff so we're scouring several university research reactors trying to scrape some together, but even if we can get that worked out, the next element we need to come up with is Rutherfordium, which has a half-life of only ninety minutes. Somehow, I don't think Mason's going to let us whip that up on-site."

"I suspect," Teller says, "our friend is probably counting on exposing our technical limitations with these exotic elements as that will give him a yardstick to determine how advanced we are."

Anderson runs his hand over his goatee beard as he speaks.

"Yeah, he's going to see us struggling with the heavyweights beyond a hundred. In principle, we can get as far as ununoctium at 118, but no further. And then, that's only ever been a handful of atoms in a particle accelerator. The darn stuff decays in a fraction of a second. There's just no way we can feed this stuff to our hungry friend."

"Exactly, and he knows it," Teller says. "It's going to be an interesting evening."

"Hey," Anderson says. "Mason said you should be getting..."

Suddenly, there is a loud, authoritative, thumping knock on the door.

"Well, how's that for timing. Looks like your ride has turned up."

DARWIN

Mason doesn't take any chances. The whole neighborhood is in lockdown with armed soldiers stationed at each intersection.

The Marines that pick up Cathy, Teller and Davis, drive three blocks to an inner-city school where several adjoining basketball courts have been converted into a helipad. Sawn-off basketball poles with their nets still attached lie carelessly on the ground. From there, Corporal Davies is flown to a military hospital in Jersey, while Teller and Cathy are flown to the park beside the U.N.

Teller is glued to the window of the military helicopter as they come in from the north. He wants to make the most of the opportunity to see the anomaly from the air.

It's a little after eight in the evening as they approach the U.N. building. Spotlights light up the anomaly from numerous angles. The concrete intersection sits high in the air, facing down to the west. The underside of the concrete is exposed to the night sky. The core team is at work on the inverted slab, walking about as though it were natural to defy gravity in such an extraordinary way. The flags inside the anomaly have passed their zenith. They look surreal, floating freely as they're suspended against the skyline. The wind up high is strong, causing them to flap madly in the evening breeze.

After landing, Teller and Cathy are checked over at the

medical center, where they shower and are given a fresh set of clothes. Mason even commandeers an electric golf cart from somewhere so they don't have to walk back to the research center.

Teller jokes with Cathy that he is so pumped full of painkillers he could spin upside down like the anomaly. And yet, he walks with a limp.

Mason makes sure they get something to eat and then briefs them on the progress so far that day.

Teller asks about the riots in the city, but Mason assures him that the National Guard has squashed the unrest. Mason says it's an isolated incident, but Teller can tell from the look on Cathy's face that she isn't so sure. One of the monitors in the research trailer displays CNN. There are images of Paris in flames. Cathy wanders over, wanting to hear the commentary.

"...coming to you from the Arc de Triomphe. The Champs Élysées is in flames. The rioting, which began in the northern suburbs of Paris, has spread to the iconic western quarter, destroying some of the most expensive real estate in the world."

Footage of Prada, Versace, and Louis Vuitton stores, ransacked and in ruins, flashes up on the screen. Broken glass and smoldering cars line the streets.

"The French government has deployed troops to protect the Louvre, blaming the unrest on the United States. Ambassador Carter was summoned to appear before French President Jacques Lebarre just a few hours ago, and was formally asked to leave the country in protest at the exclusion of the International Community from the anomaly research.

"Here in Washington, the Laver Administration is downplaying the incident, stating that Ambassador Carter flew to London for security reasons and will return to Paris once law and order has been restored."

Teller walks up beside Cathy. He too is alarmed by how little attention the news broadcast generates. No one cares. The work they're doing here is tearing the world apart, but no one around them seems to notice.

"Is it just me?" she asks.

"No," Teller says. "I see it too. We're getting tunnel vision."

Cathy moves slowly.

"It sounds bad," she says. "But, honestly, I'm sick of caring. We're doing this to ourselves. I just want the world to come to a halt. I want the madness to stop. Why is it like this? It doesn't have to be this way. Why can't we get along?"

Teller suspects she already knows the answer, but he says it anyway. "We've never been able to get along. The anomaly hasn't done anything other than expose the weaknesses that have always been there."

Teller points at the screen showing images of protests in South Africa.

"They don't trust us because we're different. We don't trust them because they're different. Oh, if only we could see how similar we are."

Cathy rests her hand on his shoulder, saying, "If only we could see anything at all."

To which Teller laughs. Together, they hobble over to the lounge in front of the anomaly. Someone has put a pair of binoculars, a copy of the New York Times, and a couple of tablet computers on the worn, wooden table in front of the couch.

"Now, this is what I'm talking about," Cathy says, dropping onto the soft couch. "You go do your science thing. I'm going to have some 'me time' and unwind for a bit."

The couch hasn't aged well. There are stains on the cushions and tears along the seams. Teller watches as Cathy slumps into the couch with a sigh. She leans back, slouching as she looks up at the anomaly. There's a vacant expression on her face.

Teller is in two minds. Part of him feels numb from the events of the day. He wants to flop on the couch next to her, but not to talk, just to be near her. With all they've been through from the very first day, he feels a bond with Cathy. She's so different to him. Seeing her go through all the same things he has provides him with another perspective on his own life, one that seems more grounded. That she's the one that has propelled him through all this escapes his mind, and he sees only their common, shared experiences. But she needs some time alone to clear her head and recharge her batteries, so to speak. He figures he'll sit in one of the armchairs and not say anything, perhaps have a cat nap, when he sees Anderson walking up to them.

"Your timing is impeccable," Anderson says, oblivious to all Teller and Cathy have been through. "We're making great progress. We just passed radium."

And with that, Teller finds himself swept up in the anomaly research again. He loses himself in the science, talking passionately with Anderson and Bates.

A row of monitors set up beneath the awning of the nearby research trailer displays all kinds of readings from the various instruments set up around the anomaly. None of them make any sense to Teller. They're plotting trends over time, noting the subtle changes when each new element is introduced, but what it all means is lost on a grade school teacher. Teller knows the graphs are probably telling the real scientists a great deal about the anomaly, but he'd rather turn around and watch the anomaly itself.

After milling around for a while, talking to the contact team, Teller notices Cathy again, still sitting there alone on the couch. He looks at a clock, it has been the best part of two hours since they watched the vision of Paris in flames. Anderson is rushing from one group of scientists to the next, so Teller figures he'll stay out of his way and keep Cathy company.

Sitting on the couch, they are less than twenty feet from the open pit carved out by the anomaly. Teller is surprised Mason has allowed even the scientists this close. If anyone fell into the broad hole, they'd fall up to the concrete intersection, wherever that may be as it rotates over the course of a day. It is as though they are sitting on top of a building with no railing along the edge. The view of the anomaly is awe-inspiring.

"Are you okay?" he asks.

Cathy nods but doesn't say anything. He holds her hand, warming her fingers. She responds to his touch, snuggling up against him for warmth.

"It's a lot to take in, isn't it?" he says.

"Yep," is all she can muster in reply.

They sit there in silence for a few minutes.

She breathes deeply before saying, "It's not just the anomaly—the whole world is turning upside down."

"Yeah," is all Teller can say.

"Why is all this so difficult for everyone to accept?"

"I guess it's change," Teller says, putting his arm around her. "We tend to get in a rut, in a rhythm. We expect life to unfold the same way, day after day. And as boring as that may be, we feel comfortable with mundane routines. There's security in repetition—going off to work each morning, watching a soap opera at night, taking the dog for a walk on the weekend. And then, along comes a visitor from another planet, from another galaxy, and, well—there goes the neighborhood."

Cathy laughs. Teller laughs too. There's something about

belittling such a radically disruptive concept that if you didn't laugh, you'd cry.

"You know the U.N. wants this thing?" she asks. "They're claiming jurisdiction over it. They claim we're illegally occupying the site."

"I don't understand politics," Teller confesses. "It's never made sense to me."

"Me neither."

They chat idly for a while before Cathy drifts off to sleep, snuggling up to him for warmth.

Teller is sore, but it's nice having Cathy leaning against him as the cool of the evening settles around them. After watching the swarm of activity around the anomaly for a while he dozes off as well.

Bates walks up to them with two cups of hot chocolate.

"Thought you two might like this," he says. Cathy stirs at the sound of his voice. She smiles, accepting the warm drink. Teller sips at the hot chocolate. It tastes sweet, with a rich, milk froth on top.

"Is this from the mess?" she asks.

"They've brought in a barista," Bates says, sitting down in one of the armchairs next to them. "I guess there's only so far you can push a bunch of civilians without decent coffee and some fancy hot chocolate."

"Yep," Teller says, warming his hands on the cup.

"So, what do you think of our setup?" Bates asks, seeing Teller staring at the activity on the intersection above them.

"I just don't know if I can ever get used to that," Teller says, watching the core team walking around upside-down on the inverted concrete slab. For him, it's mind-bending to watch people climb down the scaffolding from his perspective, but up the scaffolding from their perspective. And the orientation of their bodies, with their hands lowest and their feet above them, it's a lie perpetrated against physics, betraying the instinctive notion humans have of up and down. He keeps waiting for them to fall, but is grateful they don't.

"Yeah," Bates replies. "I know what you mean. It's one thing to understand that the anomaly is stationary in its orientation, while we're moving, spinning around the Earth's axis, but it is another to see it that way. It feels like we're standing still and it's the one that's moving. How do you get your head around that?"

"To be honest," Teller says, "The anomaly does my head in."

Cathy bursts out laughing, almost choking on a mouth full of hot chocolate. She scoots forward on the couch and turns to look at him, her hand poised to catch any drops of drink running from her lips as she swallows. "You're kidding, right? I thought it was just me! You guys are always so confident and assertive. I just figured I was the only one that felt intimidated by all this."

"Oh, no," Teller replies. "Don't let the macho act fool you. When it comes to what Anderson is doing, well, I've heard of these elements but I couldn't spell half of their names."

"Me neither," Bates says, leaning over the back of the couch.

"If I ever get to name an element, I'd like to call it absurdium," Teller says.

"Ha," cries Bates. "I like that."

"I'd call mine ignorantium," Cathy jokes, leaning back against Teller.

"Mine would be have to be wackium, or ium-ium," Bates says, being recursive.

Mason walks over with Trissa and Anderson. Cathy sits up, which surprises Teller. It's as though she feels like she is doing something wrong by snuggling up to him. Mason swings a regular desk chair around and sits backwards on it, facing them as he straddles the seat. Anderson sits on the arm of a plush armchair while several other NASA scientists mill around, sitting on the coffee table or just standing in the background. Finch angles for the best shot.

"So," Mason begins. "What do you think of our progress so far?"

Teller looks up at the anomaly. Yet another injection is under way. He's not sure which chemical element they've reached in the Periodic Table, but it is in the process of being dropped upwards from a canister on the scaffolding above the center of the anomaly.

A clump of silvery metal roughly the size of a tennis ball falls up toward the slab. It floats for a second or two upon reaching the center of the anomaly before continuing up into the catchment basket. Only, as the ball falls up toward the basket, it seems to change. It has a slightly different hue.

"That was the Fermium drop," Anderson says. "It's a fascinating process. The anomaly catches our offering, somehow adds a proton to all the individual atoms within that mass, and the next element in the periodic table drops out the other side. So that would be Mendelevium coming out of there with the green tinge."

"Incredible," Teller says, lost for words.

"You should have seen the platinum drop," Anderson says. "We released a one kilogram glistening silvery sphere only to watch just over a kilo of gold drop out the other side. There is more than one technician that wanted to see that one again. Astonishing. Alchemy in action."

"So what's next?" Mason asks. "What kind of machine is this thing likely to build?"

"No idea," Bates says.

"I can't think of any machine that would use all these elements," Anderson replies.

They look at Teller.

"You're asking me? Your guess is as good as mine."

Teller corrects himself, pointing at Trissa, Anderson and Bates, saying, "In fact, their guess is significantly better than mine. These guys understand the physics—they're operating on a whole other level to me."

Trissa says, "I don't know if we're going to be able to preempt the next step. We may just have to wait and see."

"Got any more helium balloons?" Bates asks. "Any ideas?"

"Well," Teller says, stalling for a second. He is sore and tired, but he pushes his mind through a sense of lethargy. "Let's look at what it knows about us. It knows we're able to isolate a continuous string of periodic elements through to the heavy radioactive metals like uranium and plutonium. So it knows we're in the atomic age. It knows we have nano-tech and can form buckyballs and sheets of graphene. So it must figure we've stumbled upon relativity and quantum mechanics, at least at a basic level, as without that knowledge we wouldn't be able to come up with these things."

Mason nods in agreement.

"So we've passed Astro Chemistry 101, probably not with an A+, but I think we would be given a strong B. We certainly didn't flunk. It knows we're out of the Dark Ages and should be in the Space Age."

"So what's next?" Anderson asks. "I'd love to see some advanced physics, string theory or something like that? Astrophysics maybe? Astronomy?"

"Too specialized," Teller says, liking his thinking but realizing there are other possibilities. "I mean, this is just a guess, but I think it's going to branch out and establish a broader base of understanding before delving too deep on any one specialist subject. You've got to remember, we're still at the trading-beads-for-blankets stage. We've got to expand our shared scientific vocabulary before we can get into some of these other topics. Perhaps delve into some of the fundamental concepts for life."

"So what?" Trissa asks. "You're thinking biology?"

"It's possible," Teller says.

"Really?" Anderson replies. "Not a particle accelerator or something like that?"

He seems disappointed.

"Hey," Teller says, qualifying his comments. "I may be completely wrong on this. I was wrong on the whole Vega thing, so it wouldn't be the first time I've been wrong when it comes to this thing. But my guess is biology because any kind of mechanical device is going to be so far beyond our level of understanding it would be meaningless. And, picking up on the point Dr. Anderson made, life is the only thing that uses a majority of the lighter elements in the Periodic Table."

Mason looks intently at him, not saying a word.

Teller continues, saying, "It's just an idea. I mean, imagine trying to teach Archimedes how to build his own computer tablet. Imagine taking an iPad apart and trying to explain to Plato or

Aristotle what each of the components are, how they work, how they are built, and how they all fit together. Let alone trying to describe software. And these guys were highly intelligent. I just think the anomaly's tech is going to be so far beyond us, we'd never get it. And besides..."

"Besides what?" Trissa asks, clearly not wanting that thought to slip away. Teller can see the sparkle in her eyes. She's an astrobiologist at heart. There's probably some wish fulfillment at play, and it's all guesswork on his part, but she seems more interested in the possibility of the next steps being biological than either Anderson or Bates.

"I think it's curious about us. We've exchanged chemical elements. Elements make up molecules. Molecules make up DNA. DNA makes up life. It's here because we're alive. I think it's going to want to know what makes us tick. Remember, this isn't just about what we want from the anomaly. It has goals too. It's going to want to examine life on Earth."

"So what?" Mason asks. "We start dropping animals and people into the damn thing?"

"Not quite," Teller replies. "Just samples of their DNA."

Trissa is excited. She says, "And we'll need to do it sequentially, traversing the phylogenetic tree of life as best we can. Something with this level of sophistication is going to quickly work out the pattern of inheritance and link species together by common ancestor."

Bates groans. "And I thought the periodic table was tough.

Where the hell am I going to get sequential biological samples from? Good God, most of it's microbes. Where do I start? At a zoo? At a university? At a garden nursery? For that matter, I could start in a garbage can!"

Teller laughs, saying, "How about all of the above."

"And?" Mason asks, suspecting there are more ideas bouncing around in Teller's head.

"And if the anomaly holds true to form, there will be another exchange."

There's silence.

"Ah, what do you mean by that?" Mason asks.

"It's guesswork on my part, but the whole premise of interaction with the anomaly is based on exchange. It presented hydrogen, we responded with helium."

"So we give it some of our DNA," Bates says.

"And it gives us some of its DNA," Trissa says. "Or whatever its equivalent is."

"Maybe," Teller says. "It's just an idea. We'll find out soon enough. But I suspect it's not going to be interested in seeing our computers or electronics or any other kind of machinery. It's going to want to see what chemicals make us tick."

Mason's phone begins vibrating. He looks at the caller ID.

"Let me guess. It's the Big Guy on the phone," Bates says,

knowing the President's advisers would have been watching the live broadcast along with everyone else. "Make sure he understands this is speculative. We could be way off base on this, but it makes sense."

"Tell him progress will be slow," Anderson says. "It took us decades to decipher our own DNA. Anything the anomaly shows us could take decades more to unravel and map out. Making sense of it could take even longer still."

"Yeah," Bates says, agreeing with him. "I suspect the days of sensational news events are over. Now is when the serious science begins."

"Absolutely," Trissa says.

Teller says, "And maybe once the anomaly has sat here for four or five years, slowly conversing with us about the mysteries of the universe, we'll finally figure out there's no reason to get all upset and feel threatened."

"Where's Charles Darwin when you need him?" Trissa asks, to which Anderson, Bates and Teller smile, appreciating the sentiment.

Mason walks away, taking the phone call from the White House. Finch follows him with his camera, catching his every word.

NEPTUNE

As the others disperse, Cathy asks Teller, "Did you say all that stuff about biology just to set the cat among the pigeons and get everyone out of your hair?"

"No, but that would have been a great idea," Teller laughs.

She leans into him on the couch. Teller slips his hand over her shoulder. They both quietly appreciate how natural and comfortable it feels to sit together. The events of the past day seem to fade like some distant dream. Talking about aliens and watching people working upside down leaves Teller feeling overwhelmed. It's the little things, like a hug, that keeps him grounded.

"I don't know why everyone wants to know what I think. Who am I? I'm a grade school teacher."

"You have some great ideas," Cathy says.

"What happens next?" Teller asks rhetorically. "Who knows? For all I know, its next step could be a game of Parcheesi."

Cathy laughs.

Teller likes her laugh. He continues, saying, "Or Checkers. Or Chess."

"You really think it's going to move from chemicals to

biology?"

"If I was setting up something like this, it's what I'd do next. After all, the whole reason for coming to Earth is to seek out intelligent life, so the anomaly must be intensely curious about us. It's at least as curious about us as we are about it, so yeah, I think cycling through the periodic table of elements is a prelude to the main event. At least, I hope so. But I'm not ruling out Parcheesi."

She rests her hand on his thigh.

They chat idly, watching the hive of activity on the inverted slab. The concrete slab is almost directly overhead which means it's getting close to midnight. Hundreds of feet above them, soldiers and workers move around, their feet seemingly glued to the concrete slab. After a while, Cathy drifts off to sleep with her feet curled up on the couch. Teller leans back, getting comfortable himself before falling asleep while wondering what they'll see next. Someone must notice the two of them asleep as they cover them with a blanket.

Finch gets a shot of the two of them curled up together.

Cathy opens her eyes, hearing the familiar sound of the zoom lens moving. She startles Teller, and he wakes briefly.

Finch speaks softly, saying, "Human interest shot, Cath. There's only so much people can take of hydrogen, helium, and lithium."

Teller keeps his eyes shut, pretending to be asleep, not

wanting to give that tidbit away to Finch and his audience.

"I'll give you human interest," Cathy growls, shaking her fist at him.

Finch laughs and wanders off. Cathy gets herself comfortable, curling up against Teller, and drifts back to sleep. Teller tries to get back to sleep, but in his half-dreamy state he's aware of distant conversations going on around him.

Shortly after midnight, the core team runs out of elements to exchange with the anomaly. Mason makes the call to pull everyone off the intersection. He wants to send a message, to let the anomaly know they are finished. And besides, he comments to Trissa, no one knows what's next, so it makes sense to be cautious.

The members of the contact team on the slab ascend the ropes one by one, being hoisted up/down from the ground using climbing harnesses, carabiners and pulleys. They've become used to twisting around in midair once they feel the pull of normal gravity just past the three-quarter mark. It makes for great footage, Finch says, capturing their descent on camera.

It is almost one in the morning before the team is back on firm ground. Mason and the others turn in for the night, leaving the graveyard shift to just a handful of scientists and engineers.

Bates wakes Teller and Cathy so they can get some proper sleep in the air-conditioned tents. Truth be told, Teller is a little disappointed at being woken. He would be quite content to stay there all night, although he realizes being woken by the rising sun would have cut his sleep cruelly short. He aches as he gets up, his muscles sore from the events of the day.

Teller stretches. He is a little dehydrated. The bruising on the side of his head throbs slightly. He stops by the medical tent for some ibuprofen before turning in. Cathy is just as lethargic as he is.

The two of them look up at the anomaly. Nothing has happened. The scaffolding sits there idle. There is no visible activity at the heart of the anomaly. If it wasn't for the scaffolding, Teller wouldn't be able to pick out the center. All is quiet. It's a bit of an anticlimax.

"Maybe alien probes need their beauty sleep too," Cathy says as they wander off to bed.

Neither Teller nor Cathy rise before noon. They run into each other while heading for the showers.

Neither of them looks respectable, and looking at each other, they both know it, but their looks do elicit a smile. Cathy's hair looks like she's stuck her finger into a light socket, while Teller's looks like something out of a 1970s punk band. With knowing glances and coy smiles, they go their separate ways and enjoy relaxing under a hot shower, washing the aches and pains away. Teller finishes first, and sits outside waiting for Cathy, which she seems to appreciate.

"How are you feeling?" he asks as she walks out into the sunlight.

"A lot better," Cathy replies, messing with her damp hair. "It is amazing what a good night's sleep, a shower, and a fresh change of clothes can do."

The anomaly is almost perfectly aligned when they wander up to the NASA trailer with coffee in hand. The noonday sun makes it a bit hot for coffee, but Teller feels he needs the caffeine kick to jumpstart his brain. Cathy barely touches her latte.

Bates and Anderson are busy chatting with the contact team over to one side and don't notice them, which is fine with Teller.

The anomaly looks as it always has—a fractured segment of reality. Nothing is glaringly out of place at this time of the day. It is the subtlety that makes the anomaly unnerving. The slow moving slab, the ragged sections of the State Department and the flags look almost normal as they approach their original positions, but that they are in motion at all is unsettling. The mind demands that these artifacts remain stationary, but they move gradually in an arc in defiance of expectation. The abandoned equipment on the slab looks chaotic, out of place on what should be an unassuming road cutting north through New York City.

Finch sees Cathy and Teller walking down the road toward the anomaly and yells out, "Hey, Teller. Looks like you were wrong again."

"Yeah, thanks for that," Teller replies, not appreciating Finch and his caustic humor. So much for his theory of progression, with the anomaly moving on to a biological conversation.

Quietly, he says, "Why did I open my big mouth last night?"

"Don't worry about him," Cathy says. "Mouthing off is a kind of compliment for Finch. It means you have his attention."

"Great," Teller says, feeling a little low.

Cathy wanders off to talk to Finch, probably to tell him to pull his head in.

Trissa talks with some of the engineering crew, pointing at a schematic diagram.

Mason is sitting alone on the couch with his laptop and phone, madly typing on the small computer keyboard.

"Morning," Teller says, sitting in one of the armchairs.

"Afternoon," Mason replies cheerfully.

"You don't seem too bothered nothing's happened?" Teller says.

"Oh, I'm not. This is perfect. Finally, I have a chance to clear my backlog of emails. Given all we've observed, we can do with a few days to catch up on analysis."

Teller nods. Makes sense.

"You wouldn't believe some of the requests I'm fielding. There are countries wanting to take samples of the concrete slab. We've already done that. It's concrete. But I suspect what they really want is an Apollo moon rock or something physical to show their citizens they're doing something."

"Huh," Teller replies, regretting sitting in the blinding sun.

He gets up, wanting to find some shade, when he notices Trissa and a couple of the guys from the engineering team walking toward the anomaly to collect their equipment.

Something's different.

Something isn't quite right with the anomaly, but Teller isn't sure what. At first, he doesn't think too much about it, but out of the corner of his eye he notices the rest of the trees stretching out along 1st Avenue. Their foliage is rich and full of vibrant summer greens. He looks back at the one, lone tree on the edge of the slowly moving slab. It looks different. For lack of a better word, the tree looks tired. The limbs and branches sag a little. The leaves lack luster. The branches have curled downward.

"Maybe it's not getting enough water," he says.

"Huh?" Mason replies, looking up from his laptop.

"The tree," Teller says, pointing at the anomaly. "Maybe the roots are drying out."

"Maybe," Mason says, going back to work on his laptop.

But the traffic light is sagging as well.

The engineering crew are too busy talking with each other to notice.

Trissa walks up to within fifteen feet of the gently sloping intersection, approaching the invisible boundary between Earth and this alien phenomenon.

Teller drops his coffee, spilling it on the ground as he bursts into a sprint, running over toward the engineering crew yelling.

"Stop! Hey, Trissa. Stop! Don't go in there. Stay right where you are."

"What?" Trissa cries in response. Her legs freeze. She stands perfectly still, looking at the ground around her as though she were standing in a minefield.

"Don't move," Teller yells again.

Mason, Anderson and Bates all stop what they are doing and look up. Nothing seems out of the ordinary.

Teller is in pain, even just a short burst has exposed how sore his body is from the day before. Half-running, half-limping he makes his way over to Trissa and the engineering team. For their part, they stand there baffled. The slab barely moves, creeping onward at an almost imperceptible rate. The spherical shape of the anomaly means their heads are within inches of breaking the invisible perimeter that defines the gravitational influence of the alien environment, but none of them seem to realize that.

The slab making up the intersection within the anomaly is almost level with the ground. Walking onto it would be like walking down a slight ramp. Trissa can't see any threat. She goes to step forward.

"No," Teller yells, jogging up to her with his arms out. "Don't."

She looks out across the intersection, saying, "I don't understand."

The trash in the gutter is crushed. It looks as though the loose candy wrappers have been ironed flat. Some of the leaves on the tree have been stripped off, along with most of the smaller twigs. Instead of lying on the ground, they have been compressed against the slab. The flags are hanging straight down even though there is a stiff southerly breeze blowing along the avenue. The traffic light sags under a heavy load.

"Don't go in there," Teller says, hobbling the last few feet over toward Trissa. "Step back."

She backs away slowly.

"What is going on?" she asks.

Teller is out of breath.

Mason, Anderson and Bates run over.

"I don't know for sure," Teller replies. "But something is not right. I think the strength of the gravitational field may have changed."

Teller picks up a small stone and tosses it into the anomaly. The stone should fly a good twenty feet, but it doesn't. Instead of following a casual arc through the air, it dives straight at the ground as though it were shot down out of a cannon.

"If you'd gone in there, you would be crushed."

A large branch breaks off the tree, crashing to the ground in less than a second. It doesn't bounce. It slams hard against the pavement as though it has been dragged down by a chain.

"What the?" Mason cries.

They all back away slowly.

"Well, you are right about there being a new phase," Anderson says.

"But wrong about what that would be," Teller adds. "This isn't what I imagined at all."

As ever, Finch is their wingman, broadcasting their reactions to the world.

The scaffolding within the anomaly falls, crumpling to the ground. But it doesn't end up in a pile of steel rods poking out at various angles with gaps in between. Instead, the various pipes and cross-members spread out, being crushed hard up against the concrete.

A few seconds later, the traffic light snaps and crashes into the concrete intersection.

"Did you notice that," Bates says, raising his hand up near his ear.

"The sound," Trissa says.

"It's delayed," Anderson replies. "And at a low pitch. There's nothing in the higher frequencies."

"What is going on?" Mason asks, wanting answers.

"It must be the density of the medium," Bates says. "It's dulling wave propagation. Teller?"

"Ah, yeah," Teller replies, as surprised by all this as everyone else.

"Tell me this is not something I should be worried about," Mason says.

"Well," Teller says. "It's contained, so whatever's happening, it's limited to the anomaly, just as it has always been."

"That's good," Mason replies. "What else?"

Cathy walks up to them. The look on her face is quizzical. She's not sure what she's missed but she must realize there is a sense of alarm rippling through the scientists.

"Why is it blue?" she asks, pointing up at the heart of the anomaly.

"Blue?" Trissa asks, squinting as she peers up hundreds of feet above them, looking through the anomaly at the sky above. Teller joins her, trying to pick up on what Cathy has spotted, but the sky makes any tinting impossible to detect.

"From back there," Cathy says. "The anomaly looks blue. Well, those buildings on the other side look bluish."

Teller hobbles over and picks up the binoculars sitting on the coffee table. He looks toward the center of the anomaly. That's where the action has always been. He fiddles with the focal ring.

"Well," he says, handing Mason the binoculars. "It's moved on to another phase, all right."

"What the hell?" Mason says, staring through the binoculars. "What the fuck am I looking at?"

He hands the binoculars to Trissa. She takes a quick peek before handing them on to Anderson.

"So what is it?" Cathy asks. She's dying to get her hands on the binoculars, but Teller suspects she is quite a way down the pecking order.

"It's hard to tell," he says. "But it's asymmetrical. Finch, can you zoom in on that?"

"Sure."

"Get as close as you can," Teller says. "But whatever you do, don't go in there."

Teller hobbles over to the NASA trailer where the broadcast is being displayed on a large external screen. Finch moves to within a few feet of the anomaly, kneeling down so he can get a steady, close-up shot of the heart of the anomaly.

"Look at the color," Anderson says, noting the build up of a distinct cerulean blue tinge within the sphere. "It's denser toward the center. That has to be an illusion, an artifact of the spherical shape, but, damn, the density must be increasing."

"Nitrogen? Oxygen?" asks one of the other scientists standing beside them.

"I'm picking up both, and lots of methane," another scientist says, looking at a spectrometer.

"Interesting," Anderson replies. "We're starting to see pressures and atmospheric mixes similar to a gas giant. Can anyone get me a temperature reading?"

"On it," someone cries.

Bates is over by Finch, standing near the anomaly. He calls out, "Temperature's dropping. Must be well below zero."

He's got his hands within a few inches of the now distinct barrier between the two worlds, saying, "The moisture in the air out here is condensing, forming a fine mist just before the smooth blue edge of the sphere."

The tree gives way, collapsing and crashing to the ground. Finch pans down, zooming in on the crushed metal scaffolding and then over at the flattened tree.

"Finch," Cathy yells. "This is no time for candid shots. Stay on the core."

Teller has his fingers up by the screen, moving his hand back and forth as he looks at the blurred object in the center of the anomaly. He covers the object and then slowly draws his hand back, trying to stimulate his thinking, trying to see things from a different perspective.

"Can you hold the image still?" Teller calls out.

"Someone get him a tripod," Cathy cries, and one of the technicians jogs over with a camera stand in his hand.

Finch takes shallow breaths. With the zoom on full, even the slightest movement is amplified through the image. He rests his elbow on his knee, trying to steady the camera. The backup cameraman sets up a tripod beside him.

"It's in motion," Teller says.

"As in, turning with the slab?" Mason asks.

"No." Teller says, moving his hand back and forth over the fuzzy image. "Any movement from Finch is only going to be in two dimensions, shaking the image about. But this bit, right here, it's receding. It's moving on the z-axis, away from us. That's not Finch. And it's not in the direction of rotation."

Teller drops his hand and stands back, squinting at the hazy image.

"Look at the irregular patches, the smooth edges, the dark blobs," Anderson says as he examines the video feed. Bates comes up beside them, looking intently at the fuzzy glob on the screen.

Bates asks, "Can we get a high definition camera on that?"

"At a guess, I think it's organic," Teller says.

Trissa says, "You think this is—"

"—alive," Anderson says, completing her sentence.

"I thought you said this was a probe?" Mason cries. "You told me it wasn't alive."

"I was wrong," Teller replies. "I seem to be wrong quite a bit these days. But, actually, it's not that surprising, if you think about it a little."

"What do you mean it's not surprising?" Mason says. The expression in his voice indicates he thinks Teller's gone mad.

"Spam in a can?" Trissa asks.

"Something like that," Teller says as Finch jogs over. He leaves his backup cameraman with the main camera still focused on the heart of the anomaly, and has a secondary camera. Damn, he takes his role seriously, Teller thinks, noting Finch doesn't want to miss any of the discussion.

Anderson answers Mason's question, saying, "If we were going to send an interstellar mission to another star system, it would take generations to complete, so we couldn't send people. We'd want to, but it's just not viable."

"So what would we send?" Cathy asks, intrigued by the concept.

"DNA. Sperm and eggs," Anderson says. "It'll be cheaper, easier and more humane to simply make people at the other end."

"Spam in a can," Trissa repeats with a smile. "It's not very romantic, but it's practical."

"Exactly," Teller replies. "If you think about the astronomical cost of propelling something from one side of the galaxy to another in terms of energy expenditure, it's going to be orders of magnitude easier to send the blueprints for life instead of sending life itself. The absurd amounts of time involved make it impossible to send living creatures between stars. This thing could be traveling for millions, perhaps billions of years. So the freeze-dried option is really the only option for life."

"So that," Mason asks, "That is some kind of test-tube alien?"

The image goes blurry as the backup cameraman switches to a long range lens. It takes him a few seconds to adjust the filters and balance the light before the image is displayed in greater detail. Although the edges are blurred, they see a central mass curled up in a ball with several appendages along with what appear to be veins and some kind of pulsating muscle.

"So that's a fetus?" Cathy asks.

"Maybe," Teller says. "If it is, then like us, the embryonic stage is probably full of vestigial elements that are nothing like the fully formed creature. Our own children tend to look more like a lizard or an alien than a human in the first trimester."

Anderson smiles at the irony, saying, "Yeah, it's going to take some time before we see its final form."

"How much time?" Mason asks.

Teller loves the way Mason assumes there are answers available on tap.

Bates says, "It could be days, weeks, months, or even years."

"There's no way to tell," Anderson says, slapping Mason on the back as he adds, "But it looks like you're going to be a daddy."

Cathy laughs.

"Biologists are going to pore over these images for years to come," Teller says. "The anomaly is giving us a glimpse into its evolutionary past, a snapshot of millions of years of alien evolutionary development from the other side of the universe. Fascinating."

"I hope it doesn't expect the same kind of show-and-tell from us," Cathy says.

Teller laughs.

"I hate to sound like I'm paranoid," Mason says. "But tell me why this thing isn't breeding some kind of clone army to conquer Earth?"

Mason doesn't look worried by the concept. He gestures toward the permanent camera mounted on the side of the research trailer, saying, "For the folks at home. Hollywood has a way of molding popular opinion. Tell me why we shouldn't be worried."

Teller looks up at the camera. He's known it's been there for a couple of days, but it is only now he notices the microphone mounted below it. He hasn't given any thought to audio being recorded, assuming the only sound being captured was by Finch, but all of the cameras broadcast audio and video. He wonders what inadvertent conversations have been captured with this camera, and he remembers standing here looking at the images of Paris burning the previous evening. He can't remember what he and Cathy had said about that at the time, but whatever they said has gone global. There is nothing like being caught unawares to show one's true colors, and he hopes he hasn't said anything indiscreet, only to have foolish words broadcast around the world.

"I don't think there's anything to be alarmed about," Trissa says. "To start with, the pressure difference between in there and out here is extreme. Even here on Earth, organics tend to be fine-tuned to the environment. Take snailfish from five miles below the surface of the ocean, deep in the Marianas Trench, and bring them to the surface, and they'll die. Their bodies have evolved to deal with certain tolerances. For that thing, being out here would be fatal, so I don't think it's going anywhere. It really is a bit like hauling up deep sea squid. The pressure difference will be lethal."

"To put it in context," Bates says. "If the same difference was applied to us, it would be worse than standing atop of Mt Everest or being caught unprotected in a decompressed plane. We'd die in minutes, if not seconds. As pressure changes, the intricate chemistry associated with cellular life changes—the interactions are all different. It just won't work. The inside of the anomaly changed for a reason, because that's what this alien needs to survive."

"And it's all wrong," Anderson adds, "You generally don't start your quest for world domination by being polite. You don't go out of your way to be considerate and courteous only to then crush the natives underfoot."

"Yeah," Bates says, thinking about it further, "If you are invading the Earth, you don't give your enemy the chance to study you in such a vulnerable fetal state."

"Hah," Trissa says, laughing, "These guys clearly haven't seen Independence Day. Epic Fail. This is not the way you do it."

"And one alien?" Anderson says. "That's hardly an invasion force."

"That's right," Teller says. "From the look of what we're seeing here, the most ideal planet for our intergalactic friend would probably be Neptune. If he's looking for a new home, he'd be moving in a little bit further down the road, he'd be looking at the next suburb, so to speak. Earth is just too small, too hot, and too lightweight."

Mason smiles. They are relaxed, confident, joking around.

Given the chaos and upheaval Teller has seen elsewhere in New York, he hopes common sense will prevail over panic when these images are viewed around the world. There isn't anything to panic about. These are exciting times.

Teller adds some more of his thoughts.

"It's quite interesting to realize how deliberate and controlled all this is. The anomaly is methodical. We may not know what's next, but whoever built this thing has clearly planned the interaction out ahead of time and knows how to proceed. They're taking us on a journey. All we need to do is go along for the ride."

He hopes the rest of the world agrees with that sentiment. Somehow, he doubts it.

CABLE TV

Teller loses himself in various discussions with the NASA scientists. He barely notices the hours floating by. It is dark when he comes out of the research trailer with rumbles in his empty stomach.

Cathy is having a late supper, sitting on the couch staring at the massive blue sphere rising up over a hundred meters before her. Floodlights light up the anomaly. She picks at a piece of chicken breast and is content to squish some salad between two slices of garlic bread and make an impromptu sandwich. Teller sits down next to her.

"Hungry?" she asks, offering him some chicken, which he happily accepts. She's looking at the latest news on her tablet computer as she eats, trying not to make the screen greasy.

"Anything interesting?" Teller asks.

"Anything interesting?" she replies. "Are you kidding? The world is falling apart out there. It's hard to find something that's not interesting. Oh, for the days when we longed to know what Brad Pitt's wearing, or what Angelina Jolie's eating. These days, it's all so darn intense.

"Everyone hates us. There's very little in the way of positive commentary on the work we're doing here, and what little is positive tends to have a hidden political agenda, trying to push some left-wing or right-wing ideology. They're a bunch of rats, the whole damn lot of them."

"You're being a bit hard on the media, don't you think?" Teller asks.

"You forget," she replies. "I work in the industry. I know exactly what kind of back-room conversations are going on and how they're favoring the more sensational aspects of these stories. It's like pouring gasoline on a fire."

"Seems Mason was right," Teller says, conceding ground. "We're living in a cocoon, insulated from the world outside."

"You're not wrong. There was a riot in Washington D.C. this afternoon, so it seems the madness is spreading."

She flicks a virtual page as she continues.

"The U.N. is trying to impose sanctions on the U.S. for not complying with its mandate for access to the anomaly. The Russians have followed the French lead and have expelled their U.S. ambassador, while Germany, Poland and Austria have withdrawn their diplomats from Washington, supposedly for their safety.

"The Chinese are stirring the pot, calling for military action. Even the Canadians are getting in on the act. They've closed their borders with the U.S. What is it with all these guys? They've gone mad. It's like they've got rabies."

Teller rubs his eyes. He is tired, but not just from the day—the pressure of all they are dealing with weighs on him.

"Maybe they think we're the ones with rabies," he replies.

"Do you think Mason is right to insist on this being a U.S. led effort?" Cathy asks, putting the tablet to one side. "As that seems to be the thing that's stuck in their throats."

"I don't know," Teller replies. His mind is exhausted. "We're supposed to have some European scientists arriving soon, but it's a token gesture.

"I can see Mason's point, though. Science isn't about consensus or equal representation. Science is about facts and theories. It really doesn't matter who comes up with them, so long as they're open and transparent, so long as they can be verified by others. But it seems that's not good enough.

"I know it sounds selfish, but I agree with Mason. I just want them to go away and leave us alone. They need to let us get on with the job and stop the bickering and politicking."

"Fat chance," Cathy replies. "I wonder if you'd feel that way if you were in Brussels or Moscow."

"Yeah. Probably not."

"Probably?" Cathy asks, keeping him honest.

Teller grins as he picks at the food on her plate.

"What happened to the concrete?" she asks, staring out at the swirling blue orb before her.

"Best we understand it," Teller says, talking with his mouth full, "The slab was dissolved or absorbed. Who knows? This thing plays with atomic structures like they're play-dough. It could have rearranged the molecules for some other purpose, converted them into other elements, or into raw energy, we really don't know. But it's all gone—the slab, the building fragments, the tree, the flags."

"Is it still rotating?" Cathy asks.

Teller shrugs his shoulders as he bites into a cold drumstick.

"I think so."

Finch sits down on the arm of one of the chairs, turning his camera on them.

"Is this really necessary?" Teller asks, covering his mouth with one hand as he speaks, trying not to talk with his mouth full.

"The anomaly's not the only thing living in a fishbowl," Cathy adds, picking up a small plastic cup filled with chocolate mousse.

"That looks good," Teller says.

"It is," Cathy replies, licking the spoon after her first mouthful. "But you're going to have to get your own."

She laughs. Teller enjoys her banter.

Finch pipes up, saying, "So, what can you tell us about this next phase?"

"Not much," Teller says. "But I recommend the chicken. It's

got a nice peri-peri coating and isn't too dry."

"Can't you leave us alone?" Cathy asks.

"Come on," Finch says. "I need something for the late edition."

"You always need something for some edition," Cathy replies dryly.

"Okay," Teller says, figuring the only way he is going to get some peace and quiet is to comply. "But if I give you something, you've got to promise to leave us alone for the rest of the evening."

"I promise," Finch says. The tone of his voice implies this is a promise he actually might keep. But Teller understands that all bets are off if there are any more unforeseen developments.

"All right. We've been able to figure out that there's roughly ten tons of pressure per square inch within the anomaly. That's like balancing a fully laden bus on your finger, although, it's not an unheard of pressure. There are about eight tons per square inch at the bottom of the Marianas Trench in the Pacific, and there's life down there, so we're able to draw some good parallels from that."

"So it's like crabs and stuff?" Cathy asks.

"No, the pressure is too great for hard shell creatures, but there are tube worms and other soft bodied animals in the Marianas. From what we can see at the center of the anomaly, the alien has a similar composition. It's the size of a bottle cap at the moment and appears to be growing quite slowly. We'd love to get closer, but the general agreement is we need to give it time and avoid anything invasive. Like it or not, we just need to wait."

"So it's like a snake?" Finch asks, pointing at the heart of the anomaly.

"No," Teller replies. "At a guess, what you're looking at there is something like an umbilical cord. There's a kind of sac around the creature, like a transparent egg. That winding cord connects the two. But we're pretty sure the thing in the middle is the alien, everything else appears to be life support. It's a bit like a chick in an egg."

"Okay. So the alien is like something from a deep sea trench?" Finch asks, peeking out from behind the camera for a second.

"Not quite," Teller replies. "But that's the closest parallel we have. The animals we see in the Marianas Trench are on the very fringe of life on Earth. For our alien, however, rather than being on the edge of what's survivable, these kinds of pressures are probably the norm, so it's a very different ecosystem.

"If we assume evolutionary pressures are the same, which they probably are as they all revolve around survival to reproduce, then we know that intelligence arises primarily in second-string predators and omnivores."

"You're going to have to explain that one," Finch says.

"Okay. Think about sharks and lions. They're apex

predators. They sit at the top of the food chain with no real threats. Their numbers are only contained by disease and the abundance of prey available to them because they have no predators feeding upon them. They don't have any real, tangible threats to deal with, so their intelligence only extends so far. They only need to be smart enough to catch their prey.

"But if you take second-string predators, like a cheetah, or a leopard, or an octopus, a cuttlefish, or a monkey, you'll find they sit well below the apex. They're predators, but they are vulnerable to other predators, so for them intelligence is a necessity—it's a survival trait.

"One of the main reasons Homo sapiens developed such a vast degree of intelligence was because we're so darn vulnerable that, without it, we'd go extinct.

"So when it comes to our alien, we're expecting to see something similar. It's going to occupy a mid-range position within its ecology. Rather than an invulnerable acid-dripping monster like you see in the movies, it's probably going to be more mid-range."

"Is there a point to this?" asks Finch, clearly regretting asking for more information.

"Yes," Teller says, forgetting what the original question was for a moment. "It means the pressures we see within the anomaly probably represent the norm rather than the extreme, as they do here on Earth. And that means we know how big the home planet must be. It would have a mass of 5-8 times that of Earth. It's probably what we call a super-earth. Based on what we can observe, the temperature suggests their planet is on the outer edge of what we call the Goldilocks zone around their star. If it were in our solar system, it would orbit somewhere out near Mars."

"That's good stuff," Finch says. "Giant blue planet that looks like a marble. Out by Mars. Got it."

"Oh," Teller says. "There is one other thing, but you're probably not going to like this."

"What?"

"Well, both the low temperature and high pressure indicates a creature that is likely to have a slow metabolism. It's not going to be warm-blooded like us."

"So?" Finch says, from behind the camera.

"So it's probably not going to move around that fast. Now, we're speculating that this is why it evolved intelligence as it needs some kind of advantage to survive in such a harsh environment, one in which speed and strength are going to be largely negated. But it also means that it's not likely to have a rapid gestation."

"And that means?" Finch asks.

"That means we could be here babysitting for quite some time. Even once it matures, it will probably be quite slow from our perspective. It's going to look at us like a bunch of ants scurrying around on a hot summer's day."

"First you're comparing us to chimps, now to ants," Finch says. "Doesn't seem that flattering."

"Nope," Teller says. "But that's reality for you. Reality is never flattering. When it comes to the alien inside this thing, we're going to have to be incredibly patient. A conversation that might take us a couple of minutes could take hours, days. And that's if we can figure out how to talk to it."

"Great," Finch says, with sarcasm dripping from that one lone word.

"That's all I've got. I swear. Now, can we have some privacy?"

"Sure," Finch says, and he heads back to the research trailer to see who else he can nab.

"Soooo," Cathy says. "It's... going... to... talk... real... slow..."

"I guess," Teller replies, smiling. "Actually, I quite like the idea."

"Really?" Cathy says, surprised.

"Yeah. It'll bring some normalcy into the equation. Rather than a mad rush to cover as much ground as possible, we're going to be forced to take our time. We're going to have to pace ourselves. And I think that will be good for us all. Things have been racing along far too fast. I'm not sure anyone can keep up. I know I can't."

"You think this will calm things down?" Cathy asks,

balancing her dinner plate on her knees as Teller continues to snack on her leftovers.

"I hope so," he says, eating an extra bread roll she left on the plate. "We can't go on shooting tear gas canisters at crowds, or staring at the TV screen for twelve hours a day waiting for the next installment in the anomaly saga. Maybe this way people will chill out a bit. Relax and take it easy. You know, let life get back to normal."

"If you're right, then this thing is going to become a tourist trap," Cathy says, messing with her hair. "A novelty item rather than the focus of everyone's attention. Something to get your photo taken in front of when you visit the Big Apple."

"Hah," Teller replies. "I wonder what our friend will make of that. I don't know about you, but I'd like to get my life back to normal. For that matter, I'd like the world to get back to normal."

"I hear you," she replies, although she pauses just a little too long before saying that. Teller can tell something he said has struck at her heart.

"What's the matter?" he asks.

"It's nothing," she replies, tucking her hair behind one ear.

"It's something," Teller says, looking her in the eyes. "Hey, it's okay. You can tell me."

Cathy swallows, looking down at her lap as she speaks.

"It's silly, really," she says. "I mean, this whole thing is like a roller coaster ride. As a journalist, this is a once in a lifetime opportunity, and what am I making of it? Nothing. I'm avoiding the camera rather than seeking it out. What is it with that?"

"Hey," Teller says. "You were caught in the middle of a riot just yesterday. It's okay to have a bit of downtime."

Cathy wipes away the tears as she speaks. "Is it?"

Teller is silent. He holds her hand, but doesn't say anything. Now is the time to be quiet, to listen. She pulls away, not wanting to be touched. Mentally, her wounds are still raw.

For Teller, being able to immerse himself in the anomaly provides a distraction, something to allow the passage of time to soothe the aches, but Cathy has no such placebo. Her fingers pat his hand, but she doesn't want to be held.

Teller's not offended. He knows she doesn't mean to pull away, it is just too soon for her to let go of what happened. Sitting there, he feels as though he's staring into a deep well, unable to see the bottom.

"I mean, at least you belong here. Me, I'm a hitch-hiker. You fit in. But what do I add to these things? Nothing. If I don't show up for a day or two, I don't think anyone would notice."

"I'd notice," Teller replies softly. "And you're forgetting, I'm as much of an anomaly as that thing. I'm no scientist. I don't have a doctorate or anything like that. Hell, I barely made it through college. I don't deserve to be here either, but here we are."

She sighs, her eyes unable to meet with his.

"I keep seeing him," she says softly, wringing her hands together and squeezing nervously at her fingers.

Teller is quiet. He knows who she's talking about.

"I can still see the rage in his face in those last few seconds. And then, nothing. Just the violent crack of the pistol firing. The recoil slammed the gun back into my palm, throwing my hand up for a fraction of a second, and I lost sight of him."

She pauses, lost in memories.

"I think I shut my eyes. I'm not sure. But when I looked again. He was gone. I could see an overturned bus, a burned-out car, but I couldn't see him. Tear gas cylinders curled through the air, leaving a trail of white smoke behind them as they bounced down the street. I could see the bright sun beating down upon us, but I just couldn't see him anywhere. He was gone. I fired again, and again, and again. It was instinctive. I don't know what I was shooting at, I was just shooting. Shooting at ghosts, I guess. Trying to scare away the ghouls. But I didn't see him, not until I lowered my outstretched arms, and there he was, lying on the street in a pool of blood."

She reaches out and squeezes his hand.

A knot forms in Teller's throat as his mouth runs dry.

"You don't appreciate how red blood is until you see it spilt on the pale, white concrete of a road."

Cathy is curiously detached as she describes her recollection of that afternoon.

"He was twitching, clutching at his chest, but not really moving as such. Just sporadic impulses. There was nothing fluid, nothing smooth. Just jerking motions as his life faded."

Cathy pauses, pursing her lips, drawing them in tight. Her eyes look into the distance, as though she is staring back in time. Her face is pale, bleached of any color.

"I remember the smell. Isn't that funny? I don't remember any sounds after the gunshot, but the smell. Oh, it was overpowering.

"People were running and yelling around us, but I couldn't hear them. I remember you tugging on my arm, urging me on. I could see your lips moving, but I couldn't make out the words. All around me there was silence. There were police in the intersection. They had helmets on. Their riot shields were battered and scratched, scarred from where bricks and rocks had pelted down upon them. They were yelling. I could see them calling to each other as they were attacked from the side. But it was like watching a movie with the volume turned down.

"Oh, but the smell. There was the smell of burning rubber from the Hummer. The smell of smoke, pungent and acrid. I could smell sweat, like musk, slightly sweet, but with the scent of a wild animal tainting it. The oil-stained concrete smelled like a wrecking yard. It came in waves, radiating with the searing heat of the day. Gasoline hung in the air, like the smell you get at a gas station when you're filling up the car. But it was the gunpowder that lashed at my nostrils. The discharge from the gun stung my eyes. The charred, burnt smell of gunpowder scorched my nostrils, cutting at my lungs. For me, it was the smell of death."

Cathy's eyes glaze over. Teller reaches out and squeezes her hand in support, but there is no response.

"He had brown eyes," she says, her head turning slightly to one side with that realization. "Dark brown hair and hazel brown eyes."

She tries to put on a brave face, sitting up slightly and composing herself, but she's still looking beyond Teller, looking into the past as she relives those few fatal seconds.

"He had a bandanna over his nose and mouth. I can still see the horror in his eyes.

"And he was wearing a New York Giants t-shirt. A white one, with a blue football helmet printed on it. My brother has a t-shirt just like that."

Cathy sobs, burying her head in his shoulder. As she does so, she knocks her plastic dinner plate on the ground. Scraps of food and a couple of chicken bones roll across the rough concrete.

"Oh, look at what I've done," she says, being jolted back into the moment. She wipes her eyes and runs her hands up through her hair. "I'm so clumsy. So stupid."

"Don't worry about it," Teller says, kneeling down and cleaning up the mess. He puts the plate on the coffee table, saying, "You're not stupid."

"I must look a mess," Cathy says, sniffing.

Teller smiles. He takes her hands in his, but she pulls away again, much quicker this time. Her eyebrows narrow as she says, "Eww."

"What?" Teller asks, confused.

Cathy hands him a napkin, saying, "Greasy fingers."

Teller laughs, wiping his hands. He reaches out again, asking, "Is this better?"

"Yes," she replies, smiling and then laughing.

"Is it wrong?" she asks. "Is it wrong to just go on? I mean, life goes on. To see a life end like that, and then to have a glass of water, or something to eat, to go to sleep, or to watch TV. It just seems weird. You know? It feels wrong."

"It wasn't your fault," Teller says. "You did what you had to."

"I know, but knowing that doesn't help."

Teller puts his hand on her knee.

"It's okay to feel bad. It means you care."

Cathy wipes her nose. "Oh, I hate feeling like this. And look at me, I'm a wreck. Make sure Finch doesn't see me like this. I don't want to be his next human interest story."

Teller looks up. Finch is nowhere to be seen. "I think he's over on the other side by the mess tent. He's probably getting some coffee or something."

Cathy sniffs, trying to gain some composure.

"I know it's hard," Teller says. "But try to focus on the positives. Look at the wonderful things around you."

She turns her head, taking in the anomaly. The swirling eddies of blue and white form marble patterns rising up hundreds of feet above her in a smooth arc, slowly blending into each other.

"Well. It sure beats covering World Education Week."

"Oh," Teller says. "It's been an education."

"Hah," Cathy says. "Yes, it certainly has."

"So what do you make of all this?" Teller asks, waving his hand toward the giant blue sphere towering over them, trying to help her bury the past few minutes.

"I don't know," Cathy replies, sniffing. "I haven't really stopped to think about it too much. The last few days have been a blur."

Teller is quiet. He wants Cathy to talk. It will be good for her to talk about something other than the riot.

"For me, the anomaly is a curiosity," she begins. "I mean, it's interesting and all, but if I was at home, if I hadn't been caught up in all of this, I'd probably be watching re-runs of Gilligan's Island by now."

Teller bursts out laughing. It's such an unexpected proposition that he isn't sure what to say in response. He is overacting a bit, trying to shift her frame of thinking. Cathy's outlook on life is outrageously different to his, but that's something he loves about her—she never ceases to surprise him.

"As fascinating and impressive as it is to hear about a super-earth, it only holds my interest for so long, and then I find myself wondering about whether I could go home for a while and catch up on some laundry. I'd love to pick up my iPod and head off to the gym for an hour. Just be normal for a bit."

Teller is taken back by the notion. "I'm sure you could," he says, thinking about it. "We're not prisoners."

"Oh," she says, pushing him playfully, "I know. But you guys take it all so darn seriously. I mean, you can barely pull yourself away after an eighteen hour day. I'd feel as though I was betraying everyone if I went off and did a bit of shopping at the mall."

Teller smiles.

"Maybe that's what we need," he says. "A little bit of perspective—a reminder of reality. Maybe we should organize a day trip to JC Penney's for the whole team."

Cathy laughs. Her demeanor has changed. Her cheeks, which looked so pale just minutes before, are full of color, blushed and radiant.

"To me," she says. "The idea of talking to an alien is like walking on Mars. It just seems so far from reality as to be absurd. But here we are, making it happen. Well, you're making it happen. I'm one of the cheerleaders."

"You're more than that," Teller says. "Perhaps the most remarkable thing about the human race is its diversity. And you bring diversity to the team. You may not have a Ph.D. in physics or astronomy, but neither do I. And you're a much needed counterweight to the rest of us geeks."

"Are you saying I'm fat?"

Teller laughs. "Not at all."

She is coy, playing with him, which is something they both enjoy.

"At some point," she continues, "You realize you're going to have to introduce your friend to a real American."

Teller looks at her sideways.

"You know—someone normal."

"Normal?"

"Yeah. Your average American Joe. We can't have an alien thinking we're all a bunch of geeks. You're going to have to introduce him to the American stereotype. The white-collar office clerk punching invoices five days a week to pay off a mortgage on some aging, converted trailer home. You know the type, never made it to college, dreams of being a center for the Chicago Bulls, enjoys a few beers with his friends while watching the play-offs. That kind of stuff."

"You've got a point there," Teller concedes.

"Not everyone's a super nerd," she adds. "No offense. I mean, I love you, but you're hardly the typical American guy."

Love?

Teller didn't expect that word to slip in quite so casually, but he knows she means it in the social sense. It is nice, though, to hear her say that so naturally.

"And what about the rest of America? We're a multicultural country. We've got Mexicans, African Americans, Native Indians, Chinese Americans? For that matter, what about the Fighting Irish, or the Italians? And what about the rest of the world? What about the ethnic and cultural groups that define the Africans, the Indians, the Chinese, the Polynesians, and South Americans? At some point, you're going to have to parade them all before the anomaly."

She has a valid point.

"Look," she continues. "Here comes Bates. Ten bucks says he's got some esoteric geeky quirk to tell us about, something like they've detected pimples on the alien's ass and that's a sign of uber-intelligence."

Teller tries not to laugh as Bates walks over, handing both of them a couple of high resolution images of the alien embryo. Teller looks at Cathy. She seems to know what he is thinking. Without saying a word, the look in his eyes says, "See, Bates doesn't take you for granted, he gave both of us a copy of the image." But Cathy raises her eyebrows as if to say in reply, "Is that a pimple on its ass?"

Bates is oblivious to the interplay going on between them. He is too excited about the image.

"They're quadrupeds with bi-lateral symmetry. Four digits on each limb, Teller. Four digits!"

Teller looks up at him, not understanding the significance.

"Computers are built on bits—binary values that naturally group into numbers like two, four, eight, sixteen, thirty-two, sixty-four, etc."

"Ah," Cathy says, pretending to understand.

Teller knows exactly what she is doing, she's joking around with him, but without Bates realizing what is going on. Teller's mind is torn between the non-verbal banter going back and forth between them and the concept Bates is putting forward.

Bates misses it entirely. "For five fingered creatures like us, everything revolves around the number ten, so we struggle with concepts like an octal base system or hexadecimal arithmetic. When it comes to working with computers, we have to abstract all that away and hide it in the background, but for these guys, it would be natural, they're already speaking the same numeric language as any computer."

Cathy hands the image back to Bates with an emphatic, "Brilliant!"

Bates is taken off guard by her burst of enthusiasm and misses the sarcasm in her voice. He takes the photos from them and walks off, saying he has some ultrasound images Teller should look at.

Cathy puts her hand on Teller's thigh, rubbing it gently as she says, "Duty calls, my dear. But, as for me, I've had enough of squiggly little alien embryos for one day. I'm going to go and find myself a TV with cable and watch something mindless, like how to renovate a bathroom, or cooking adventures in Patagonia. Call me a couch-potato, if you want."

"They've got tubs of Ben & Jerry's ice cream over at the mess tent," Teller says, figuring a bit of comfort food is probably of interest.

"Well, why didn't you say so earlier?" she cries.

Cathy leans over and kisses him briefly on the lips before getting up and walking off. There isn't much in it, but it feels wonderful. She is quite something, he thinks, enjoying their quirky, blossoming, whirlwind relationship.

MALL

Teller slept in.

Again.

Sleeping in seems to be a regular occurrence.

Getting out of bed, his body aches. Yesterday, he was a bit stiff and sore in the morning, but once he warmed up he felt fine. This morning, though, he feels as though he was hit by a truck. If anything, he feels worse today than he did the day after the riot. Lactic acid causes his muscles to seize, and he forces himself to get up and have a shower.

After almost forty minutes standing under a stream of hot water, relishing the gentle pounding of multiple thin jets of pressurized water, the skin on his hands start to wrinkle, so he figures it's time to move on. He dresses and then grabs a bagel for breakfast, walking over to the research trailer.

The anomaly towers over the research center. A swirling mass of blue and white, the anomaly looks considerably larger than it did when the slab moved within it. The NASA scientists say this is an illusion, but the massive sphere, reaching up over thirty stories in height, looks intimidating. The gases within the anomaly have cleared a little since yesterday, and the sphere is somewhat transparent. Teller can see the faint outline of buildings on the other side. The creature growing within is still too small to be seen clearly at a distance, but the umbilical cord, if that's what it is, stretches and snakes, winding off to one side. The cord appears to be the thickness of the hose on a vacuum cleaner.

Teller is surprised by how far it reaches out from the center of the anomaly, extending almost three-quarters of the way to the edge of the sphere. And it is in motion, slowly rotating. At a guess, Teller wonders if it terminates at the outer edge of some egg-like sac surrounding the alien embryo.

"Dangerous, isn't it," Trissa says, walking up beside him and seeing him staring at the anomaly. "We read our own assumptions into this thing."

"Yes," Teller concedes. "I guess we do."

"There's a few people saying that's an umbilical cord," she says, and Teller wonders if she's politely correcting him for running off with speculation in front of the cameras last night. Science isn't about guesswork. Science takes hard work. He's wrong to constantly throw ideas out that are completely unsubstantiated, and he can sense Trissa gently correcting him. "An umbilical cord would feed nutrients from a larger parent body to a smaller, developing body. This thing, though, seems to be growing out of the center, working its way toward the edge."

"I don't know what it is," he confesses.

Trissa smiles warmly, saying, "Neither do I."

She stands beside him, staring at the phenomenal sight before them, but leaving him to his thoughts.

Secretly, Teller hopes there isn't going to be an alien growing to fill the massive space occupied by the anomaly, as the size alone would be enough to terrify people with visions of giant killer creatures invading the city. If the thing inside the anomaly turns out to be something out of Godzilla or Cloverfield, people would feel threatened and panic. He'd like to ask Trissa what she thinks, but she has more discipline than he does. He suspects she'll quite happily admit she doesn't know. Godzilla, though? Not likely.

"Fear distorts reality," she says.

For Teller, Trissa is a paradox. She's roughly the same age as him, but she has maturity beyond her years. She's talking to him as though she can read his mind.

"Makes it difficult to see beyond the end of our nose."

If he's honest with himself, regardless of his bravado about how exciting and adventurous it is to be in contact with an alien species, there's a part of his mind that fears the worst.

He says, "I guess we've all had nightmares about being chased by monsters."

Trissa nods, looking at the anomaly rather than him.

"It's silly," he says. "But that's human nature. Fear is stronger than reason."

"We've got to be careful with what we say," Trissa says. "We don't want people to be afraid."

"No," he concedes. "You're right. We don't."

Cathy comes bouncing up to them as Trissa says, "You're a good man, David Teller. Glad to have you on our team."

Teller feels as though he's just been spun around in a washing machine. Trissa has a soft touch, but she knows how to cut through the crap and get to the heart of the matter.

"Thanks," he says as she walks off, knowing she'll recognize the greater meaning intended by that one word. Thanks for having me. Thanks for keeping me focused.

Cathy bounces around like a box of birds.

"Has someone changed your batteries?" he asks, struggling to make the transition from the sobering conversation he just had with Trissa to Cathy's unbridled enthusiasm. The difference between now and last night surprises him. Perhaps she just needed to get things off her chest. Once the air was clear, it must have been easier to move ahead.

She kisses him on the cheek, and he feels like he was suddenly shot full of painkillers. All the aches and creaks in his body fade.

"Thanks for listening," she says. "I really needed that."

"Hey, I think it helped both of us," he replies. "Did you find any re-runs of Gilligan's Island?"

"Nope. But there was a reality show about cooking."

"And what is it you like about cooking shows?" Teller asks

as they walk into the shadow of the anomaly. He isn't really that curious, but he wants to show some interest in the things that interest Cathy. If she found a particular show interesting, there has to be something to it despite his stereotypical masculine misgivings about the subject.

"It was called Cooking for Lazy People," she replies, having a laugh at herself. "It's all over within an hour and there's little or no clean up."

"But you don't get to taste anything on TV," Teller says.

"Oh, the dishes they cook probably don't taste as good as they make out anyway. The way the judges carried on last night, you'd think the chocolate dessert gave them an orgasm."

"Ha!" Teller cries, being taken completely off guard by Cathy once again. He isn't sure, but he figures he's probably blushing at the thought. Teller is a bit of a prude when it comes to sex, whereas Cathy is easy-going. And he likes that about her—she brings him out of his shell.

She pushes him playfully, laughing as well.

Anderson calls them over to one of the monitors on the side of the NASA trailer.

"Look at this," he says, pointing at the screens. "What little we thought we knew yesterday seems to be wrong today."

Teller catches Trissa looking at him out of the corner of her eye. She has a smile on her face.

"This central area, here, at the heart of the anomaly, has remained roughly the same size. What we thought were appendages have turned out to be recursive, arcing back within the organism."

Teller is beginning to regret sleeping in. He's missed more than he realizes. Anderson continues to explain their observations.

"Rather than being a separate entity, like a fetus in a womb, this looks more like the anchor point of the cord stretching out to the wall. The cord is tethered here, at the heart of the anomaly. Look at the radar imaging."

Anderson flicks through a few screens and brings up a false-color image showing pulsating fluids pumping outward within the cord. Bates comes over, as does Mason.

"Rather than being the focal-point for a growing alien embryo," Anderson says. "It appears the entire organic structure originates from here and provides nutrients or cellular material to the outer wall. The cord appears to be feeding the growing egg-sac surrounding the core, but it's constantly expanding. Give it a few more hours and it will be the same size as the anomaly itself."

Teller looks at the anomaly, then back at the screen.

"So it's empty?" he asks. "That whole vast sphere is empty?"

"Well, it's full of fluid, but yes, it's void of life," Anderson says. "The end-node, where the umbilical cord attaches to the outer wall of the egg-sac is easily a hundred feet across and still growing. Any ideas?"

Teller looks at Trissa and shrugs. Finch hovers in the background, trying to record the conversation without distracting them.

Anderson brings up the image of the outer wall of the supposed empty egg-sac as he continues describing what they've been able to observe. "Look at how the cord fans out when it reaches the sac-wall. It branches out with what looks like arteries and veins. That placenta-like mass must be about five feet across, but then it fades, and all we have is the semi-translucent sac-wall."

Bates asks, "Why would they build an empty biological environment? Why wouldn't they fill it with something other than fluid?"

"And what could it sustain?" Teller asks. "I mean, look at it, that inner sac is dozens of stories high in itself. It dominates a significant proportion of the whole anomaly."

"There has to be a purpose," Trissa says. "But we need to be wary of guessing and running to conclusions we'll later regret. Whatever the anomaly is building, it requires time, effort and energy to construct. This has to be deliberate."

"Can you tell anything about its construction?" Teller asks Trissa.

"Without a sample, it's impossible to determine composition, but the xenobiologists are saying it's most likely carbon-based organic chemistry, given what we can determine from the environment."

"Is there anything at all in that egg-sac?" Cathy asks.

"Not that we can tell," Anderson says. "There's fluid equalizing the pressure, but we really have no idea why it's there. It seems to be a structure without a purpose."

"Could it be building something that's transparent to our eyes?" Cathy asks.

"Yeah," Teller says, liking her question.

Anderson rubs the stubble on his chin before replying.

"We're observing this thing at every wavelength, looking for the most subtle variations, anything that would reveal the internal composition, but there's nothing there. Anything invisible to our sight would still show up in either infra-red, ultra-violet, or x-ray wavelengths. Any time you introduce something with a slightly different density, it distorts the electromagnetic spectrum in one way or another. It's just not possible to make something entirely invisible at all wavelengths."

"We don't know that," Mason says. "After all, up until a week ago, we would have said it was impossible to defy gravity."

"It's not likely," Bates says. "It would be inconsistent with everything we've observed so far. The anomaly has made no effort to conceal its activities. From ripping up a New York intersection to burning lithium, and then to transforming a section of the Earth into something from a gas giant—everything we've seen has been overt. There's no reason for the anomaly to suddenly pull some hocus-pocus magic act on us now and cloak its activities. I think the answer is simple. It is empty, and that's deliberate on its part."

"But why?" Mason asks.

"Why indeed," Bates replies. Finch zooms in on his face, capturing his expression.

Trissa looks as though she wants to say something but she's tightlipped. She's clearly not comfortable with everything being caught on camera and presented as gospel.

"It's following a preset path of action," Teller says, weighing his words carefully after his conversation with Trissa. "Bates has a good point. From day one, the anomaly was invasive and intrusive. Everything we've seen suggests the anomaly is deliberately disruptive, wanting to catch our attention. But it's important to note that it is not here to satisfy our agenda."

"No, it's not," Trissa agrees.

Anderson adds his thoughts. "We know the alien entity is modifying the environment within the anomaly to suit itself. This may just be another phase, another prelude. Perhaps it's still establishing an environment in which it can propagate its biology."

"After almost two days?" Bates asks. "When it could turn platinum into gold in little more than a nanosecond? No, if it's taking its time, it's for a reason. If it's empty, it's for a reason."

"But what reason?" Teller asks.

"I have a serious problem with this thing," Trissa says. From the tone in her voice this is something that's been bothering her for a while. That she uses the term 'thing,' instead of 'anomaly,' is ominous. Teller has no doubt this remarkably astute woman is about to drop a bombshell. "What would have happened if this thing turned up in Berlin in 1939?"

Teller listens to her, thinking carefully about the concept.

"What if ET began spilling the secrets of the universe to the Nazis? Or to Stalin? Or Saddam?"

"You've got a good point," Teller says. "Science rarely overlaps with morals, and yet the two concepts are inextricable. What is the knowledge of nuclear fission without a moral compass?"

"Wholesale murder," Anderson replies.

"Exactly. Perhaps that's why the anomaly has slowed its pace," Teller says. "Perhaps it wants to be sure about us and our intentions before taking things further."

"Maybe," Bates says. "We may not understand the reasoning, but the anomaly has chosen to take its time."

Trissa says, "We have to respect that it is slowing things down and be patient. We should be wary of forcing the issue."

Cathy stands so she can take in most of the anomaly as the backdrop to the conversation. She looks at the winding umbilical cord within the sac deep inside the swirling blue orb.

"Whatever ends up growing inside that thing," Cathy says, "it sure is going to be big."

"Should we be worried?" Mason asks.

"We shouldn't," Teller says. "We don't even know if that is an umbilical cord. It could serve some entirely different purpose, one we can't even imagine. We've got to be careful to avoid speculation."

Trissa nods, acknowledging his acceptance of her earlier point made in private.

Teller says, "The whole tone of our conversation with the anomaly has revolved around science. I'm betting that will continue. It's not aggressive. It's not threatening. It is self-restrained. We need to be patient."

Again, Trissa nods. She's clever. She must have known this conversation was coming. She probably discussed some of this beforehand with the others. And she sought out Teller to get him on-side before the discussion got underway in earnest. Teller has a deep sense of respect for Trissa.

Cathy points at Finch with his camera as she says, "You might be patient. I doubt they will be. I bet the pundits out there are already having a field day with this, trying to out-guess you guys. The armchair experts will be whipping up a frenzy. The media isn't good with patience."

Trissa says, "They can out-guess us all they want. For us,

it's important not to guess. We can't afford to guess and be wrong. We need to study and observe and be correct."

"She's right," Teller says, more so for the audience at home than any of the scientists standing there. He's acutely aware their conversation will be dissected by millions. "We need theories, but these need to be testable and, importantly, falsifiable. We need to pursue ideas and examine concepts, but we need to be equally ready to discard any ideas that don't fit the evidence."

"It would be nice if we had more to go on," Mason says, turning toward Finch and his camera. "There's considerable anxiety out there, but it's important to emphasize this thing is going slow for a reason. As alarming as that might seem, the anomaly appears to be taking its time so it doesn't freak us out."

"So don't be freaked out," Teller says kindly, facing the camera. He smiles, hoping that conveys a sense of calm confidence.

"Absolutely," Bates says, also turning toward the camera. "Remember, this thing is able to instantaneously transform elements. If it wanted to build something in the blink of an eye, it could. We have to look at its current actions as a deliberate effort to slow things down, to avoid any misunderstandings, and give us time to observe it in action. We've just got to do the one thing no one likes to do, and that is, wait patiently."

"So what now?" Mason asks.

"We wait," Anderson says. "Like Trissa said—we watch and observe. And when it's ready, it will let us know. Any speculation beyond that is really not helpful."

Trissa smiles faintly.

"Okay," Mason says, walking off. "I'll tell the President it's time for patience."

Finch looks disappointed. He spots a few scientists setting up what looks like a satellite dish, something to eavesdrop on the anomaly, and walks over to find out what they are up to. His camera is constantly streaming video out to CERN in Switzerland, and then on to the Internet at large, so Teller feels much less self-conscious as he walks away.

"Looks like we get a nice quiet day off," Cathy says, turning to Teller. "It would be a great day to go to the beach."

Teller laughs.

"Yes, it would," he replies, feeling the warmth of the sun on his face. "Hey, were you serious last night about wanting to go shopping?"

Cathy looks at him sideways. She instinctively knows he has something else in mind, and that seems to bother her. Teller calls out after Mason, jogging off after him. Cathy follows along.

Mason stops, his hands resting firmly on his hips with his suit jacket open and his tie loosened.

"What is it?" he asks. For all the talk about patience, he's distinctly impatient.

"I'd like to go shopping," Teller says.

"Shopping?" Mason says, rather abruptly. "Am I hearing you right?"

"Yes," Teller says before Cathy can stop him. She has her hand out, almost at the point of pulling him back. She must think he's gone mad.

"Make out a list of what you want and I'll get the quartermaster to pick up whatever you need," Mason says.

"I can't do that," Teller says.

"Why not?" Mason asks, clearly not amused. The scowl on his face shows he has more important tasks to attend to.

"Because I don't know what I need."

"Then why do you want to go shopping?" Mason asks.

"Why does anyone want to go shopping?" Teller asks rather innocently. "I want to look for something, but I don't know quite what."

Mason shifts his weight. He doesn't look impressed. Anderson walks over, listening in.

"Think about it," Teller says. "We're looking for innovative ways to interact with the anomaly. I'd like to get in an environment where I can think outside the box."

"In a shopping mall?" Mason asks, surprised by the concept.

"Yes. I've got a few ideas. But I suspect they'll become more concrete if I can get my hands on stuff."

"And how is going to a shopping mall going to help?" Mason asks. "Couldn't you just go online, pick out what you're after, and we'll get one of the Marines to run out and grab this stuff up for you?"

"It doesn't work like that," Teller says. "It's about stimulating thinking. It's about seeing things from a different angle. It's about escaping this bird cage."

"The last time you did that," Mason replies, "I had to flood New York with troops to get you back!"

Mason turns toward Cathy, asking rather aggressively, "Did you put him up to this?"

Cathy holds her hands up denying any responsibility.

Teller ignores him. "Listen. We're divorced from reality in here. We're in an artificial environment. Everything's regimented. It's contrived. I think that by getting out in the real world, it will open up other possibilities for consideration. The human brain works best when it's stimulated."

"He's got a point," Anderson says, offering his unsolicited opinion.

"He's got a point?" Mason cries. "Are you kidding me? The real world doesn't consist of shopping malls. The American world might, but not the real world. Find me a shopping mall in Afghanistan. Find me one in Malawi. Find me a Wal-Mart in Tierra Del Fuego. Find me a goddamn Costco in Mongolia. Come on. Don't play me for a fool. What is this really about?"

"Okay," Teller says, swallowing a lump in his throat as he speaks. "I want to go shopping for toys."

"Toys?" Mason cries, looking at Cathy and Anderson with disbelief. He's looking for some kind of support from them for his sense of exasperation. Teller grimaces, this is worse than he expected.

"Bear with me," Teller says. "Toys stimulate and educate the mind at the same time. They teach us how to interact with our world. I think they could be invaluable in providing a stimulus for lateral thinking when it comes to communicating with the anomaly."

"Toys?" Mason repeats, somewhat hung up on the point. "Have you gone mad?"

Teller doesn't reply.

Mason says, "What? Like Lego?"

"Wait a minute," Anderson says, turning to Mason. "A couple of days ago, you would have thought releasing a balloon inside this thing was a dumb idea, and yet it was just what we needed to kick start things. Maybe Teller's got a point."

"Toys," Mason says, shaking his head. "Okay. Talk to Sergeant Davies. He'll arrange transport and a protective detail. But I don't want you going more than a couple of blocks. Okay?"

"Fine," Teller says.

"What about Grand Central?" Anderson asks. "It's over on Park Avenue, less than three blocks from here."

"Okay," Mason says. "But no further. And you stay in constant radio contact. And you move with an armed guard. Understood?"

"Understood," Anderson says. That takes both Teller and Mason by surprise.

"What?" Mason asks. "You're going with them?"

"Absolutely," replies Anderson. "I think our grade school teacher has a valid point. We need to stop thinking like scientists stuck in a basement somewhere, never seeing the light of day. We're too close to this thing. We need to start looking at how to simplify our approach. Sometimes, you can get blinkered working with the same experiment over and over again. Sometimes, you've got to step back so you can see the forest among the trees."

Teller smiles.

"All right," Mason says. He points a stern finger at Teller, adding, "But no more riots. Okay?"

Teller laughs. "Yes, dad."

Mason walks off, shaking his head and mumbling under his breath.

Anderson saying, "I'll get Davies to arrange transport."

"What do you think you're doing?" Cathy asks once they're alone.

"Getting you your day trip," Teller replies. "And, besides, I really do think there's some value in a change of scenery. I've got a couple of ideas, but I think just being there will help to stimulate some alternative concepts about how to communicate more effectively."

"You're kidding? Right?" Cathy asks.

"No," Teller replies. "I'm quite serious. After all, what are kids but someone learning about our world afresh? I think if we look at the anomaly like that, we might be able to simplify our approach and move things along."

"You sure are weird," Cathy says, shaking her head, but she has a smile on her face.

It takes almost four hours before the Navy SEALs are ready to go. Although reports of violence within the city have subsided with the National Guard out on the streets in force, the SEALs aren't taking any chances. They arrange a convoy of three Hummers. The SEALs weld what looks like a cow-catcher on the front of the lead vehicle—a series of pipes welded into a V-shape so as to form a slanted, plow-like structure stretching across in front of the Hummer radiator. One of the SEALs explains it's intended to break down barricades and push aside any disabled vehicles. The rear vehicle has a 50 caliber machine gun mounted on the roof. What started as a casual outing has turned into a major military exercise.

Anderson, Cathy, and Teller sit in the middle vehicle, while armed troops ride along outside their Hummer, standing on the sideboards and holding on to the roof. The convoy barely breaks 25 miles an hour as it drives down East 47th Street bristling with armament. Those few blocks are a ghost town. There are no pedestrians, no traffic. The streets have been cleared by the New York Police Department. Squad cars block off the intersections, giving them a straight run to the mall. People peer nervously out of their apartment windows, curious as the convoy rolls slowly past.

"Lady Gaga doesn't get this kind of treatment," Cathy notes as they pull up outside the mall. Teller is feeling more and more stupid with each passing moment. Nothing is ever simple. It should be, but at each point the sense of overkill dismays him.

"So much for blending in with shoppers," Anderson says.

"I didn't mean for everyone to go to such efforts," Teller says. "This was supposed to be something easy to do during our downtime."

"You had better find something of value in there," Cathy says sternly. "If they find out all you wanted was a doughnut, it'll be the Navy SEALs starting the next riot."

Anderson laughs. "She's right, you know."

The sight of armed SEALs walking around inside the mall with their fingers poised alongside the triggers of their M4 rifles is unsettling to the few shoppers brave enough to venture out, especially those with children. Although the kids don't seem to mind.

The soldiers are friendly enough, but the stark reality of their presence is upsetting.

"Can you and your team wait here?" Teller asks the sergeant as they stand outside a department store on the second floor.

"I'm not supposed to let you out of my sight," the sergeant says.

"It's a dead end," Teller says.

The sergeant doesn't look convinced.

"I tell you what. If we run into any trouble in the toy department, we'll have plenty of Nerf guns to hold out until you arrive."

The sergeant laughs and says, "Okay. Deal."

The store manager served in the Marines, so he brings out a case of Pepsi for the soldiers. Nobody complains.

"Funny," Cathy says, as they walk inside the store. "No one else wants to come in here while there are armed soldiers stationed outside. You'd think they'd feel safer."

"Would you?" Anderson asks.

"I guess not," Cathy says.

Teller heads for the toy department. His mind is already kicking into overdrive, thinking about the possibilities, and looking for fresh ideas.

"So, what are we looking for?" Cathy asks, grabbing a shopping cart and heading off after him.

"This," Teller says, picking up a packet of 64 colored markers and handing them to her.

"Would you like a coloring book to go with that?" she asks. "Perhaps some crayons as well?"

"Oh," Anderson says, ignoring Cathy. "I see where you're going with this."

Cathy screws up her face a little.

"It's a spectrum," Teller says. "Look at the way the colors slowly vary from red to blue."

"So?" Cathy replies.

"It's a sample—a thin slice of the electromagnetic spectrum," Anderson says, instinctively picking up on Teller's point. "The entire spectrum is incredibly vast. There are radio waves that span several miles in length, while visible light is squeezed into a narrow band between 380 and 700 nanometers, the tiniest fraction of an inch you could imagine. X-rays and gamma rays are even smaller again. The orders of magnitude that lie on the spectrum would make it difficult for any alien species to know what we see, or if we see anything at all."

Anderson rolls his hand, mimicking a wave, trying to help her picture what he's describing.

"Okay," she says. "I know I'm going to regret asking, but,

what is a nanometer? Other than ridiculously small?"

Teller opens his palm, gesturing toward Dr. Anderson. Teller has a fair idea, but isn't exactly sure, and doesn't want to mess it up. He feels a bit of pressure to be right, but the reality is, he is more instinctive in his thinking than someone like Anderson with his decades of scientific experience. And Teller feels a little intimidated by that, realizing he is a bit of a citizen scientist, full of ideas, but lacking any real depth.

Anderson picks a bag of marbles out of a display stand. He holds them up, saying, "A nanometer is one billionth of a meter. If we use the Earth as a point of comparison, it would take roughly a billion marbles laid end-to-end to circle the planet. Imagine trying to see that line of marbles from outer space. A nanometer is so small as to be invisible to us."

"And it brings up an interesting point," Teller says. "We live in moderation. And I don't mean in terms of economics or anything like that. Our daily experience of the universe is limited, being extremely narrow and restrictive. We don't see things that are super big or super small, super fast, super hot, or super cold. Everything about life on Earth is moderate by comparison with the universe at large, and that's quite deceiving. The universe is anything but moderate."

Cathy listens intently, intrigued by the concept.

"The smallest thing we can see with the naked eye is something like a strand of hair, and yet that's not that small at all. It's at least a hundred thousand nanometers wide. We live in temperate, moderate climates. Our coldest day is nothing compared to how cold it gets in the shadows of the moon. We fly in an airplane at hundreds of miles an hour and we think we're going fast, when our world is hurtling around the sun at almost seventy thousand miles an hour. We look at the sun and it seems tiny, yet it is over a million times bigger than Earth.

"We are so isolated and insulated from the reality of the cosmos around us. It's like we've lived our entire lives in a religious cloister and have never seen the world beyond our small courtyard."

Standing in front of an inflatable bouncy castle by the toy section, the idea of a small courtyard seems almost comical.

Teller adds, "Imagine spending your whole life in that and thinking your bouncy castle represents reality. That's us here upon Earth."

Neither the attendant nor any of the kids that would normally be swarming within the castle are anywhere to be seen. A small electric pump whirs away, continually pushing air into the flimsy structure.

"And the anomaly?" Cathy asks, looking at the colorful, soft, plastic padding on the castle.

Anderson says, "Extending the analogy, the anomaly has searched everywhere from the Sahara to the Himalayas looking for us playing in our bouncy castle."

"And it's trying to figure us out?" she asks.

"Exactly," Teller replies, picking up a box of Monopoly and looking at it, wondering if there's anything inside the game that might be useful. He puts it down and moves on to look at something else.

Anderson picks up a basketball, saying, "If the Sun was the size of this, then Earth would be smaller than a peppercorn. And yet, our sun is tiny in comparison to other stars. But to us, the stars are immaterial, almost irrelevant to daily life. They're just tiny sparks of light in the night sky, twinkling before our eyes like jewels."

Cathy says, "We have such a narrow, sheltered view, huh?"

"We miss a lot," Teller says. "And when it comes to talking to our extraterrestrial friend, there's a good chance we'll miss anything he has to say if we don't make sure we're both talking on the same frequency."

"He?" Cathy asks.

"She," Teller concedes, grinning. "But you see my point. We need to establish a baseline, to let him or her or it know what we can handle, what the limits are for our senses, while trying to understand the range in which they operate."

"And a bunch of markers is going to do that for you?" she asks. "Surely NASA can do better than that."

"Oh, yes," Anderson replies. "But it's a good starting point for planning. It sets the upper and lower bounds of what we can and cannot see. The rainbow of color defines a set range."

"We think we see all the light there is," Teller says, "but we see only a fraction of the light that is emitted by a star like our sun. UV light, as an example, can burn you on a cloudy, overcast day, even though it doesn't seem that bright outside. We miss UV light entirely."

"And here I was thinking you were buying a present for Susan," Cathy jokes.

Teller is too focused, talking himself through the logic. Whether Cathy or Anderson is there seems irrelevant in the moment. He's talking to himself more than anyone else. It's a bad habit. His sister has chewed him out about it on more than one occasion. She's told him he needs to listen more. She's told him he's especially prone to rambling during those long Thanksgiving afternoons sitting around watching the Macy's parade. Cathy reminds Teller of his sister. She calls him a geek. When he goes off on tangents at family functions, she throws grapes at him, or popcorn, anything to snap him out of his introverted focus. Cathy, though, is far too polite, so Teller continues. In the back of his mind, though, he knows he's waffling.

"We communicate via our senses. When it comes to communicating with the anomaly, we need to show it what our senses are capable of detecting. A bunch of marker pens is crude, but right here, in these sixty-four colors, you've got roughly the band of light we see every day."

Cathy says, "Yeah, I've heard bees see different colors, and cats too. They see things we can't see. Like seeing in the dark."

"Yep," Teller says. "For all we know, the creatures that created the anomaly could be just like them, seeing some other portion of the electromagnetic spectrum. A rainbow of colors like this will allow the anomaly to understand the limits applicable to us."

"Are we certain our alien friends even have eyes?" Cathy asks.

"Oh, yes," Teller says. "When the anomaly started to mimic its home world the atmosphere appeared like a shallow sea. Sight would be a crucial evolutionary development in such an environment."

"Why?" she asks, not convinced.

"Well," Anderson replies. "Evolution is all about exploiting opportunities. The cycle of day to night would give a distinct advantage to any creature that has even the most basic sensitivity to light. It could have started with simply feeling the warmth of the sun on your skin as opposed to the cool of the evening, as that distinction helps even blind animals forage and survive. And that tendency would slowly become refined over numerous generations into a greater sensitivity to light. We've seen the same thing here on Earth, with over twenty different evolutionary paths converging on the formation of the eye.

"The day-night cycle conveys a specific advantage to sight, allowing animals to detect threats. Predators exploit sight, so to survive you need good eyesight to see them coming. If you're the hunter, you need better eyesight to catch your prey. And so an arms race develops. That shallow sea is going to favor any organism with sight. And so, given time, they should have evolved eyes, just like fish did on Earth."

"And to reach the stars," Teller adds, "you have to be able to see them. From those shallow seas, they would have had their curiosity piqued just as ours was when Galileo first watched moons in orbit around Jupiter. They must have some kind of sight, but it's probably on an entirely different portion of the electromagnetic spectrum to ours."

Cathy holds the packet of coloring-in pens in her hand, looking at them as she speaks. "So they can see, but they can't necessarily see this? What colors would they see? Red but not green? Or something like that?"

"It sounds crazy," Teller says. "And you're probably going to think I'm making this up, but there is no red or green. All the colors we see are artificial—they're illusions, constructs of our minds. This beautiful rainbow of colors you see here on these markers is, in reality, nothing more than different shades of gray."

Cathy looks suspiciously at Teller.

"I can't believe you're telling me there are no rainbows," she says. "Next you'll be telling me there aren't any unicorns either."

Teller laughs, "Oh, no. There are definitely unicorns. We like to call them rhinos."

"But rainbows?" Cathy asks, smiling, clearly enjoying the

conversation.

"Color is contrived," Anderson says. "Our eyes evolved to detect various frequencies of light as something more than shades because there is an advantage in distinguishing between these subtle hues, but there is no red, no blue, no green, no yellow. Somewhat surprisingly, those that are color-blind see colors for what they really are—shades of grey."

"Oh, please," Cathy says. "As in Fifty Shades of Grey?"

Teller says, "Not quite, but without our minds adding a little bit of extra pizzazz to the scene that cries out as indigo, or violet, red, yellow, or blue, we wouldn't be able to tell when fruits were ripe, things like that."

"I hate you guys," Cathy says, with a grin.

"What?" Teller asks, surprised.

"You take all the fun out of life."

Teller laughs, loving the way she's able to absorb all his geeky ideas and take them in her stride.

Anderson picks up a child's atlas.

"Yes, yes," Teller says, looking over his shoulder at an image of North America, with the continent depicted as a swirling mass of green and brown blending together. The Rockies and the Appalachian mountain ranges are visible, as are the Sierras. On either side of the United States lie the blue oceans of the Atlantic and the Pacific.

"Are you thinking what I'm thinking?" Anderson asks.

"I think so," Teller replies. "This is a nice abstraction. It takes generalized colors, a generalized geographical shape, easily recognizable from orbit, and portrays three-dimensions scaled down into two. If they get it, they'll instinctively understand we use paper as a medium for communication. I like it."

"Me too," Anderson says, closing the book and tossing it in the shopping cart.

"I thought you said they can't see color?" Cathy asks, a little confused.

"Oh," replies Anderson. "They won't see colors as we do, but they'll recognize the different wavelengths. They'll correlate that with the markers. And they'll be able to see how we simplify complex concepts, like the variety of colors in the oceans or on land, reducing them to just a few dominant shades set in stark contrast to each other. They'll realize these distinctions are meaningful to us, and they'll understand why, because they describe the land mass we are on—a land mass they've seen from outer space."

"But more importantly," Teller says. "They'll begin to appreciate how we communicate with each other. How we transmit ideas and concepts from generation to generation."

"They?" Cathy asks. "So there's more than one of them?"

Anderson laughs, saying, "Oh, I don't know. Just easier than him or her."

"Ah."

"These things are primers," Anderson says. "They're signposts, appetizers, setting the direction for what's to come."

Teller pulls a dictionary off the shelf. It is intended for children, probably from the ages of 10-12, with large print and broad coverage of common words. "Too much?" He asks.

"Too much, too soon," Anderson replies.

"I was thinking there might be some value in this," Teller says.

"How so?" Anderson asks.

"Well, they're not going to be able to read it, but they'll be able to conduct some kind of meta-analysis on its contents, and that might act as a bit of a Rosetta stone for them."

Anderson's quiet.

"So long as their sight isn't in the x-ray portion of the spectrum, they'll pick up on these markings of black on a white page and realize that they're not symbols. The repetition and methodical mixture forming words should indicate they're not depictions, like cave paintings. They should recognize them as language in written form—a means of using a limited set of characters to communicate an unlimited amount of information by reusing recognizable components. Even if their sight is shifted toward x-rays, I think we can safely assume they'll scan anything we give them using the entire electromagnetic spectrum, and so they'll pick up on the deliberate distinctions made by our characters and words."

Anderson lets out a slight hum in agreement.

Cathy says, "I'm lost, but don't worry about me. I'm just along for the ride."

"Look at the structure. The contents are sequential. The word being defined is highlighted in bold. The definitions are indented. Variations on each word are included under the broad definition. They won't understand it, but they'll understand what it is. They'll see the order, the patterns, the structure, and they'll know there's a depth of meaning behind the words."

"I like it," Anderson says. "They're going to see a distinction between a dictionary and an atlas, and it won't be as confusing as exposing them to a novel or a textbook, where the terms and concepts are more contextual. What's more, they'll recognize the same symbols from the atlas, and will see that this book is devoid of images, that it's the words formed by the characters that are important, not the pictures."

"But they're not going to understand this, right?" Cathy says. "They're going to need a point of comparison, a means of translating it."

"Yes," Teller says. "But they'll learn the size and sequence of our alphabet—they should appreciate the range of words we use and something about our grammar. They'll be able to detect conjunctions as opposed to nouns and verbs, simply by the frequency of their use."

Anderson purses his lips together. "It's ambitious."

"It is," Cathy says.

"They're smart," Teller replies. "They've just traversed seventy five million light years to get here. They're going to love something like this, where there's an organized structure surrounding information. They won't understand it, not right away, but it will become a reference point for them as they decipher our mode of communication moving forward."

Teller flicks through the dictionary, looking at the words and their definitions, trying to see things from the perspective of an alien.

"Think about how communication occurs in the animal kingdom," he says. "Communication is about projecting ideas, either through sound, through visual clues, or even the use of pheromones. But in all cases communication is about projecting information. Humans are the only animals that use an intermediary form for communication, something static that forms a kind of intellectual echo, whether that's a book, or text on a computer screen, art hanging in a gallery, or a play shown on the television, the principle is the same. The act of capturing communication, storing it, and reusing it is a hallmark of intelligence, and I think they'll appreciate that."

"Cave paintings," Cathy says.

"Yes," Teller replies, liking her thinking. "That's where all this started, I guess."

"Although, for all we know," Anderson says, "they may communicate with an entirely different medium, something like light. Think about cuttlefish and the beautiful array of colors glistening off their skin as their pigments change in response to their thinking, flashing up blotches and patterns rather than speaking words.

"Or think about the way spiders communicate by tapping on a web in a kind of primitive Morse code.

"They could use infrasound, like whales and elephants, low resonate thumps we can barely register but which carry for hundreds of miles.

"Or they may have electromagnetic sensitivity, like sharks and rays sensing the muscle spasms of their prey.

"There's a host of possible mediums for communication, but it would be helpful if we can show them where our focus lies, and that's clearly in the audio/visual."

"Yes," Teller says, enjoying the speculative discussion. "I think it's safe to say they use a variety of senses, just as we do. If we can steer them toward what's convenient for us, it's going to make things easier."

Anderson shrugs his shoulders, looking at the dictionary, saying, "Might as well take it. Can't hurt."

Teller drops the dictionary in the cart.

Cathy wanders over to the electronics section as the two grown men keep looking at toys and books. It takes some time before Teller notices her slowly wandering up and down the aisles in the distance, looking at music from various recording artists. After a few minutes he joins her. Cathy really does remind him of his sister. By ignoring him, she has subtly reminded him that he can become too self-absorbed and distracted.

"Who's going to pay for all this stuff?" Cathy asks, looking at the items Teller and Anderson have gathered in their shopping cart.

"Uncle Sam," Anderson says. "We'll probably only use a fraction of this. We'll come up with something a bit more robust than a bunch of markers, but it's the principle that's important, the ideas behind all this."

Cathy has a hand basket. Teller starts helping himself, looking at the contents of her shopping.

"Do you mind?" she asks.

"Perfume?" Teller says, squeezing the lid and sniffing at the fine mist that floats in the air. "What a great idea! I hadn't thought about olfactory senses. They'll be able to detect chemicals in suspension. They'll understand the molecular complexities, but I'm not sure how we could communicate what's desirable and what's not."

"This isn't for the alien," Cathy says dryly, taking the perfume from him.

"Oh," Teller replies, feeling a little stupid. "Of course not."

Anderson laughs.

"Music, though," Teller says, switching gears. "Music's a good idea. There are natural harmonic relationships inherent in the notes of each key, rhythms that correspond to our heart beats, repeated patterns slowly developing in complexity, it's a wonderful way of communicating aesthetics. We should get some instrumental, some music with singing, both male and female. Some modern music, some old."

Teller looks at one of the music discs, reading the list of songs on the reverse side. Cathy runs her hand along a row, knocking one or two copies of each music artist into her basket randomly as she says, "They're not going to care about which album they listen to, right? A bit of Jazz. A bit of Hip Hop."

"Ah, no. You're right," Teller replies, seeing a pile of twenty-odd discs in her basket.

Cathy drops a small music player and a set of speakers into the shopping cart Anderson is pushing, saying, "And if they don't like your selection, I'll have them."

Cathy is curious about what the men have collected. She pulls out a third-grade mathematics study guide.

"Math? Really?"

"Oh," Anderson says. "This is probably our only rational choice. There's some trigonometry, right-angle triangles, equilateral triangles, stuff like that. It's pretty basic, but it's universal as math transcends language. Our aliens may never have heard of Pythagoras, Newton, or Einstein, but they'll recognize their equations."

"Does it bother you that there's nothing in there?" Cathy asks, shifting the subject. "Nothing inside the anomaly. I mean, there's just a big empty sac, right?"

"Well, the sac is full of fluids, but yes. It's empty," Teller says, feeling like he's admitting to a mistake. "Yeah, it does bother me. I don't understand it at all. We thought we were looking at something like a womb, but we're not. We have no idea what its function is."

"So all this speculation," Cathy replies. "It's based on the assumption that something's going to grow inside the anomaly. But …"

"But," Anderson says, completing her sentence. "Maybe there is never going to be anything inside the anomaly?"

"Yeah," Cathy says. "I mean, this thing takes us by surprise at every turn. It's still taking us by surprise. We may have entirely the wrong expectations. Perhaps we want too much."

Teller is quiet, as is Anderson.

"I know you guys want to talk to ET, and it's fascinating to hear how all this could potentially unfold, and how the simplest of things, like a packet of markers, could help us bridge the communication gap, but I wonder if we're reading too much into the anomaly."

Teller goes to say something, but stops himself. Anderson has the sense of composure to listen as Cathy continues.

"I can't help but wonder if we're too close to this, so close we can't see the anomaly for what it really is. I mean, this thing just appears without warning one day and starts turning our world upside down. And we've been waiting for this, this is what we want. For hundreds of years we've waited for someone to drop out of the sky, and now, here they are. But maybe all that speculation has blurred our thinking. All those science fiction books and movies have led us astray. Our culture is shaped by stories of first contact, from Martians invading with heat rays to creatures bursting out of someone's chest.

"We're obsessed with a desire to find alien life. And there's no doubt this is alien, but maybe we want too much of it, more than it wants to give us.

"I don't know, but maybe this thing is more like the Maytag repairman. Rather than being a flagship, it could be the cable repair guy of the universe, or the plumber, here to install the alien equivalent of a new shower head or something, and it's just stroking our egos."

"Hah," Teller cries, laughing at the thought.

"You might be right," Anderson says. "We're assuming a lot. But that's not a bad thing. Science is about proposing ideas and testing their validity. There's nothing wrong with assumptions, so long as they're modified or abandoned as soon as evidence is shown to the contrary."

"What he's saying," Teller says, "Is he agrees with you. And you're right. We're over excited."

"You're like kids in a candy store," she says, "Speaking of

candy, how do you explain this?"

She drops the math textbook back in the cart and pulls out a couple of chocolate bars.

"How are aliens going to relate to chocolate?" she asks. "And dark chocolate at that?"

Teller grins. "Oh, these are for me."

TRUST

As they arrive back at the grounds surrounding the U.N., Teller looks up at the anomaly. The sphere spans hundreds of feet, like a giant blue marble resting on a New York street, towering over the nearby buildings. He finds himself thinking about Cathy's comment earlier. There are so many assumptions they're operating on. Perhaps it takes someone without a scientific background to see their position for what it is—folly.

The sac within the anomaly has grown to almost the same size as the anomaly itself, filling most of its volume. Teller sees what he had assumed was some kind of umbilical cord snaking out from the center of the anomaly and connecting to the transparent sac wall. Veins appeared to branch out from the cord, weaving their way over the inside surface of the sac. A slight blue tinge makes it impossible to see all the way through the thickest parts of the sphere, but toward the edges, the outline of the buildings behind the anomaly are apparent.

The anomaly isn't what Teller or anyone else expected in regards to first contact with an intelligent extraterrestrial species. They were all so convinced they'd be conversing with an alien intelligence in English. Surely, there's some kind of universal translator? And yet the anomaly is silent. It's just a big ball of slush, full of prebiotic material and a single snake-like appendage, but no intelligent life. It doesn't make any sense.

Teller racks his mind, wanting an answer, desperate for

some kind of meaning, but he has no more ideas. That realization scares him more than being caught in the middle of a riot. As much as he doesn't want to admit it, anticipating what the anomaly would do next gave him a sense of control, or at least the illusion of control. It made him feel confident and self-assured. And yet deep down he knows all his bluster in the mall with Anderson and Cathy was a cover—a facade.

The reality is, Cathy is right. The scientists want the anomaly to be more than it is. When they were swapping elements, Teller felt so sure, so confident that he knew what was coming. Even though the specifics of the next phase eluded him, he felt sure the alien species would want to communicate at a biological level, but this—this isn't part of the plan. They aren't following the path they should, and that unsettles him. All the talk about marker pens and dictionaries personifies where he wants things to go, and not the reality that confronts him. The reality is, the anomaly doesn't fit with any of their expectations.

Cathy and Anderson take the bags of shopping over to the research trailer, but Teller excuses himself. He wants a bit of room to think. It's funny, just getting out of the research group for a couple of hours and wandering around the mall has allowed him to distance himself once he got back, making it easier to be honest with himself.

Teller turns his back on the anomaly and walks away. It's as much a mental act as it is a physical one. Cathy joked about the anomaly stroking their egos, and she was right. Certainly, the attention of NASA scientists has flattered his.

Perhaps the Reverend Stark was also right, he thinks, recalling the debate in lower New York. Perhaps the anomaly is an idol, not in the religious sense of being worshiped as a god, but in the sense of attracting blind admiration.

And Cathy knows, she's seen what the anomaly has done to Teller, filling him with an unwarranted sense of overconfidence while the world burns around them. Here they are, grappling with an intelligence thousands, perhaps millions of times more advanced than their own, and what's their response? To act like children. What was the phrase Cathy used? "Kids in a candy store?" Teller wonders if it is more like rich kids in an exclusive club. They're the cool kids, not willing to share their toys. And so the world burns. Paris is in flames. The streets of Washington D.C. are barricaded off. Smoke still drifts on the breeze above New York City. But he's ignored all this. The NASA team has ignored the protests from the rest of the world because they are convinced they are sharing, when they are actually teasing everyone else, tormenting them, whether they mean to or not.

Teller is disgusted with himself. Too damn self-absorbed.

He kicks at pebbles on the road, walking past one of the makeshift tents. A soldier coming the other way stands to attention, recognizing him.

"I'm a school teacher," he says by way of explanation, but the soldier looks at him confused as he wanders on toward the outer barricade. He shouldn't be here. He has no right. None of them do.

Cathy's passing comments have stirred something deep within him. The roller-coaster ride was fun while he was on it, but now the ride has come to an end, reality is returning.

"Goddamn movies," he mumbles, talking to himself. "Movies are to blame. From the silver spaceships of the black and white classics to the monolith in 2001: A Space Odyssey. Movies have had more influence on us than science."

It's a startling realization. From mysterious black slabs hidden on the moon to bugs and critters, spiders the size of an SUV—we've done it all, imagining every conceivable combination that could constitute an alien species.

"Tribbles, Vulcans, Klingons," he mumbles, walking past the mess tent. "Cute and cuddly aliens that just want to phone home, and those with acid for blood we'd never want to bring home."

"Are you okay, sir?" another soldier asks, seeing him talking to himself.

Teller looks up.

"Oh, me? Yes. I'm fine. Never been better."

"Is there anything I can get you, sir?"

"No, I'm good. Thanks."

What he really wants is to stop being called "sir."

Teller wants to go home. He's not someone special. He's not someone to be revered. He's a grade school teacher. He wants to see "his kids," as he affectionately calls them. He wants to leave the ego behind.

He walks up to the outer barricade. It's unusual approaching the barricade from the rear. Although the barricades have moved back hundreds of yards since the early days, police still dutifully man their stations behind the wooden structures. There are police cars off to one side. A couple of medics sit beside an ambulance, on standby in case they're needed in an emergency.

"Hey," a familiar voice says. It takes a few seconds for the face to register, but Teller smiles when he recognizes the officer that wouldn't let him go and get Susan. Teller's not bitter or resentful. The man was doing his job. And now he greets Teller like a long lost friend.

"Is there anything I can do for you?" the officer asks. Everyone wants to do something for him. Why? Why him? What makes him so special? His damn ego?

"Just taking a walk," Teller replies, stopping to talk to the officer for a moment.

"So what's it like?" the officer asks, his face lighting up. "I saw the footage of you on the slab. How trippy was that?"

"Yeah, it was pretty wild," Teller replies, his mind still wandering.

Giant prawns, aliens that breed and evolve at a breakneck pace, body snatchers, shape shifters, but always monsters. And yet truth is stranger than fiction. Damn you, Hollywood.

The officer doesn't say anything. He's waiting. He wants something more than, "pretty wild."

"Ah," Teller says, not sure what the officer wants to know beyond all that's been televised. Teller doesn't think there's anything that hasn't been captured on film.

"We got it wrong," he says, seeing the officer's surname is Zachmann. "We've imagined this day for decades, and we finally meet an alien intelligence, but it doesn't play by our rules."

The officer looks confused, as though he's walked into the middle of a conversation and is trying to make sense of the context. In some ways, he has.

"But does that bother us?" Teller says. "No, we keep trying to fit the anomaly into one box or another. We're trying to pigeonhole another kind of intelligence, but we can't."

Not what the officer was after, but it feels good to talk.

"Oh," the officer says, not sure what to say in response.

"Doesn't matter," Teller says. He holds out his hand. The officer accepts his open gesture and shakes his hand vigorously. Teller says, "Thank you for everything. You guys have done a great job out here."

He's saying what he thinks the officer wants to hear. That being on the outer perimeter hasn't been a waste of time. It probably has, but it's best not to tell him that.

Teller walks on. It's strange to wander down the middle of an empty road instead of walking on the sidewalk.

Trissa was right to pull him to one side. His intuition might have helped on a couple of occasions, but it was guesswork. He's batting below the Mendoza Line. Sure, the crowd stands when he knocks the baseball out of the park, but how often does that happen? And Trissa nailed the real problem—good science tests ideas, it doesn't go flying off on tangents.

His mind casts back to the religious debate. He isn't sure what triggered that memory as he walks along, kicking pebbles and rocks and scuffing his shoes on the concrete. Rather than a few days, it seems as though the debate happened years ago. Not only in another time, but to another Teller, a different Teller, one brimming with confidence, blinded by enthusiasm.

"Lying signs and wonders," that's what the preacher had said, "a strong delusion." Only the preacher was talking about the anomaly.

"He should have been talking about us," Teller mumbles.

"So many assumptions," he says to himself as he walks past the paramedics, "and all of them biased toward what we want the anomaly to be. But it's not what we want it to be."

The irony of that moment is not lost on Teller, not now. All the participants in that debate had gone to the Town Hall to discuss the moral and religious implications of alien contact, but neither side was ever going to move on their initial position. Teller felt attacked, but the reality was, so had each of the religious leaders, only for them the assault was through the media, through endless speculation and the posturing of supposed experts on TV giving them no right of reply or rebuttal. It's no wonder they took their frustration out on him. But could he hear what they were saying? No, he was as entrenched as they were.

As critical as Teller feels about Reverend Stark and the Archbishop, their position was predictable, and they had a point. No consideration was given to the ethical, moral, or religious implications of alien contact. NASA simply ran headlong into the investigation, assuming there were no other considerations beyond the science. But now, Teller isn't so sure.

Cathy struck a raw nerve, probably without realizing it. The anomaly is empty, just a shell waiting to be filled, and that has spurred Teller to the reality of what they are dealing with—something that's forever beyond their control.

"Huh," he says, walking down the abandoned street, already almost fifty yards from the barricade.

That should have been obvious from the very first, with the concrete slab turning over through the night. Physically, the lack of human control was always apparent, but somehow it never translated to their own sense of hubris spiraling out of control. And it wasn't until neither he nor anyone else had any answers that he finally began to see what had troubled the preacher. Oh, it's not the same concern from a religious sense, but it is the same desire for caution, for prudence, for level-headed thinking. It's—

Teller's concentration is shattered by the sound of gunfire.

Cracks resound through the air, echoing off the buildings. As he turns, he sees a cloud of dust kicking up from the far side of the anomaly. Automatic machine gun fire rips through the air, a staccato breaking around him. Instinctively, he ducks.

He runs, but not for cover.

Pumping his arms and driving with his legs, he pounds on the concrete, running back toward the barricade. Several police officers call out for him to stop, but Officer Zachmann waves them off. That he could have been shot barely registers as he sprints past the police line. Zachmann follows hard behind him.

Cathy.

Soldiers run through the maze of tents. For the first time in days, they're carrying rifles. Police swarm in toward the anomaly as the crack of gun fire lashes out again and again and again. On the far side of the anomaly, a bus topples, sliding on one side and stopping just shy of the gigantic sphere. Smoke pours from its shattered frame. The concrete crash-barriers have been smashed aside, crushing police vehicles as they were tossed backwards by the force of the impact.

"Contact heavy," is the cry over the radio waves as soldiers sprint past him. "Perimeter breach south. Commence lockdown."

Teller wants to see what's happening, but Officer Zachmann grabs him, pulling him away and yelling something about his safety.

"Let me go," he cries. "I've got to get her out of here."

Teller tries to wrestle free, he has to find Cathy, but the officer's grip is too strong. Two soldiers grab him and shove him hard into the sheet metal of one of the support trailers.

"I need to—"

"You need to stay put," the soldier says, forcibly pinning him against the back of the trailer. Another soldier speaks into a radio microphone slung over his left shoulder, saying, "This is Bravo 4-5, I have Sierra Tango intact. No injuries. Repeat, Sierra Tango is one hundred meters north and secure. Over."

Sierra Tango—school teacher.

"Copy that," comes the reply. "Evacuate Sierra Tango. Rally point helo. Over."

"Copy. Bravo 4-5. Out."

Teller goes to say something, but the soldier grabs him by the scruff of the neck and runs with him toward the helipad. It is only then he realizes the soldier is bleeding, blood seeps from a wound in his left shoulder, but he will not be deterred from getting Teller to safety.

"Concentrate response south," is the call on the radio. "Civilians down. Watch your fields of fire."

Two other soldiers from the helipad run in to help them. One of them, a woman, takes Teller while the other goes to the aid of the injured soldier. In the blur of the moment, Teller doesn't realize quite how submissive he's become to their sense of authority.

Over the radio he hears, "Bravo 4-2, I have Delta Mike. We are skirting the U.N. building, heading north to rally point helo. Over."

Delta Mike must be Director Mason.

"What is going on?" Teller asks, pleading with the female soldier.

"I'm sorry, sir. I do not know," the woman replies with a sense of formality ringing in her voice. She checks him for injuries, pulling at his clothes and looking to see if he's bleeding.

"I'm fine. I'm fine," Teller repeats, trying to reassure her.

A Blackhawk helicopter, some thirty feet away, lifts off the ground, kicking up a storm around them. Small stones and flecks of debris are kicked up and sent hurtling out at them like hail. Teller grimaces as the tiny pebbles sting his arms and face. The helicopter rises swiftly, its blades thrashing at the air, thumping as it clears the buildings. A machine gunner leans out the side of the helicopter, opening fire on their attackers.

"No," Teller yells, waving his arms. His reaction is irrational. He's concerned about the anomaly, afraid the gunner will strike the vast swirling mass rising up hundreds and hundreds of feet in the air. But in the chaos of the moment, there are probably dozens of other soldiers firing as well, each one just as likely to hit such a huge target with a stray round.

As the chopper departs, circling out over the river and around to the south, Teller finds himself huddled among a troop of soldiers. They surround him with their M-16s pointing outward in all directions. He catches sight of Mason being bundled toward him.

Mason sprawls into the middle of the soldiers. Several other soldiers crouch beside a forklift. They're bristling with weapons, daring their adversaries to approach. A small team of soldiers turns a diesel generator over on its side, using it to provide shelter for the main group.

"What the hell happened?" Teller asks, hearing the sporadic gunfire in the distance. The shooting is subsiding, but violent cracks still jar the air as shots ring out.

Mason falls in a heap beside him. His jacket is torn. His tie has been twisted to one side, while the collar on his white shirt has been ripped, torn at the neck.

"I don't know," Mason cries, gasping for breath. "We were attacked from the south."

"Blue on blue," comes the cry over the airways. "Avoid East 44th, we have troops there. Concentrate on the vehicles south. Over."

There are other cries on the radio, but most of them are inaudible to Teller over the crack of gunfire.

"They used a bus," Mason says. "Knocked the barricades around like they were made of balsa wood. There were two minivans following hard behind the bus. They overwhelmed us before we knew what was happening."

"Only two?" one of the soldiers asks. "I heard reports of more vehicles."

It is only then Teller realizes Mason is talking to the soldier and not to him.

"There's not that many of them," Mason says. "For all the shooting, I think there were only a couple of dozen in the attack. It's hard to tell. But yes, there were only two vehicles behind the bus."

It takes fifteen minutes for the gunfire to subside. Once it becomes clear the attackers have hostages, a stalemate is reached. It's another hour before anyone is able to confirm that Cathy and Anderson have been caught in the crossfire, pinned down in the research trailer.

Finch escapes, leading a group of scientists with him to the southern rally point.

Trissa and Bates make it to the police line, but they're wounded. Paramedics rush them to a hospital.

As the afternoon wears on, Teller grows exceedingly impatient. The soldiers want to remove him entirely from the scene, but he sticks close to Mason, demanding that he be allowed to stay.

Negotiators move in, trying to reason with the terrorists; at least, that's what they are calling them on the television. The reality is, no one is sure what faction they represent. They're men, mainly of European descent, but a couple of them appeared to be Middle Eastern, or that's what the news reports claim. None of them are over the age of thirty, if the news reports are to be believed. At first, they don't make any demands. They simply hunker down, fortifying their position and setting up a stronghold around the research trailer.

Smoke drifts on the breeze. Helicopters circle overhead. Snipers line the rooftops of the neighboring buildings, but they have orders to hold fire.

"What about the anomaly? Mason asks Teller. "How will it respond to this?"

"I—I don't know." Rather than guessing, it feels good to be honest and admit he has no idea. "It had to have been hit in the crossfire. It's simply too big to escape at least one stray bullet."

"Damn thing's bigger than the proverbial side of a barn," Mason says as they look at the NASA research trailer from behind a hastily established cordon.

"It has to have taken hits," Teller says. "Probably multiple hits, but the thick atmospheric layer surrounding the sac should have stopped any rounds from going too deep, in much the same way a bullet fired into water never penetrates more than a few feet."

"What will this mean to the aliens?" Mason asks.

"I have no answers," Teller says. "Only questions."

It has taken him some time to get to this point, and perhaps it's too late, but he doesn't know and won't guess.

Mason persists, saying, "Give me something to work with. Give me options. Ideas. How has the dynamic changed?"

Teller points out the obvious.

"It is still there. The alien entity undoubtedly has an awareness of what has happened, although I doubt it understands why. Hell, we don't even know why.

"To the anomaly, this is probably seen as some kind of power struggle among the natives, and in that regard, it probably expected something like this sooner rather than later."

From the look on Mason's face, that's not what he wanted to hear.

"What will it do now?"

"I don't know. We have to rethink our assumptions about the anomaly. It simply doesn't fit our stereotypes of what an alien encounter is supposed to be. And now, with this, all bets are off. "

As the heat of the afternoon slowly gives way, the leader of the group appears in front of the bullet riddled NASA trailer wearing a vest with an array of explosives attached to it. In one hand he holds a gun, identified by the police as a 9mm Glock. In the other, he holds a switch with a wire leading back to his vest.

"What is that?" Teller asks, standing beside Mason at the perimeter.

"It's a dead man's trigger," Mason says. "A positive-pressure switch. He's wired himself with enough C4 explosive to take out a city block, and there's not much we can do about it other than try to talk him down. If a sniper was to take him out, he'd release the pressure on that switch and boom!"

Teller swallows the lump in his throat.

Mason says, "What will an explosion of that magnitude do to the anomaly? And don't tell me you don't know. Give me an educated guess."

"Ah," Teller says, his mind scrambling for answers. "C4. At a guess, it's a highly exothermic reaction releasing vast amounts of nitrogen and oxygen as gases. It's the speed and ratio of solid to gas decomposition that's the killer."

"Speak English," Mason growls, but Teller's simply talking himself through the chemistry.

"You're looking at an expansion rate of anywhere from 20,000 to 30,000 feet per second. Given the anomaly is no more than 30 feet away, it's not good."

"And?" Mason asks.

"I don't know," Teller says. "Something is maintaining the integrity of the pressure inside the anomaly, keeping it from spilling into our world. Could the C4 rupture that? Maybe. If it does, the C4 will be the last of your worries. That C4 will act like a detonator inside a grenade. The sheer volume of highly volatile gases inside the anomaly would be enough to flatten most of the

East Side."

"Fuck!"

"It might not rupture," Teller says.

"But if it did, what would be the blast radius?"

Teller isn't sure. He doesn't know, but Mason doesn't want to hear that. Again.

"Well, in terms of volume, there's over a million cubic meters of volatile gases and pressure-induced liquids inside the anomaly—oxygen, methane, various nitrates. That's roughly four hundred Olympic sized swimming pools compressed under ten tons of pressure per square inch. Without doing the math, I'd say three, maybe four miles."

"Sweet Jesus," Mason says. "That's pretty much all of lower Manhattan and a good portion of Queens."

Teller tries to run the sums in his head, but the analytical part of his brain is still reeling in shock. He talks through the practicalities of such a massive, rapid decompression.

"The buildings will absorb and deflect some of the blast, but they'll crumble like sand castles. They're built to withstand vertical weight, not a horizontal shear. And the streets are going to channel and concentrate the blast, funneling it out into the city at large."

Mason turns to the woman beside him, saying, "Evacuate all non-essential personnel from this site. Get the National Guard to start evacuating the island, starting with 45th, spreading north and south from there. We've got to get as many people out of the city as we can."

"The whole of Manhattan?" the woman asks.

"As much as you can," Mason replies.

"But we don't know that a C4 explosion will rupture the anomaly," Teller says. "The alien craft may be able to withstand the shockwave. We just don't know."

Mason replies. "But if it doesn't, we lose New York City."

"Yes," Teller says with grim determination. "If it ruptures, it'll happen so quickly, no one will know. This won't be like the movies. Blink and the city will be gone. If the anomaly ruptures, it will pretty much go off like a nuke."

"Wonderful," Mason says sarcastically. "Just what I wanted to hear."

He walks off, raising his phone to his ear, presumably to brief the President.

Police negotiators talk with the man, pleading with him to allow them to remove the injured and dead. Most of the injured scientists and soldiers have managed to crawl behind some kind of cover, a barricade, or a trailer, or a police vehicle on the perimeter, and from there soldiers have managed to get them to safety, but there are several lying in the open, within twenty feet of the research trailer. From their clothing, Teller can see they are NASA scientists, with their bright blue polo shirts soaked in deep red blood. A couple of them are moving, with just the odd twitch of an arm or a leg. Most of them are still.

Teller tries to spot Cathy, but he can't remember what she was wearing. She has to be wearing one of the polo shirts, but he can't remember for sure. He spent that whole morning with her and Anderson, and yet his mind is blank, unable to recall any details.

After roughly an hour, there's been no progress with negotiations over the phone.

A negotiator walks out with his hands raised high in the air. He's dressed in jeans and is wearing an "I love New York" t-shirt.

"We just want to talk."

"And we just want honesty," the terrorist leader yells in reply. His head has been shaved, with a neatly cropped goatee beard reinforcing the stark features on his face. His dark facial hair marks a harsh contrast with his pale skin and bald head. The faint outline of a tattoo sits low on the right side of his neck—a swastika that has faded and stretched slightly with age. The lines on the tattoo are no longer crisp, and its color has turned a dull blue.

He points his gun at the negotiator. At that distance, Teller hopes he struggles with accuracy, but that the negotiator is walking out there without a bulletproof vest is alarming. He's either stupidly brave or absolutely crazy, but he's trying to gain the man's trust, trying to mentally disarm this radical.

"Is he mad?" Teller asks.

Mason explains, "The stakes are too high for anything less. The longer that guy holds down that kill-switch, the more likely it is he'll become fatigued and let go. Time is not on our side.

"This is a deliberate choice by the police. They want our man to appear vulnerable, to give the terrorists a sense of control. By being compliant, he's trying to be seen as a facilitator, not a roadblock."

"It's a big gamble," Teller says, not sure if he'd be quite as courageous.

"It's a big boom we're trying to prevent. And he knows it. He volunteered."

Mason sips at a water bottle and says, "In this kind of scenario, a bulletproof vest is more of a comfort blanket. It doesn't offer any real protection as a shot to the head, neck or thighs would be fatal, especially as we can't get to him."

Regardless, Teller would rather have the comfort blanket.

"Listen," says the negotiator. "I'm here to help you. I'm here to listen to you, to assist you in any way I can, but I need you to work with me. Okay?"

"You see this?" the man cries, holding the trigger above his head, his hand wrapped tightly around the switch. "This says, 'Fuck you. Fuck all of you.' If anyone tries anything stupid, I'll blow this whole fucking place sky-high. Fuck you and your anomaly. I want the truth."

"Okay, okay," the negotiator replies, holding his hands out and trying to calm the man. He bends slightly at the knees, trying to make himself seem that little bit smaller as he speaks. "What do you want? What do you need?"

It is a good question, Teller thinks as he watches from behind a police car. Everyone needs something, and this guy's needs and wants drove him to this act of aggressive desperation. He's fanatical about something, and understanding that may be the key to defusing this situation.

"I told you, stupid," the man yells. "What are you? Fucking dumb? I want the truth. I want the truth about Roswell. The truth about the cover-ups. The truth about this fucking monstrosity."

Mason speaks softly to Teller. "Listen to how he's talking about himself and not his team."

"What does that mean?" Teller asks.

"Classic egomaniac. Everything and everyone is subordinate to him. This is not going to end well."

Mason hands Teller a photo. On it, he sees a picture of the terrorist leader standing in front of a police mug-shot station, holding a clipboard with a processing number on it. Someone's written on the back of the photo.

James Johnson Phelps the third.

Born and raised in rural Texas.

White supremacist.

"I want the truth about these fucking aliens," Phelps cries out.

Spittle sits on his beard.

He bares his teeth as he speaks.

The veins on his neck are pumped.

"You've been talking to them for decades. Selling us out. Apollo, the shuttle, the space station, they were all a lie—a cover. This is nothing new, this is old. These are the same fucking lies you've been shoving down our throats for decades. But this time you screwed up.

"They weren't supposed to come down here, were they? They weren't supposed to be seen in public. They're supposed to appear as they always have, out in the desert, down in 51. But you fucked up.

"I think they got too pushy. They wanted more. They wanted control too soon, before you could enslave us, before you could take our guns, before you could take away our rights and freedoms. They want to invade us right now, and you can't stop them."

The negotiator tries to say something, but Phelps points his gun at him, thrusting it forward repeatedly, almost willing it to fire as he yells at him.

"We will not be your slaves. Today is the day we fight back. My brothers have fallen, their blood has been spilt, but the truth is out now, you cannot put the genie back in the bottle."

Mason whispers in Teller's ear. "We make six of them in and around the research trailer, four of them are wounded. There were originally close to thirty in the assault, but we were able to neutralize over twenty of them. We've traced most of them to an extremist group called Purity, along with an outlaw motorcycle gang that goes by the name of Hell's Own."

"What happens from here?" Teller asks, noticing the police are setting up blast screens behind their squad cars on the outer perimeter. The screens are transparent panels of bulletproof Plexiglas, rimmed with steel and designed to protect against shrapnel and flying debris. Built in sets of three panels, they're free-standing, but Teller isn't convinced they'll do any good. They might provide protection from the C4, but if the anomaly ruptures, it's game over.

"I don't know for sure," Mason says. "Control is being handed over to the Delta counter-terrorist squad, but they're still coming on site. Over the next couple of hours, they'll replace the police and soldiers we have here, but they'll wear the same uniforms to avoid raising the alarm and giving away their presence."

"I don't see how they can tackle a dead-man's switch?" Teller says. "That's an impossible scenario."

"The problem is time," Mason says. "And it's a problem for

Phelps as much as it is for us. He has to keep his fist clenched. Even if the pressure setting is minimal, that constant need for load is going to cramp his muscles within a few hours.

"There has to be a safety catch. He cannot have got here without one. My guess is the team will be watching his hand like a hawk, waiting for him to tire and engage the safety. That's when they'll move. And when Delta attacks, it will be quick. It will be like a dozen lightning strikes happening all at once, and the counter-strike will be over before you know it has even begun."

Teller appreciates Mason's confidence. He isn't so sure. It seems risky, but the alternative is unbearable. If they do nothing, Cathy will die.

What will become of the anomaly? Could it absorb such a blast? Maybe. But the ramifications beyond the blast are unknown. How would the alien entity interpret such violence? Would it react? Would it suffer damage? Would it see this as a hostile act taken by humanity as a whole? Would it depart? Or attack?

There's some commotion over by the research trailer but Teller can't make out what's going on. Mason has a small portable TV screen and can see from the other angle. He brings up the sound.

Cathy is marched out of the trailer by one of the terrorists. Anderson is with her, hanging from her shoulder and clutching a dark, bloody patch on his stomach. Blood runs down his trousers. His footsteps are marked in brilliant shades of scarlet. Someone is shouting at Cathy, screaming at her, telling her to stop, but she staggers forward, out into view, shuffling onto the road in front of the anomaly. Anderson's head hangs low, his feet barely move as she pulls him on. She's trying to reach the police cordon, but she's too far away, moving far too slowly. She's in shock.

"Get the fuck down," Phelps yells, charging over toward her. "Get the fuck on the ground."

Cathy is defiant. Blood stains streak her clothes. Black soot mars her face.

"I can't. He'll die."

Phelps raises his gun, pointing it at her head, "I said get down, bitch."

"No," Cathy yells as she staggers on in a daze.

"Not good," Mason says, turning to one of the soldiers beside him. "Defiance is never good. Just, go to ground, Cathy. Please."

Cathy stumbles forward, pulling Anderson on with her. Phelps is enraged, his face is visibly red. He steps forward and strikes her with the back of his hand. His pistol rakes across her face and she falls to her knees.

"He'll die," she cries. "Don't you get that?"

"I decide who lives and who dies," Phelps yells. "Me! I decide that, not you."

"And yet you let us live," Cathy pleads. "You didn't kill us.

You kept us alive. But he's sustained a life-threatening wound. If he doesn't get medical treatment, he's going to die. Is that what you want? Is that really what you want?"

Phelps is unusually quiet. He raises his gun swiftly. The look on his face is cold, his eyes don't even blink as he squeezes the trigger. The shot is astonishingly quick, startling Teller.

From the look of horror on Cathy's face, she expected Phelps to pause, to threaten them further, to continue with his bluster, but he kills Anderson without a second thought.

The bullet strikes Anderson in the center of his chest. Teller watches helplessly as Anderson reels to one side. He convulses. Spasms rack his body as he falls away from Cathy, crumpling lifeless to the ground.

The negotiator runs for cover, falling back behind a police car.

Cathy kneels on the bloodstained concrete road, shaking as Phelps holds the barrel of his gun just inches from her forehead. She quivers, closing her eyes, waiting for the inevitable.

Teller isn't sure how the next few seconds unfold. Somehow, he finds himself halfway across the concrete road before he knows what's happening. He's running toward Cathy, and yelling at Phelps, screaming at the terrorist leader incoherently.

The road seems so wide, so long. Teller feels as though he is running through mud, as though each step holds him back, slowing him down, making it harder and harder to push through. Although he's running fast, his body feels slow and sluggish. His heart pounds in his chest. His mouth goes dry, and the world falls silent around him.

Searing jolts of pain tear through his body, first through his right shoulder, then a sharp, stabbing pain rips into his left arm. An invisible knife cuts along the side of his right thigh, tearing the muscle open. It is only then he realizes he's being shot. He looks up. Spent shell casings fly out of the gun being fired by Phelps. Shots echo off the surrounding buildings. The gun runs dry and the slide on top of the 9mm Glock remains open.

Teller staggers forward the final few yards, falling to his knees before Cathy.

With a tightly clenched fist, Phelps holds the bomb trigger in his left hand, squeezing it with a vengeance. He's yelling something at Teller, but Teller's ears are ringing from the shots. He can't make out the words.

Phelps tosses the gun to one of the other terrorists, who drops the empty magazine out of the grip and slams another magazine in place. In those few seconds, Teller grabs Cathy, wrapping his bloodied arms around her. They cling to each other, sobbing as Phelps gets his gun back.

"It's okay," Teller says. "Everything's going to be all right." He runs his hands through her hair and feels her trembling beneath his fingers.

The hot barrel of a gun pushes hard into the back of his

head.

"What have we here?" says a voice from behind him. The burnt smell of gun powder hangs in the air. The barrel slides around the side of his head, across his hair, and then on top of his head, always pointing into his skull.

"What kind of idiot runs at a man firing a gun?"

Teller turns slowly, getting his first good look at Phelps. His eyes aren't quite blue, more of a light gray. His goatee beard has been dyed black to make him look younger than he is, and the regrowth betrays his age with flecks of gray that match his eyes. His nostrils flare. Phelps bares his teeth, pulling back his lips as he speaks.

"What do we have here? A goddamn all-American hero? A lover or a fool?"

Phelps is strangely quiet, almost subdued as he speaks, just as he was before he killed Anderson. He brings the barrel of the gun down, running it around the side of Teller's face, pushing it hard up against Teller's cheekbone and then down under his chin, lifting Teller's head slightly as he raises the gun.

"A fool," Teller says, and he means it, knowing how stupid he has been. For Teller these words aren't simply the admission of a stupid act in running to Cathy, but rather the culmination of the past few days. He feels as though his entire life has been little more than a stupid dream.

"Get up," Phelps says, gesturing with his gun and signaling

for them to move apart. They comply meekly, getting slowly to their feet. Phelps backs Teller over toward the lounge suite, barely twenty yards from the anomaly. His eyes glance up. Although Teller's back is to the anomaly, he knows Phelps is staring at the gigantic marble sphere in awe. The anomaly has that kind of hypnotic effect up close. The slowly swirling blue environment is semi-transparent, allowing Phelps to see the outline of the vast fluid sac within.

"What is it?" Phelps asks. "What does it do?"

"I don't know. I don't think anyone knows. I thought I knew, but honestly, I was guessing. The truth is—no one knows."

Strangely, that seems to satisfy Phelps. His lips show a hint of admiration for Teller's response. For all his talk about conspiracy theories and alien invasions, it seems reality has a numbing effect on Phelps.

Teller staggers a little. The tear in his thigh throbs with each step. He clutches at the wound. Blood seeps down his leg.

"You have nine lives," Phelps says.

Teller doesn't answer him. He keeps his gaze down, away from the terrorist's eyes.

"Three shots, and not one direct hit. I'm not normally that sloppy."

Teller leans against the back of the lounge, supporting his weight. Cathy circles out wide, not wanting to come too close to Phelps, but wanting to stay close to Teller.

"What is all this?" Phelps asks, kicking the bags of shopping that were left by the lounge. Toys and books, music discs and a packet of colored markers lie scattered on the concrete. Teller feels himself slipping down the couch. He's weak from blood loss. He's going into shock. The adrenaline of the moment has worn off and his injuries sap his strength. His shoulder aches, and his arm feels as though it was slashed with a red-hot iron.

Phelps kicks one of the books over to him as he slumps on the ground, his back up against the couch.

"Math."

The terrorist leader says. "I hate math."

"Me too," Teller replies, half laughing. "And I'm a teacher."

Teller picks up the thin, paperback textbook and thumbs through the pages, looking at the equations and diagrams awaiting an answer—the blank lines await some intelligence to complete them. Answers, that is all anyone ever wants in life. As sick and distorted as Phelps is, he's predictable—he wants answers. That is what they all want. But what has the anomaly given them? Nothing but questions.

Cathy moves in from the side with her hands out touching at Teller's shoulder, trying to stem the flow of blood. He drops the math book and the pages flay open before him on the ground. Bloody fingermarks stain the white paper.

Phelps kicks the dictionary to one side. The cover is open. The pages flutter in the breeze. He looks at the music discs, kicking them around with his steel capped boots.

"What is all this for?" he asks.

"They are a fool's errand," Teller says, not expecting him to understand. Teller watches as Phelps flexes the fingers of his left hand, rolling them slightly and relieving the pressure for a moment. Phelps follows his gaze, seeing Teller's eyes settling on the bars of explosive strapped to his jacket. Thin wires run between the bars of C4.

"You have to be prepared to die for what you believe in," Phelps says. "Or you don't really believe in anything. There's no progress without sacrifice."

He pauses, thinking for a moment before continuing,

"You're a learned man. Do you know of Henri-Frédéric Amiel?"

Teller shakes his head, still not looking up.

"Amiel coined the phrase, 'Sacrifice is the passion of all great men.' But you understand that already, don't you? You ran in here. You were prepared to die for her."

Teller is silent.

"I respect that," Phelps says, his fingers flexing on the deadman's switch.

He is not going to apply any safety catch. Mason must know it too. He would have heard everything Phelps said, but there's nothing he can do.

There is only one way this is going to end.

They're going to die.

Phelps turns to walk away.

"Why?" Teller calls out after him.

Cathy drops down beside Teller. She's alarmed that he's called Phelps back.

"Why did I come here?" Phelps asks in reply, facing Teller with his arms hanging limp by his sides—a gun in one hand, the detonator in the other.

"No," Teller says. "Why are we still alive? You're going to kill us anyway, right? You're going to sacrifice us. Why haven't you killed us already? Why wait? Why haven't you blown us up?"

Phelps laughs. His head rocks back and his eyes look up at the vast expanse of the anomaly.

"I am mad," he says, pointing at his own heart with the gun, making as though he was about to shoot himself. "Do you not know that? Does a mad man need a reason? And yet you ask for a reason as though I were sane. Ah, but perhaps it is you that is mad and I am sane."

Teller doesn't say anything. For the first time, he looks Phelps in the eye, refusing to be intimidated in the final seconds of his life.

"Madness is a matter of perspective, my friend. Hitler was mad. Truman was sane.

"Or was he?

"Hitler never unleashed the horrors of nuclear weapons on innocent, unsuspecting women and children. Hah, no. That takes a sane man.

"You see, madness exists only from another's point of view. We are all mad. And madness only needs impetus, not reason."

Phelps holds the dead-man's switch up so Teller can see the wires spiraling down to the explosive vest.

"This is not madness," Phelps says. "This is power. This is control. This demands respect."

He points at the police barrier, adding, "You see, they have controlled us all our lives, they have held all the power, but not anymore. Power is based on fear, and now they fear me, now I have the power."

Phelps steps forward, pointing the gun at Teller as he speaks. It is more as a gesture than a threat, but Cathy grimaces.

"You see this?" Phelps continues. "You see this monstrosity? This anomaly? They would have you think this is the first encounter, but it's not. They would have you think this is unknown, but it's not. They've been working with these aliens for decades.

"Think about it. The Wright brothers could barely fly a couple of feet above a beach in North Carolina for less than a hundred yards, and yet in half a century we were flying to the Moon! Doesn't that strike you as strange? We spent thousands of years climbing out of the Stone Age, the Bronze Age, the Iron Age, the Dark Age. And then in less than a century we're walking on the Moon?

"The Wright brothers flew for twelve seconds, just twelve seconds, and we called it powered flight. Hell, I can hold my breath longer than that.

"And you want me to believe we went from twelve seconds to putting men on the Moon, sending probes to Mars, flying by Jupiter, Saturn and out of the solar system, all within a century? All by ourselves?

"Somebody's lying.

"I defy you to show me how that is logical. I defy you to show me how that is realistic."

Phelps waves the gun at the anomaly and, for a moment, Teller thinks he might start shooting at it.

"Now, I don't know what this fucking thing is," Phelps says, "but I know what it is part of, I know what it is here for. It is part of the continued alien investment in our economy. Don't you see? They're propping us up. They're giving us all of this tech, these computers and microchips, these inventions, these rocket ships. But it's a bribe. They do it so they can control us. And the government's been in on it all along, since Truman at least. Roswell was just the beginning."

And with those last few words, Teller finds his mind reeling.

"Roswell," he says, caught off guard.

"Yes, yes," Phelps says, egging him on, but Teller's mind is casting back to the debate in downtown New York. The placards carried by the protestors. One of them read: Roswell was just the beginning. It was Phelps and his team. They were there.

Phelps leans down toward Teller, saying, "They want our minds. They want our allegiance, our loyalty. They mean to enslave us."

The wind picks up.

A chill cuts through the air.

Shadows grow dark as the sun sets behind the New York skyline.

The pages of the math textbook flick over in the breeze and Teller's heart stops. Phelps seems to pick up on the change in Teller's focus, seeing his eyes looking intently at the textbook.

Complete the following binary sequence 0, 1, 10, 11, 100

<u>*101, 110, 111*</u>

Convert the value of the dice into a numeric equation [::] [:.] = ?

<u>*4 + 3 = 7*</u>

There are answers. But how? These books have never actually been inside the anomaly.

All this time, they've only ever considered the anomaly as confined and constrained to the sphere, but that was an assumption. The anomaly, it seems, is impatient to proceed.

All of the questions, equations, and diagrams in the book have an answer written next to them. The writing is neat, the characters and numbers are crisp and consistent, as though they were printed as part of the book, but they weren't.

Phelps doesn't understand. He sees the page. He doesn't see the answers.

Somehow, Phelps realizes Teller has seen something important, but to him it is just a math book. It's something to be despised.

Teller fights not to give anything more away with his facial expressions, knowing he's already said too much with his look of surprise. Phelps kicks the book, twisting his boot on one of the pages and tearing the corner off. A dark smudge mars the rest of the crumpled page.

"What is it? What do you see?" he demands.

"Nothing."

"You're lying. You're fucking lying to me. What is it?"

"It's just a kid's book," Teller replies, trying to downplay the situation. "I'm a grade school teacher. I see books like this all the time. It's somewhat ironic that this is the last book I'll ever see."

Phelps doesn't buy his explanation. He flies into a rage, kicking Teller with his steel capped boots. He crushes both the textbook and the dictionary under his feet, stamping on them and bending the spine of the books back. Torn pages scatter across the ground.

Teller looks away, locking eyes with Cathy. Tears stream down her cheeks. He wants to say something. He wants to tell her, to let her know what he's seen, to let her know there is hope, but he can't.

"Nothing can save you," Phelps says. "You must know that. Nothing. You're dead. You hear me? You are a dead man!"

Out of the corner of his eye, Teller sees Phelps holding the gun out at arm's length just inches from his head. Teller refuses to look at him. If he is going to die, he isn't going to give this madman the satisfaction of terrorizing him. Teller holds Cathy's hands, keeping his eyes focused on her.

"Close your eyes," he says, not wanting her to watch, but he cannot close his eyes. If he is to die, he wants to see her right up until the end. She's beautiful. She wouldn't think so at the moment, but she is. Beauty is more than makeup, more than styled hair, more than lipstick or pretty earrings. True beauty is a connection between two people that reaches beyond mere looks.

The muscles in his body seize as he squeezes her fingers, clenching his teeth and waiting, wondering how quickly he'll die, hoping it will be instant, leaving nothing but darkness.

Seconds pass like hours.

"Any last words?"

Teller doesn't take his eyes off Cathy. He says, "Answers. That's all we ever wanted."

She opens her eyes, realizing he's talking about the anomaly, but the look in her face suggests she hasn't seen them written in the math textbook. He smiles at her, hoping she'll make it out of this alive, hoping one day she'll understand.

"You're a fool," Phelps says, leaning down and yelling in his ear, screaming, "You're a goddamn fool!"

"I am," is all Teller can say, still looking deep into Cathy's eyes. Tears run down his cheeks.

Phelps shoves him against the back of the couch and walks off in disgust.

"You are so stupid," Cathy whispers, crying as she hugs him. "You should have never come for me. You should have left me. You're so silly, so stupid."

Teller simply holds her tight as she sobs. There is nothing he can say.

Cathy leans back, looking at his wounds. He reaches out and picks up a page torn from the textbook. Blood has soaked into the paper, deep red fingerprints stain the page. His shoulder aches, throbbing with the pulsating rhythm of his heart, but there are answers. And those answers take away the pain.

Complete the next four prime numbers: 2, 3, 5, 7, 11, 13,

<u>17, 19, 23, 29</u>

Convert the Arabic number 25 into Roman numerals

<u>XXV</u>

"I don't understand," Cathy says, not seeing anything significant.

"Answers," Teller says softly, holding the paper low so as to avoid attracting attention. "The anomaly is giving us answers. In the midst of all this chaos, the anomaly wants to answer our questions."

He puts down the page and picks up the dictionary. The damaged spine has caused the book to fall open in a strange manner. There, in the margin, he sees a large red asterisk next to the definition for one particular word.

* **Trust** — *Noun: Firm belief in the reliability, truth, ability, or strength of someone or something. Verb: Believe in the reliability, truth, ability, or strength of someone.*

"What does it mean?" Cathy asks.

"I don't know," Teller says. "The anomaly is trying to talk to us. Trying to tell us to trust it."

"But how?" Cathy asks, tearing at the loose threads on her shirt, trying to rip some material to use as a bandage. "How can we trust it if we don't know what this means?"

Teller doesn't say anything. There is nothing to say. All his conjecture, his opinions, his speculation, what have they accomplished? Nothing. Somehow, he stumbled upon the nature of the anomaly using a gyroscope. A bit of guesswork helped him figure out why there was hydrogen at the heart of the sphere, but that feels as though it happened years ago.

Back at the mall, Cathy uncovered the truth—it felt good to be important, to be needed, to be valued. And all he had to do was sound convincing, but he was shallow, hollow. He bathed in the thrill of working with NASA.

Bates was right. He wasn't qualified and shouldn't have been there. Being part of the anomaly investigation team stroked his ego.

Cathy believes in him; he can see that. She trusts him, even now when they are about to die. She shouldn't. Like him, she shouldn't even be here.

Teller looks at that one highlighted word on the page—Trust.

Trust has so much depth of meaning, so much application in life, but all too often trust is misplaced. Trust has to be earned.

Teller doesn't believe he's earned her trust.

She looks into his eyes, looking for hope. He has to be honest.

"I'm sorry," Teller says. "I wish I knew what this means, but I don't."

Phelps rages before the cameras, yelling at the police. He's taking advantage of his moment in the spotlight, and Teller knows what's coming next. Phelps holds his left hand high above his head, as though he was reaching for the sky, exalting the dead-man's trigger as he cries out in anger at the world.

"Trust," Teller mumbles.

If only he could.

Trust. Such a simple word, but the intention is unclear. How can he trust the anomaly? What should he do?

Frustrated, he tosses the child's dictionary to the concrete. Even at a distance of a few feet, the large font is easy to read.

A gust of wind swirls around them. Cathy tugs at his arm, gesturing toward the dictionary as the pages turn in the wind. Teller looks down. Another word has a large red asterisk next to it.

* ***Now*** — *Adverb: At the present time or moment*

Teller's heart leaps in his throat.

"Do you trust this thing?" he asks.

Cathy doesn't hesitate.

"Yes."

"I don't know if I do, but we have no choice," he replies soberly.

Grabbing hold of the lounge, Teller struggles to his feet. The gash on his leg aches. The searing pain causes him to grimace, slowing his motion. The bullet wound in his shoulder throbs.

Cathy helps him stand.

"What are we going to do?" she asks.

"Something really stupid," Teller replies, making his way around the side of the lounge while keeping his eyes on Phelps. "I think I finally know why this thing is empty."

"Why?" Cathy asks, taking his arm over her shoulder and helping him as he limps toward the anomaly.

"Because it's waiting to be filled."

One of the terrorists sees them and calls out in alarm, saying, "Hey! What the hell do you think you're doing?"

Phelps turns.

"Run," Teller cries, as he pushes his body on, half limping

and half running toward the anomaly. The swirling mass rises up before them, bulging out and towering hundreds of feet over them.

Teller can hear Phelps yelling. Gunshots ring out, but it doesn't matter. In just a few feet they'll run into the hazy blue of an alien world. But the pressure inside is thousands of times greater than the pressure at sea-level on Earth. Either way, they're dead. For Teller, the risk is worth it. The anomaly is trying to communicate something to them, imploring them to trust it. He only hopes this is what it means.

Bullets tear through his shoulder blade, causing the bone to shatter as they fragment and ricochet within his body. Splinters of metal puncture the top of his lung and he gasps in agony. He falters, his fingers reaching out to within inches of the swirling blue mass. Another bullet collides with his spine, sending him crashing to his knees. He can't make it. The pain surging through his body is overwhelming. He falls to his hands, unable to move any further, collapsing onto the rough concrete.

Cathy pulls at his limp body. With one hand, she reaches out to touch the anomaly when a blinding light erupts around them.

~~~

The wall of super-heated compressed air that reverberates out from the terrorist blast takes everyone by surprise, knocking soldiers and police over up to a hundred yards away.

Cameras recording the event show a visible blast wave

compressing the air as it spreads out from the point of the explosion, crushing everything in its path. The research trailer crumples like an empty Coke can as it is tossed aside and crushed against the U.N. General Assembly building.

Although the chemical reaction unleashed in that split second causes the rapid expansion of nitrogen, oxygen and carbon dioxide, the flash at the heart of the blast appears as a burst of flame, one that for a moment rivals the intensity of the sun.

In less than a second, the pressure wave spreads out over two thousand feet, dwarfing the surrounding buildings and thumping into barriers and cars, knocking them backwards. Windows shatter up to a quarter mile away. Pebbles and rocks and specks of gravel shoot out like shrapnel from a grenade, raking the cars and building facades as they radiate out from the blast. Several fragments from the lounge suite are launched hundreds of feet in the air.

The blast kills the terrorists instantly, while seriously wounding several soldiers and a police officer caught in the open. The blast barriers prove woefully inadequate, collapsing and crashing into those they should have protected. The thump of the explosion throws everyone backwards. A police car on the perimeter is overturned and left lying on its side.

The noise is deafening, leaving the survivors stunned.

The trees lining 1st Avenue flex in a split second, being thrown out by the ferocity of the pressure wave. The partial vacuum that forms in that instant collapses as the pressure dissipates, and the trees are flung back in toward the heart of the blast with the inrush of equalizing pressure.

Smoke billows into the sky. A dark mushroom cloud rises into the air, folding in on itself as it ascends into the twilight.

The anomaly is gone.

Whereas the alien structure had once towered over the area as a smooth, curving sphere set in contrast to the sharp, hard angles of the surrounding buildings, now the street is empty. In its place, a thick haze of smoke and dust hangs in the air.

Finch is one of the first to rush headlong into the street. He runs madly forward from the police line while most others are still recovering from the blast. Finch staggers like a drunken man fighting to stay upright, his arms flay out beside him as he fights to keep his balance. Blood runs from his ears and nose. For once, he doesn't have a camera on his shoulder. Cameras around the area capture his frantic motion, and this time he's the focus of attention.

With heavy steps, he drags himself forward, weaving as he pushes through the smoke.

"Cathy?" he cries, staring at the massive empty crater left by the anomaly. "Teller?"

His lone figure cuts a stark silhouette against the muddy, gray haze. Finch falls a couple of times but gets back to his feet and pushes on toward the spot where the anomaly once stood, the spot where Teller and Cathy were before the blast.

Around the area, voices call out in pain, crying out for help. The medical and police teams that were on hold in reserve on East 48th begin moving through the outer cordon, creeping forward slowly as they tend to the wounded.

Finch falls to his knees and sits there before the massive bowl shaped crater cut into the street by the anomaly. His head bows toward the ground. Tears stream down his cheeks. His shoulders are slouched. His arms hang limp by his side. For someone who has spent a lifetime behind the camera lens, this is the first time he's become the subject. Those network cameras that have survived the blast zoom in on him, catching his stoic figure from a variety of angles. The blur of helicopter spotlights cutting through the smoke gives the street an eerie, haunted, almost dreamlike quality, making his loss surreal.

A medic comes running up to him, looking to tend to his wounds. A few minutes later, the distinct silhouette of Director James Mason appears beside him, standing tall. His hand rests on Finch's shoulder. Finch is crying, that much is clear, even from the grainy video.

"I—"

"I know," Mason says, holding out his hand and helping him to his feet. For all his bravado, it's obvious Finch is devastated by the loss of Teller and Cathy, particularly Cathy, given their love/hate professional relationship. Finch has a reputation for not caring, for being bullish and brash, a hard ass, but he's shaking in the aftermath of the blast.

"She was a good kid," he says, looking Mason in the eye. For his part, Mason is tight-lipped.

"You saw how she tried to get Anderson to safety," Finch continues. "She was like that, always thinking about others. Not like me. She had some real class. She deserved better than this."

Mason swallows a lump in his throat.

"And Teller," Finch continues, struggling with his words. "Neither of them deserved this."

"No, they didn't," Mason replies.

Finch sobs.

It is over.

Humanity's first interaction with an intelligent celestial being has come to an abrupt and violent end.

Finch is distraught.

What had shown such promise, what had held such hope for humanity, has been destroyed. The dreams of those who dared are dashed. Even those that raged against the appearance of the alien intelligence are left hollow and empty without an object for their anger. It seems everyone has lost, but no one more so than Finch.

LIFE

Teller has his eyes shut in a feeble attempt to block out the blinding light. He grimaces, not sure what has happened. Was that the bomb? No. It can't be. They'd be dead. Did Cathy make it to the anomaly? He saw her reaching out to touch the gigantic marble sphere, but if she had she would have been crushed by the pressure within the anomaly. Somehow, they've survived, but the light around them is blinding.

Teller can feel rough concrete beneath his fingers. His left arm is still draped over Cathy's shoulder. They are lying on a road.

"What happened?" Cathy asks.

Slowly, Teller opens his eyes. Sunlight warms his face.

They're lying in the middle of the intersection, only there's no anomaly. There's no dismembered flags, no fractured concrete slab, no torn fragments of buildings, no broken windows, no research trailers or barricades.

"I don't understand," Cathy says, getting to her feet. "This is what it was like that day—in the moments before the quake."

There are no cars, no birds, no clouds in the sky, but everything looks real. Buildings stretch away from them in both directions. A gentle breeze blows from the south.

This can't be real. It can't.

Teller gets to his knees and then to his feet.

"Where are we?"

At first, Teller thought it was Cathy that spoke, but those were his words. He feels as though he's trapped in a dream. He has no idea what's real and what's not. He reaches out and takes her hand. Cathy squeezes his fingers gently. There's something familiar and comforting about her touch. Her motion is as smooth and unique as it was last night. Cathy is real.

Flags flutter in the breeze in front of the United Nations building. There is no disconnect, no gaps or cracks. The intersection looks as he imagines it must have a week ago.

"Where is everyone?" Cathy asks. "Is this just a dream?"

Teller walks to one side and she follows. Neither of them is game to let go of the other. He has to convince himself this is real, that he really is standing in the middle of an abandoned New York intersection next to the United Nations.

A Coke can lies in the gutter next to a fast food wrapper. Teller remembers marveling at how the crushed, empty can had defied gravity, staying inert as the concrete slab rotated through the air over the course of a day. Back then, it was hard to believe the Coke can wasn't stuck in place with glue. Without thinking too much about it, he kicks the can. There is something about connecting with reality that is important to him. He relishes the feel of his shoe making contact with the can and the noisy flight of the thin, crushed metal as it ricochets off the gutter and skids along the road. Suddenly, to his surprise, the can curls up into the air before peeling to one side and sliding back down toward him.

"Hah," he cries, recognizing the shape of a sphere from the inside.

"Do that again," she says.

"Spoken like a true scientist," he replies, squeezing her hand.

They walk toward the invisible boundary surrounding them, marking what had once been the circumference of the concrete slab within the anomaly. Although the view before him suggests there is nothing in his way, he understands this is an illusion, that they are inside the anomaly looking out, but what they are seeing is a replica, a construct of the intersection on the day the anomaly arrived.

Teller picks up the can and throws it on an angle so it skids around the inside of the gigantic sphere, seemingly curving in the air and exposing the presence of the anomaly. The can rolls awkwardly along the invisible surface before falling back to the concrete some thirty feet away over near the State Department building.

"Teller!" Cathy cries in alarm. Her eyes go wide, and his mind races at the thought he's missed some important, critical point. "Look at you. Your arms. Your legs."

She is right. He had been shot three times while making his way to her, and he was shot in the back several times as they scrambled to get to the anomaly, but he's fine. No wounds. No pain. Nothing. He feels great, so much so that he didn't even realize he had been healed.

"Huh," he says, looking down at himself. "Well, that is very cool."

"It is," Cathy says, gently running her hands over his shoulder. Blood still mars the torn material, staining his shirt, but there are no wounds. Her fingers play with the bullet holes, touching softly at his skin beneath.

"How does it feel?" she asks.

"Wonderful."

"But how?"

"I don't know," he replies. "And I don't care."

With those few words, Teller feels liberated. He had tried so hard to understand. He had tried so hard to make sense of the anomaly, but he finally concedes that the anomaly is alien to him—entirely unfamiliar and full of unknowns. It feels good to let his mental guard down. It's okay not to know. It's healthy to realize he doesn't have all the answers.

"Do you think this is real?" she asks. "I mean, this is New York. If this were real, there would be cars driving around, people bustling by on the sidewalks. It's like we're on a movie set or something, just waiting for the director to shout, Action!"

"Action!" Teller calls out.

Cathy smiles, shaking her head.

"You know what I mean."

"I do," he replies. "And I think you're right. This isn't real."

"So, it's a dream then?" she asks.

"Not a dream, at least I don't think so. I mean, honestly, I have no idea, but my arms feel normal. Somehow, this thing, this anomaly has healed me. I think that's real. But what we're seeing—I don't know. Maybe it's something familiar, something to put us at ease, to help us relax."

"Okay, Mr. Alien Dude," Cathy calls out, looking up at the bright blue sky. "If you're listening, I have one word for you—Tahiti. If you want people to relax, put them on a beach in Tahiti."

Teller laughs.

"I'm not sure it works quite like that," he says.

"So how does it work?" Cathy asks.

"I don't know, but maybe you're right. Maybe we need to ask something intelligent of the anomaly."

"Like what?"

"Like—show us where you came from. Show us your home world."

Teller blinks and suddenly there are stars bursting through a pitch black night.

Teller and Cathy are standing on the edge of a vast canyon,

looking at a spiral galaxy stretching across a quarter of the sky. Instead of the few thousand stars visible from Earth, there are millions of stars caught in a swirl of light, seemingly frozen in place as they orbit a glowing, bulbous galactic core. Jets of superheated gas stream out of the poles of the warm, yellowish galactic core, but they appear to curve overhead, reaching lengths almost twice the width of the galaxy.

"They're from a satellite galaxy," Teller says, explaining what he is seeing to Cathy. "We have these too. Miniature galaxies like the Magellanic Cloud orbiting the Milky Way, although miniature is a relative term. They're miniature in terms of their size compared to the Milky Way and yet they still hold hundreds of thousands to millions of stars.

"Sometimes they're the remnants of ancient collisions between galaxies, caught in the oscillating process of passing back and forth through the main galaxy.

"Other times, they're in orbit around the galaxy in much the same way as a planet orbits a star."

"It's beautiful," Cathy says. "I don't know if you'd ever tire of seeing that in the night sky."

"I bet they never did," Teller says. "It's no wonder they reached for the stars."

He doesn't say anything to Cathy, but this is not what he expected. This is not the quasi-aquatic environment they speculated about when they first saw the anomaly transform into a bluish marble. There's no light pollution from whatever would be the equivalent of cities. Distant mountains rise up just as they would on Earth.

Cathy squeezes his fingers; for Teller, it's a wonderfully human moment to share while standing on an alien world. The contrast between the two of them is invigorating. Teller's not sure he would have picked the word 'beautiful' to describe this sight. He would have used some superlative like 'astonishing,' or 'marvelous' but she's right.

"Yes, it is beautiful," he replies, reveling in the simplicity of those few words.

They complement each other so well.

Cathy sighs, leaning into him and savoring the view.

The landscape before them is barren. There's no grass, no trees, no signs of life as they know it, but Teller is aware that on Earth, even the most barren of dry, frozen desert landscapes harbors an abundance of microbial life despite appearances.

"We're not actually here, right?" Cathy asks, crouching down and watching as tiny rocks and fine sand run between her fingers.

"No. At a guess, what we're seeing is millions upon millions of light years from Earth. I think this is another projection, a kind of virtual reality that appeals to all of our senses, not just sight."

Teller turns over a rock with his foot, half expecting some alien insect to scurry from beneath it. In the soft light, the underside of the rock looks the same as the surface. From what little he can tell, there isn't any moisture clinging to the rock.

Various black silhouettes mark rocks and boulders and outcrops scattered across the terrain. A broad, gentle rise stretches out to one side, reminding Teller of the eroded meteor craters on Mars.

The canyon before them looks impossibly deep, something akin to the Grand Canyon on Earth. Dark shadows hide the valley floor, but the meandering nature of the canyon walls leaves Teller wondering if this too is the result of water erosion over millions of years.

As their eyes adjust to the darkness, the heavens above seem to brighten, leaving them in awe of the spiral galaxy above. It is no wonder the creators of the anomaly are a star-faring species, having watched that sky for countless generations, they must be as inspired as the ocean-going explorers on Earth were to explore new territories.

The stars are surprisingly crisp, and as there are no clouds in the sky, Teller gets the impression this must be a cold, dry, and possibly high-altitude desert on their home world, somewhere ideal for astronomical observations and not unlike the Atacama desert in Chile.

He wonders about the rest of the planet. There must be lowlands and oceans. He wonders about the chemical composition of the atmosphere, the strength of gravity, and the habitats where macroscopic life abounds. Far from the planets of science fiction, where only one environment pervades an entire planet such as the fictional ice planet Hoth or the desert planet Tatooine, there must be similar ecologies to Earth. Are there jungles? River deltas teeming with life? Rolling plains with the alien equivalent of grass? Dense forest canopies? Rugged mountain ranges? Ice-laden polar regions? He wants to see it all, to see their entire world, but he appreciates the importance of this particular view.

A soft glow emanates from behind them. Cathy notices it first and turns away from the spectacular sight before them. Teller follows her motion, reluctantly pulling himself away from the grandeur of a far flung galaxy shining down on this mysterious world.

"It seems our host has arrived," Cathy says.

Teller is well aware they are still within the spherical structure of the anomaly, and yet the concrete slab within the intersection covered a huge area, giving them plenty of room to move around within their artificial view of this alien world.

A pinprick of light appears over a hundred feet above the uneven terrain, roughly where they first saw the lithium glowing within the anomaly in what seems like another lifetime. Teller and Cathy walk over, standing beneath this tiny artificial star.

"Nervous?" she asks.

"No, I'm good."

Teller finds he can't stare straight at the miniature star. It isn't blinding like the sun, but it has the intensity of a stage spotlight, making it uncomfortable to look directly into the pulsating glow. When the light vanishes, it takes his eyes a few seconds to adjust to the darkness and recognize that something, someone is standing there facing them.

Cathy tightens her grip on his hand, whispering, "Nervous yet?"

How is she not nervous?

"A little. In a good way," Teller replies, lying. His heart thumps in his chest. At a rational level, he knows this alien creature means no harm, that through some sophisticated feat of nanotechnology it has repaired the tissue damage from his gunshot wounds, but emotionally, this is a monstrous alien lurking in the dark. He tries to come to grips with the grotesque alien before him, looking to distinguish limbs from trunk, or a head rising slightly above the torso when the creature shrinks and a familiar shape appears before him, that of a man.

"Is this form easier to accept?" the man asks.

The alien's facial features are almost plastic. Neatly combed black hair lies swept across his brow. His eyes are soft, and even in the low light it is apparent they lack the glassy reflection of real eyes, while his clothes are either skin tight or some kind of body paint.

Standing there, Teller quickly realizes that if this creature wanted to, he could replicate any living person in unquestionable detail. But he hasn't. That he produced a facsimile that could be a department store dummy modeling clothes is quite profound. He wants Teller and Cathy to be comfortable, but without being condescending. There is just enough alien in the man's appearance to retain the realization that they are talking to someone from another world.

Teller wants to say 'No' to his question. Intellectually, he wants to see these creatures for what they are, but the word that passes from his lips is, "Yes."

And that's no surprise given his racing heart. Honesty trumps bravado.

The alien has even adopted his light skin tone, subtly putting to rest the irrational tribalism that haunts the races of Homo sapiens, where suspicions arise over nothing more than skin pigment.

The alien smiles warmly from behind plastic lips. Teller can sense the degree to which this star-faring species is adapting to make the two of them feel comfortable, and they do feel comfortable, but that makes Teller feel somewhat ashamed. He's disappointed in himself, and yet he understands his reactions are natural, instinctive, human.

"Who are you?" he asks.

"To us, it is interesting that you would ask," the man replies, speaking of himself in the plural. "The anomaly, as you call it, is alive, but it is closer to a machine in your thinking than an animal. As far as names go, our name would be meaningless to you, translating to nothing more than grunts and disjointed vowels and syllables, and yet even that would be a poor interpretation. We are a representation of a species that has long since ceased to exist. What you see here is a facsimile, commissioned to search for intelligent life and learn about this vast universe."

"To what end?" Teller asks. "If your parent species is extinct, what is the point?"

"Is your parent species still alive?" the plastic man asks. "Are you not descendent from Homo habilis, Homo erectus, Australopithecus? Where are they? If they have passed into obscurity, what is the point of your existence?"

Teller laughs, shaking his head. It's a good point, and one often lost on Homo sapiens, who so often act as though humanity stands independent of the animal kingdom, when humanity is just one tiny twig on the Tree of Life. Homo sapiens are simply a species that has thrived and adapted to survive where others, like *Homo neanderthalensis* and *Homo floresiensis* have fallen.

"So you're their children," Teller replies, finding himself naturally gravitating to the plural.

"We are all children of the stars," the plastic man continues, gesturing at the magnificent view of the stars above them. "Your world is a surprising contradiction, a conflict of opposing ideals."

"Yes, it is," Cathy says, surprising Teller with her boldness. As a reporter, she's probably more comfortable than he is with being put on the spot, and Teller doesn't mind that at all. By answering, she's giving him some time to think. By agreeing, she's showing their willingness to concede to human frailty and the contradiction of scientists exploring the anomaly while others sought to destroy it.

"I don't know what you are, or where you are from," she says, "but I get the feeling humanity isn't out of high school yet."

The plastic man tilts his head slightly, as if appealing for clarification in a curious manner, and Teller marvels at the ability of this creature to perceive the subtleties of the English language. Teller is interested to note that the creature doesn't ask Cathy to clarify what a high school is, but rather seems to be interested in how that concept relates to them standing here on this alien world. His demeanor seems to implore her to explain her point.

"My young kid sister," Cathy begins. "She's seventeen. She's the smartest person she's ever met."

Teller has to mentally go through a double-take. He had expected Cathy to say, 'She's the smartest person I've ever met,' although with a hint of sarcasm. By saying, 'She's the smartest person she's ever met,' Cathy's twisting language, pushing the bounds of interpretation, and Teller wonders how difficult it must be for the alien to deal with a language like English that is so contextual and idiomatic.

He's fascinated, watching the plastic man as he listens to Cathy speak. There's body language at play, as his brow narrows and his head turns slightly toward her. He's learning. He wants to catch every nuance behind her words. He's intensely interested in what she's saying. Teller can't help wondering how concepts like age convey meaning to the creature, and he suspects the alien may not understand Cathy. Does this species even have distinct stages such as infancy, adolescence, and adulthood? How would it know that seventeen marks an often troubled age for humans seeking independence? Can the alien relate that to the implicit intent in Cathy's mention of her sister's age?

"She swears like a sailor," Cathy continues, oblivious to the dynamic at work around her. She could be describing her sister to Teller's mom. "She parties, she drinks, she smokes. That's illegal for her age, of course, and defies rationale. She drives my dad crazy."

Teller goes to put his hand out to stop Cathy, assuming she's bombarding the alien with concepts he cannot possibly hope to grasp. He begins raising his hand when the creature responds to him, holding his hand in a gesture to let her speak. The plastic man keeps his unblinking eyes on Cathy. Teller is stunned.

"So I get it," Cathy says. "For all the science buffs with their white lab coats and their Ph.D.s, their spreadsheets full of formulas and their incomprehensible graphs, I think I understand what this anomaly is. You and I have the same relationship as my sister and my dad."

She pauses.

"I, ah," Teller says, genuinely surprised by her, and not sure what she means.

A smile appears on plastic lips.

"Why would anyone smoke in this day and age?" Cathy asks, ignoring Teller, but he knows this isn't intentional on her part, she's simply engrossed in her own dawning awareness. "With what we know about cancer and heart disease, why would anyone ever smoke? And yet millions still do. I suspect this is the same, isn't it?"

"Yes, it is," the plastic man replies.

"I don't get it," Teller confesses, and for once it feels good to hear the answer and yet still need an explanation.

"The anomaly," Cathy says. "It's like graduating from high school, like getting your first job. It's a chance to grow up, a chance to take responsibility, to be an adult. It's the crossroads we all face in life—to do what we want, or to do what we should."

Teller's heart sinks.

"And we're not there yet, are we?" he asks.

"Your species is in its formative years," the plastic man says. "You have much that is admirable, much that has emerged from your scientific exploration, but you still cling to the superstitions, attitudes, and practices of the past."

"Yeah, it's a bit of a comfort blanket," Cathy replies.

Teller is genuinely surprised by her. Something in the appearance of the plastic man on the desolate rim of a vast, dark canyon has clicked for her. He isn't sure if it's the radiance of the stars, the similarity to the deserts of Arizona or Nevada, or the man standing before them, but for Cathy, all the pieces have fallen in place. Teller is still coming up to speed. Cathy doesn't need any more explanation.

"We can learn so much from you," Teller says, feeling as though the moment is slipping away from him.

The creature doesn't reply.

"No," Cathy says after a few seconds of silence, "No. We can't. We can no more learn from them than my sister can learn from me, or mom, or dad. There are some things in life you have to live through and learn for yourself. You can't read them in a textbook. You can't watch them on TV. You have to experience them and grow up by yourself."

"She is right," the plastic man says, but this isn't what Teller wants to hear. "You would seek knowledge, but what you need is wisdom. You would seek to advance, but what you need is to consolidate. You seek to run, but you must walk."

"But," Teller protests.

Cathy turns toward him, resting her hand gently on his, saying, "This is what the anomaly has always been about. Don't you see? It's a litmus test, a character evaluation, a college entrance exam. All that helium and lithium and whatever, that was just the trappings of the psych exam—they want to see whether we are prepared for the future."

"And," Teller says, unable to complete his own sentence.

"And we're not."

"Your day will arise," the plastic man says. "One day you will sail among the stars."

"But not now?" Teller says with a heavy heart.

"No."

Cathy says, "My kid sister would kill for the family car, but there's no way in hell my dad's giving it to her, she's just not ready. She'd kill herself."

Teller feels crestfallen. Cathy squeezes his hand. She senses his heartbreak at the realization that they're not ready. It's not that he's failed, or even that humanity as a whole has failed. It's that humanity needs time to mature, to learn and grow.

"So all this goes nowhere?" he asks.

"Would you give a Ferrari to a sixteen year old boy?" Cathy asks with a surprising amount of clarity.

As much as Teller doesn't want to say it, he is compelled to concede.

"No."

"There is much for you to learn," the plastic man says as the view around them changes. Suddenly, they are in orbit on the night side of a massive planet. Teller feels as though he is floating as dark clouds swirl in the atmosphere hundreds of miles below them, choking the planet. To his surprise, there's no sensation of falling, more of being suspended. It is as if they are hanging from a support harness.

Thin wisps of light catch a broad, flat expanse stretching away from the mid-regions of the dark gas giant.

"Is this Saturn?" Teller asks.

"Yes."

As they swing around into the sunlight, their path intersects with the broad ring of ice flecks spanning tens of thousands of miles. Rays of light catch the cloud tops on Saturn, casting shadows among the golden swirls.

The plane that marks Saturn's rings stretches out in golden hues, catching his eye like a rainbow. The rings dwarf the three explorers, and yet they seem wafer-thin.

Teller is in awe as they pass through one of the mid rings in the blink of an eye, briefly switching hemispheres before rising just above the plane of the rings and racing on around them. As they glide out of the shadows and into the reflected glory of the rings, trillions of tiny clumps of ice sparkle in the sunlight, shimmering like diamonds.

Their course through space changes. As the entire experience is a projection within the anomaly, Teller feels no change in his inertia. The effect is a little disorienting, as the view is so realistic he expects some kind of resistance and finds himself spreading his legs and reaching for the distant, ethereal ground to brace himself as they speed along the thin, undulating strands of thousands of rings. In the distance, a tiny moon appears as a crescent catching the light of the Sun.

The rings streak by beneath them, and Teller finds himself torn as to what he should watch. He sees the gentle arc of the distant ice moon, but it is little more than the size of his thumb at arm's length. Beneath him, the rings whizz by in thin, curving arcs, streaks of light that look as though they're made of crystal. Behind him, the gas giant looms large, catching the full strength of the sun. Eddies roll through the cloud banks, forming interrelated patterns at the various latitudes stretching up toward the pole. The subtle shades add to the mystique of the massive planet.

"It's astonishing," Cathy says.

"It sure is," Teller replies, only just realizing they're still holding hands.

Within minutes, they are orbiting a small icy moon just beyond one of the rings. Teller recognizes it as Enceladus and understands that the rings of Saturn extend even further beyond this moon, but they are so perilously thin and tenuous, he can barely make them out.

Large scars have been carved into the jagged ice field below them. It looks as though a swarm of gigantic ice skaters have scratched the surface of the moon with their blades, cutting parallel lines into the frozen surface, and crisscrossing each other as they dart back and forth around Enceladus.

From orbit, the turbulent nature of Enceladus is apparent. Chasms and fractures have been carved into the ice. The northern hemisphere is pockmarked with craters, but the southern regions are surprisingly smooth, with massive fractures separating tectonic-like plates of ice. Patches of fresh ice bleed through the surface, marking parallel stripes in the south, staining the brilliant white ice with aqua blue hues.

"Why this moon?" Teller asks. "Why Enceladus?"

"Because it is here you will mature," the plastic man replies.

"But," Teller protests. "Establishing a human presence here will take decades, perhaps the best part of a century. We can barely reach our own moon, let alone one of the moons of Saturn over a billion miles from Earth. What is here for us?"

"Life," the man replies. "And life changes everything."

"You have to help us," Teller pleads. "Tell us about dark matter, about dark energy. Help us understand the quantum world. Is M-theory correct?"

He's blabbering, but he feels as though he has to blurt out his concerns. He feels if he doesn't speak now, he's never going to get the opportunity again.

"Life," the alien replies. "That is where you must start."

"But at best, all there is on Enceladus is microbes—microscopic life. We need to learn from an intelligence like yours, not from microbes," Teller says, feeling he's losing the debate.

"Once you appreciate the simplest of life forms elsewhere, you'll understand the value of life on your own planet. Once you mature, the cosmos is yours to explore. And we will be there waiting to join you."

Teller blinks and finds himself standing knee deep in water at the base of a curved muddy bowl. Skyscrapers tower around them. Sirens sound overhead. Cathy is standing beside him, staring up at the cracked concrete stretching around the rim of this unworldly crater.

The road-base, along with the layers of stone, gravel and crushed rock that support the street crumble, sliding in minute quantities down toward them. Tiny rocks and pebbles tumble over each other, disappearing into the muddy water.

The sky is an azure blue. A flock of birds fly overhead.

"Wait," Teller calls out. "Come back." But in the depths of his mind, he knows it is too late. He knows the creature, or construct, or whatever it was has gone as quickly as it had come.

There are no shortcuts. Life is more than a quiz show question/answer session, or a multi-choice exam. Teller finally understands, the only worthwhile answers are those humanity finds for themselves.

"Hey," a voice calls from above. Finch peers into the crater left by the anomaly. "They're here! They're alive! Quick, somebody get me a rope."

Cathy waves at Finch.

"Damn, it is good to see you," Finch yells.

"It's good to be seen," Cathy calls back enthusiastically, and

Teller knows precisely what she means. It is good to be alive.

As a rope is thrown down to them, Teller can't help but wonder if there is more than microbes waiting for them on Enceladus. Perhaps when they get there, they might find a section of ice rotating carelessly through the sky in defiance of gravity, patiently waiting to continue their conversation under more civil terms.

"Do you think this is the end?" Cathy asks, turning to Teller as she grabs the rope.

"No," he replies with a smile, feeling a sense of hope and excitement for the future. "This isn't the end. This is just the beginning."

AFTERWORD

Thank you for taking a chance on independently produced science fiction and reading Anomaly.

This book has a couple of points of inspiration that might interest you.

Tor.com published an article asking where is the brainy, non-violent science fiction? I think that's a very good question. Invariably, our stories tend to focus around violent heroes. The exceptions to this rule can be counted on one hand.

We all love John McClane in Die Hard, but is he really a hero? An inspiration? Or is he a throwback to the days when violence solved every problem? Violence is the antithesis of civilization. There are times where violence is needful, such as in war, but it is never desirable. So, I wondered, where are the intelligent, thoughtful science fiction heroes? And that thought was the genesis of Anomaly.

Anomaly does have violent scenes. But, like Carl Sagan's novel Contact, they are not perpetuated by the protagonist and, hopefully, violence is not glorified. And so the main character is a bumbling teacher that loves inspiring his kids to love learning. We all need heroes like that.

Sagan's *Contact* helped inspire this novel, and not just because of its proposed contact with an advanced alien civilization, but for its mastery in stirring up intellectual conflicts and the juxtaposition of religious faith with scientific rationalism. This is something I've tried to capture in both the U.N. debate and the interfaith religious meeting within Anomaly.

Michael Crichton's *Sphere* is another inspiration. Again, it is a landmark work in terms of the fresh thinking on how an alien intelligence would struggle to communicate with humanity. And so, in honor of Michael Crichton, the shape of the anomaly is a sphere.

I wanted the alien spacecraft in Anomaly to be radically different to anything we've seen in Hollywood, and I liked the idea that the alien craft could be staring us in the face without anyone realizing quite what it is. To our senses, this particular spacecraft is all but incorporeal. The idea of the anomaly remaining stationary while facing its point of origin as the Earth revolves around it is a way of being disruptive, breaking the paradigms of what a spacecraft could be. And it gave the protagonist, David Teller, a point of entry into the story as he figures out that enigma.

How would we communicate with an alien intelligence? We can't even effectively communicate with other intelligent species on our own planet, let alone an intelligence from another world. And so, the idea of communicating via the periodic table of elements seems to be a good primer, a good place to start. Certainly, Carl Sagan thought so and used hydrogen as the key to deciphering the plaque on the Pioneer spacecraft. I think it would be plausible for aliens to think along the same lines and use hydrogen to start a conversation with us.

The original book cover is part of the plaque on the Pioneer spacecraft, showing the transition states of hydrogen (above the title), the position of our Sun relative to nearby stars (in the center), and the path Pioneer takes as it left the solar system is visible at the bottom.

For me, the highlight of this novel is the realization of what's truly important—life. I enjoyed exploring this is so many ways, but in particular when an old man shows kindness to some bloodied strangers, giving them shelter from a riot. All too often, we look outward for meaning in life, wanting something to give us meaning, not realizing we already have meaning all around us in the loved ones in our lives.

I hope you have enjoyed this speculative science fiction novel. Please take the time to provide a review on Amazon or Goodreads. Reviews are the lifeblood of an independent author as there's no better promotion than that of an excited reader.

I'm thankful for everyone that encouraged me to write this book and helped with suggestions along the way, especially my wife Fiona, Tibor Koch, and Ellen Campbell for their assistance with the editing.

You can find a list of all the books I've written on my blog, thinkingscifi. If you would like notification about upcoming books, follow me on Facebook or say hello on Twitter.

OTHER BOOKS BY PETER CAWDRON

Thank you for supporting independent science fiction. You might enjoy the following novels also written by Peter Cawdron.

WHAT WE LEFT BEHIND & ALL OUR TOMORROWS

Hazel is a regular teenager growing up in an irregular world overrun with zombies. She likes music, perfume, freshly baked muffins, and playing her Xbox—everything that no longer exists in the apocalypse.

Raised in the safety of a commune, Hazel rarely sees Zee anymore, except on those occasions when the soldiers demonstrate the importance of a headshot to the kids.

To her horror, circumstances beyond her control lead her outside the barbed wire fence and into a zombie-infested town.

"Five, Four, Three, Two—count your shots, Haze," she says to herself, firing at the oncoming zombie horde. "Don't forget to reload."

ALIEN SPACE TENTACLE PORN

A 1950s hospital. Temporary amnesia. A naked man running through Central Park yelling something about alien space tentacles. Tinfoil, duct tape, and bananas. These are the ingredients for a spectacular romp through a world you never thought possible as aliens reach out and make contact with Earth.

MY SWEET SATAN

The crew of the Copernicus is sent to investigate Bestla, one of the remote moons of Saturn. Bestla has always been an oddball, orbiting Saturn in the wrong direction and at a distance of fifteen million miles, so far away that Saturn appears smaller than Earth's moon in the night sky. Bestla hides a secret. When mapped by an unmanned probe, Bestla awakes and begins transmitting a message, only it's a message no one wants to hear: "I want to live and die for you, Satan."

SILO SAGA: SHADOWS

Shadows is fan fiction set in Hugh Howey's Wool universe as part of the Kindle Worlds Silo Saga.

Life within the silos follows a well-worn pattern passed down through the generations from master to apprentice, caster to shadow. "Don't ask! Don't think! Don't question! Just stay in the shadows." But not everyone is content to follow the past.

THE WORLD OF KURT VONNEGUT: CHILDREN'S CRUSADE

Kurt Vonnegut's masterpiece Slaughterhouse-Five: The

Children's Crusade explored the fictional life of Billy Pilgrim as he stumbled through the real world devastation of Dresden during World War II. Children's Crusade picks up the story of Billy Pilgrim on the planet of Tralfamadore as Billy and his partner Montana Wildhack struggle to accept life in an alien zoo.

THE MAN WHO REMEMBERED TODAY

The Man Who Remembered Today is a novella originally appearing in From the Indie Side anthology, highlighting independent science fiction writers from around the world. You can pick up this story as a stand-alone novella or get twelve distinctly unique stories by purchasing From the Indie Side.

Kareem wakes with a headache. A bloody bandage wrapped around his head tells him this isn't just another day in the Big Apple. The problem is, he can't remember what happened to him. He can't recall anything from yesterday. The only memories he has are from events that are about to unfold today, and today is no ordinary day.

ANOMALY

Anomaly examines the prospect of an alien intelligence discovering life on Earth.

Mankind's first contact with an alien intelligence is far more radical than anyone has ever dared imagine. The technological gulf between mankind and the alien species is measured in terms of millions of years. The only way to communicate is by using science, but not everyone is so patient with the arrival of an alien spacecraft outside the gates of the United Nations in New York.

THE ROAD TO HELL

The Road to Hell is paved with good intentions.

How do you solve a murder when the victim comes back to life with no memory of recent events?

In the twenty-second century, America struggles to rebuild after the second civil war. Democracy has been suspended while the reconstruction effort lifts the country out of the ruins of conflict. America's fate lies in the hands of a genetically engineered soldier with the ability to move through time.

The Road to Hell deals with a futuristic world and the advent of limited time travel. It explores social issues such as the nature of trust and the conflict between loyalty and honesty.

MONSTERS

Monsters is a dystopian novel exploring the importance of reading. Monsters is set against the backdrop of the collapse of civilization.

The fallout from a passing comet contains a biological pathogen, not a virus or a living organism, just a collection of amino acids. But these cause animals to revert to the age of the megafauna, when monsters roamed Earth.

Bruce Dobson is a reader. With the fall of civilization, reading has become outlawed. Superstitions prevail, and readers are persecuted like the witches and wizards of old. Bruce and his son James seek to overturn the prejudices of their day and restore the scientific knowledge central to their survival, but monsters lurk in the dark.

FEEDBACK

Twenty years ago, a UFO crashed into the Yellow Sea off the Korean Peninsula. The only survivor was a young English-speaking child, captured by the North Koreans. Two decades later, a physics student watches his girlfriend disappear before his eyes, abducted from the streets of New York by what appears to be the same UFO.

Feedback will carry you from the desolate, windswept coastline of North Korea to the bustling streets of New York and on into the depths of space as you journey to the outer edge of our solar system looking for answers.

GALACTIC EXPLORATION

Galactic Exploration is a compilation of four closely related science fiction stories following the exploration of the Milky Way by the spaceships Serengeti, Savannah, and The Rift Valley.

These three generational starships are piloted by clones and form part of the ongoing search for intelligent extraterrestrial life. With the Serengeti heading out above the plane of the Milky Way, the Savannah exploring the outer reaches of the galaxy, and The Rift Valley investigating possible alien signals within the galactic core, this story examines the Rare Earth Hypothesis from a number of different angles.

This volume contains the novellas Serengeti, Trixie and Me, Savannah, and War.

XENOPHOBIA

Xenophobia examines the impact of first contact on the Third World.

Dr. Elizabeth Bower works at a field hospital in Malawi as a civil war smolders around her. With an alien spacecraft in orbit around Earth, the US withdraws its troops to deal with the growing unrest in America. Dr. Bower refuses to abandon her hospital. A troop of US Rangers accompanies Dr. Bower as she attempts to get her staff and patients to safety. Isolated and alone, cut off from contact with the West, they watch as the world descends into chaos with alien contact.

LITTLE GREEN MEN

Little Green Men is a tribute to the works of Philip K. Dick, hailing back to classic science fiction stories of the 1950s.

The crew of the Dei Gratia set down on a frozen planet and are attacked by little green men. Chief Science Officer David Michaels struggles with the impossible situation unfolding around him as the crew members are murdered one by one. With the engines offline and power fading, he races against time to understand this mysterious threat and escape the planet alive.

REVOLUTION

How do you hide state secrets when teenage hacktivists have as much quantum computing power as the government? Alexander Hopkins is about to find out on what should have been an uneventful red-eye flight from Russia. Nothing is what it seems in this heart-pounding short-story from international best selling author Peter Cawdron.

HELLO WORLD

Hello World is a short story set in the same fictional universe as Alien Space Tentacle Porn.

Professor Franco Corelli has noticed something unusual. The twitter account @QuestionsLots is harvesting hundreds of millions of tweets each day, but never posting anything. Outwardly, this account only follows one other twitter account—@RealScientists, but in reality it is trawling every post ever made by anyone on this planet. Could it be that @QuestionsLots is not from Earth?

VAMPIRE & WE ARE LEGION

Bram Stoker wrote Dracula over the course of a decade, researching historical figures and compiling notes from scattered diary entries. What was supposed to be a work of fiction holds far more truth than he realized. Dr. Jane Langford is investigating a murder-suicide unlike anything she's ever encountered before. Sleepy Boise, Idaho, is a haven to an evil that has passed unnoticed down through the centuries.

In addition to these stories, Peter Cawdron has short stories appearing in:

- The Telepath Chronicles
- The Alien Chronicles
- The A.I. Chronicles
- The Z Chronicles
- Tales of Tinfoil

RETROGRADE

The Endeavour colony on Mars is the first step in humanity's long walk out of Africa and into the stars. Mars Alpha is heavily dependent on resupply from Earth. Where possible, colonists use 3D printing and locally grown food, but they still rely on Earth for complex medicines and electronics. The colonists are prepared for every eventuality but one. What happens on Mars when nuclear war breaks out on Earth?

WELCOME TO THE OCCUPIED STATES OF AMERICA

Seven years after the invasion of the grubs, 110 million Americans have been displaced by the war, with over 50 million dead. Ashley Kelly was crippled by a cluster bomb. While the world crumbled, she spent seven years learning to walk again, and she'll be damned if she's going to lie down for anyone, terrestrial or extraterrestrial.

Printed in Poland
by Amazon Fulfillment
Poland Sp. z o.o., Wrocław